SHADOWS OF SEASONS PAST

SHADOWS OF SEASONS PAST

Francis Roberts

Copyright 2023 © Francis Roberts

All rights reserved.

No part of this book may be used or reproduced, distributed, or transmitted in any form or by any means, including photocopying, recording, or other electronic or mechanical methods, without the proper written permission of the publisher, except in the case of brief quotations apart, embodied in critical reviews and certain other noncommercial uses permitted by copyright law. Use of this publication is permitted solely for personal use and must include full attribution of the materials source.

For Emma

Acknowledgments

There are numerous individuals to whom I owe immense gratitude for making this book possible.

First and foremost, I'd like to express my heartfelt appreciation to my partner, Emma, who patiently endured late-night writing and editing sessions, enthusiastically accompanied me on visits to archaeological sites and museums, and engaged in lengthy, inspiring conversations about prehistory during the writing process.

Additionally, I would like to extend my thanks, in no specific order, to Matthew Carless, Joseph Curry, Adam Jackson, Frank Bell, Paul Davis, and Callum. They diligently navigated through the initial drafts, providing invaluable feedback.

I must also acknowledge Dr. James Dilley and Ancient Crafts U.K. for generously offering detailed responses to even the most peculiar of questions from strangers.

Lastly, I want to convey my deepest gratitude to all the archaeologists who dedicate their lives to digging around in the dirt. Without their tireless efforts, we would have no knowledge of our prehistoric ancestors. We owe them much.

Concerning the Setting

This story takes place roughly thirteen thousand years before the present in southwestern France during a period known as the bolling–allerod interstadial. This was a brief period of warming during the ice ages that sits between the end of the last glacial maximum and the Younger Dryas. The Glaciers that had covered Europe for thousands of years began to retreat, and great birch forests crept across the continent as temperatures approached those of the Holocene. Pleistocene fauna would have collided with a more recognisable world as gradual warming began to make lives easier for the people clinging to existence in the wilds of Europe.

We know very little about the people that lived during this time. We know virtually nothing about their language, culture, religion or rituals. Time has washed away these things, leaving only mystery and speculation in their place.

However, what scant evidence they have left behind reveals a little about them. We know what kind of tools and jewellery they had, from antler-tipped spears and stone blades to ivory beads and carved figurines. From this, we can extrapolate the daily tasks they might have performed, what they wore, and how they lived. We know they had an appreciation for the natural world they inhabited, based on the beautiful Magdalenian cave paintings that can be found in France and Spain. And most of all, we know they were as indelibly human as you or I. They certainly laughed, loved, and grieved with all the same emotional intensity that a person living in the twenty-first century might.

The characters, groups, and religious elements in this story are all totally fictitious. What I have tried to do, however, is to use what archaeological evidence we do have to build a coherent picture of what life may have been like for people living in Europe during the late upper Palaeolithic.

I hope, in my own small way, through this rough and tumble adventure story, I can provide at least a small window into the life of someone living on the plains of Europe thirteen thousand years ago.

Summer

Chapter 1

The boy named Auroch held his breath and steadied his aim. The long grass tickled his legs as the warm afternoon breeze caused it to sway back and forth against his thighs. Insects had made their way onto his shins, and now they nipped and scratched at his skin as he couched, frozen in place. He waited patiently for the signal. Without moving his head, he looked out of the corner of his eye to check on the row of men crouched several paces apart in the long grass. They formed a large semi-circle, perfectly spaced apart around their quarry, ready to create a living net. If one man made a mistake, a morning of anticipation and silent stalking would all be for nothing. He directed his eyes back to the herd of grazing deer before him. On cue, he heard the imitation bird call from the Master Huntsman. The deer stopped and looked around for the source of the sound, sensing its unnatural origin. The hunters had little more than a second before they bolted. It was all they needed.

Moving fluidly from a crouched position to standing, Auroch pulled his arm back. Using a carved antler-bone spear thrower, the atatl, he released a thin wooden projectile with a sharpened antler tip hafted to the shaft. His aim was true, and it hit his deer squarely in the lower neck. Tens of spears, each with their individual target, flew from either side of him, most striking soft flesh. Auroch's deer stopped for a second, shaking the spear free. The tip came loose inside the animal, holding the wound open. The boy wondered if the poor creature had understood what was going on. It ran forward a few yards before stumbling, arterial spray dousing the grass. Auroch raced the hunting dogs to the dying deer before pouncing on it, locating its windpipe easily with his knife. The animal died quickly.

The rest of the men descended on the thirteen deer that now lay dead and dying, strewn across the glade. Those who escaped the clearing before succumbing to their injuries were hauled back out of the woodland and laid next to those who had died on the spot. Auroch, a head shorter than the rest of the men, strode to keep pace with his elders as they moved from carcass to carcass. He watched nervously as the Master Huntsman, known as Bloodied Thistle, examined the kills one by one. Running his hands over the wound on the neck of Auroch's deer, he turned to the boy, giving him an appreciative nod. A clean kill. A good kill. Auroch turned back to see his father's face standing amongst the hunters. Father, whose name Auroch shared, gave him a look of encouragement, and the boy joined Bloodied Thistle at the deer's side.

The two men swiftly began their work, first decapitating the buck with a sharpened bone knife. Then, using tiny flint microliths, they made cuts around the hooves before moving on to the animal's thighs and ankles. With a little tugging, they peeled off the deer's hide. The familiar ripping of sinew from skin caused the boy's mouth to water.

He glanced across the glade to see his father performing the same sanguine routine on another corpse. Bloodied Thistle laid the skin on the ground and the now naked deer upon it before gleefully slicing it from crotch to neck.

Opening the animal up, they took the valuable bones, cleanly removing the pelvis and ribs. Auroch pulled at the animal's throat, skilfully extracting the lungs and heart along with the trachea. He placed the heart with the good meat, adding the little innards he couldn't use to a growing pile of offal. His mentor sliced open the head to reveal the tongue before sending a runner to fetch women to strip the now detached limbs of their meat.

The women arrived and began to ferry the organs back to the main woodland camps. A soft hand touched the back of Auroch's neck. Mother. She whispered a few grateful words before taking an armful of gore back to the women's communal dwellings. Soon, everything of use had been carried from the glade, and the boy sat on the grass, proud of his work. He fed the remaining meat to the dogs, taking delight in watching them obediently wait their turn before jumping on the piles of intestines when summoned.

The men dined under the stars that night. They were handed each a wooden bowl, full to the brim with a broth containing rich deer meat, wild shoots, and berries. They danced and shouted, and the hunting dogs jumped and howled along with them. Auroch swept his sandy brown hair from his eyes and looked at the faces of the huntsmen. They were the masters of the Summer Valley, and Auroch knew he would one day lead the hunt. They danced until dawn.

It was warm when Auroch awoke. The fire had burned down to

embers, and he could already feel the night's cool air giving way to the warmth of the day. He noted that it felt colder than previous mornings and that soon, it would be time to leave the valley. The very end of the rutting season. He glanced across the camp and recognised the silhouette of Father. The details of his face and rugged physique were obscured by the shadow cast by an endless mess of birch trees that blanketed the valley floor. The sun was higher than Auroch expected, and no doubt Father would scold him for it. The days were precious. Auroch yawned and stretched, throwing off the deerskin that had covered him while he slept. Father did not look up from his work.

"You have wasted the day, my boy." Father was working with stone, striking a lump of flint with an antler hammer to shake free scraping tools. "Your mother has summoned you. One of our infants has a heat on his temple and is in distress."

Auroch stopped stretching and rubbing his eyes. He was suddenly very awake.

"What would you have me do?" Auroch said softly.

He controlled his emotions. This would be the third time in six summers that one of Mother's new children had fallen ill. He had cried when the first of his siblings had perished from sickness, and his father had beaten him for it. Screeching was for infants. As the eldest son, Auroch was expected to show fortitude. At fourteen summers old, he now performed all the work of a man. He had felt a sense of anticipation as they had travelled from the great plains, through the creeks and forests, to the valley where stags were so plentiful at this time of year. He would hunt as his father did, and then, just before the journey back, he would be inducted as a man. Upon return to the meeting of the tribes on the great plain, a suitable bride would be chosen to bear his children. The prospect excited him.

"You will not join Bloodied Thistle and the others today." Father looked up, his nervous eyes betraying his mood as worried rather than irritated. "Go and see the old woman, Morning Mist. She knows what you will need to help your brother."

A direct command from Father was not to be disobeyed. Auroch quickly grabbed his atatl and some spare projectiles from the ground and placed them in his small hide travelling sack alongside his scrapers and burins. The long thin darts were about his height and had deadly sharp antler points secured to the shaft with birch bark, heated by himself and his father until it became a sticky, tar-like substance. The bag slung around his shoulder, darts protruding above his head; he began towards the stream that led down towards the second encampment where the women and children slept in small tents made from a frame of birchwood and reeds. He felt a firm hand on his wrist, and he was yanked around to face back toward the men's encampment. Father towered over him.

"Auroch, you are my eldest, but you do not yet have the strength of most men. Take care. If you must fight, then fight. And if you must run, then run."

The young boy looked into Father's deep brown eyes, which he knew mirrored his own. A visible ripple of fear and sadness fell over Father's swarthy complexion. He placed one large, calloused hand on Auroch's shoulder and softly placed his knife onto the boy's outstretched palm. Neither man nor boy said a word. Auroch gazed at the delicate sharpness of the blade for a moment, feeling the weight of the beautifully knapped flint, its tang reaching back into a bark handle. Then the boy departed.

The women's camp was situated at the bottom of the valley, a short but noticeable walk from the men's camp. From the valley floor, the great mountain range to the south loomed over him, seemingly both distant and immediate. Here, nestled in the foothills, they were safe. The women's dwellings were comfier than the men's shelters, who in the warm summer air would sleep under the stars. He began to feel nervous as he walked past the now extinguished campfires dotted around the landscape. He made his way past the small pen where the dogs were kept, noting most of the pack had already been taken from the pen for hunting. A few pregnant she-dogs and pups remained, padding around their wooden prison, awaiting their next meal.

The woman's camp grew closer, and its occupants appeared in gradually sharper detail. The women hurried from one place to another, performing morning duties and preparing for the day ahead. There was a smattering of men amongst them, either helping the women tan hides and weave baskets and cordage or anxiously awaiting the attention of their wives so they could go and copulate in the woods, away from prying eyes. Auroch approached the communal birchwood and hide dwelling his mother and siblings shared with several other women.

Little Wren, his sister, was the first to greet him. She was now seven summers old and as inquisitive and daring as any child could be. She had been tattooed for the first time only several nights ago, and the vertical black marking that spanned both her bottom and top lips was clearly still causing her discomfort.

She hugged him, shouting for Mother.

"Auroch is here! Father sent him, just like you said!"

Auroch spied his other sibling, Boar, playing on the floor with some rocks. He was only four summers old, but his mop of sandy brown hair and dark complexion reminded him of Father. He thought back to their muted goodbye.

Mother sat in the corner with two women. She was holding one of the twin babies that had been delivered last winter at her breast, where it suckled noiselessly. The other baby was also silent, held in a bundle by a girl Auroch knew as Egret. She was the daughter of Old Heron, the leader of the Valleyfolk. Egret was a couple of summers older than him, and he felt his stomach flip as his eyes met hers. The warm season spent in the valley had been good to her, her hair was clean and neatly plaited, and her skin had darkened under the summer sun. Her figure had also changed, and Auroch found it difficult not to stare at her. She glared back at him, unamused by his gaze. Auroch was aware that this may be the last trip to the valley for her; as Old Heron's daughter and apprentice to the tribe's Spirit-Mother, she would likely be taken by the leader of another group as they all congregated on the plains for the cold, harsh winter. Mother coughed, stealing Auroch's attention away from Egret. She did not stand, but Auroch knelt and was received with a familial embrace.

"Thank you for coming, Auroch. One of the babies is sick. His head is hot, and he relieves himself constantly."

"What is he passing?" Auroch frowned. The twin children had yet to undergo the naming ceremony.

"It is watery, not firm." She sighed and looked her son in the eye. "He cannot die before the end of summer, before the ceremony. Three of my children have died, but none before naming. An unnamed child is a mark on my soul I cannot bear when I am returned to the earth. Severe punishment would befall me. I would be unable to move across the sky and join my family, bathing in the river of stars that splits the heavens at night. I cannot endure this." Mother began to weep. Through her tears, she gestured to the bundle held by Egret. "Auroch, please, I have a task for you. You are fleet of foot, and I ask that you help gather what is needed."

She motioned again with her head to the third figure, an old woman that sat beside them. Morning Mist. The old woman did not look at Auroch, nor could she. Morning Mist had been blind for as long as anyone could remember. Her milky pupils disturbed Auroch. The old woman knew things. She had a perfect knowledge of plants and fungi, far beyond any of the other valley dwellers. She knew every possible permutation, which to use on a wound, which best to treat illness of the stomach, and which to ingest to glance into the next world, to travel to the stars and communicate with the souls of the dead. And on this day, Auroch thought, which plant could save his brother. They could not perform the naming ceremony if the infant was sick. It would not be permitted.

"Young man," Morning Mist mumbled, her speech hard to understand through her toothless gums. "I can save your brother, but you must listen carefully." Auroch leaned in but recoiled suddenly as her rotten breath caught him off guard.

"Travel south from the valley…yes, yes. I remember it from when

I was a girl. I could see then. Not more than three days walk, I think. At the end of the valley, go down into the gorge. In front of you lies a second peak. Follow it with your right side to the sunset until you see a narrow pass. The gate of the Old Men of the hills."

Auroch shivered. "The Old Men of the hills?" He stammered. It wasn't a question. He knew of whom she spoke.

"All gone now! All gone since the moon was new in the sky! Before we were fashioned from mud!" She lept up, grabbing a wooden walking stick that lay by her feet before swinging it around to smack Auroch on the ankle. He almost flinched in pain but managed to maintain his poise at the last minute as he knew both Mother and Egret were watching.

"But you will see their works! Follow through the pass, enter through the caves of the Old Men of the hills! And beyond!" She cackled and turned her head so that it appeared she was looking up at him. Auroch thought she couldn't possibly be, but the lifeless balls in her eyesockets seemed to see through him, into the deep recesses of his mind. Auroch suddenly felt embarrassed about the earlier feelings of arousal when he first saw Egret.

"Beyond the caves, you will find a meadow. Oh! I remember the meadow. Beautiful. There you will find the plant we need. The red elder."

"And how should I know it?" Auroch asked. The thought that he might make the journey and not recognise the plant began to panic him.

"Egret has been learning from me for many summers now. Soon, my body will be returned to the mud, and the wriggling creatures will pass through me and eat the contents of my head and heart. She will go with you and help you find the red elder. This is why I have summoned her here today." Auroch glanced at Egret. Her expression was unchanged. Mild annoyance.

"If we leave now, we can make it out of the valley by nightfall," Egret interjected. It was the first time she had spoken. She looked Auroch in the eyes, and he had a similar feeling as he had done moments ago when he had been face to face with the blind old crone.

"Are you ready?"

Chapter 2

It was almost midday by the time Auroch said his farewells. His sister hugged him tightly, as did Mother. Blissfully unaware of the situation, Boar remained on the floor, bouncing tiny painted rocks off one another by throwing them enthusiastically with his chubby arms. The ill baby began to cry, and the loud reminder of their task cut their goodbyes short. Mother gave Auroch one last tearful embrace, and then they were parted. Egret stormed ahead, and Auroch jogged after her, up the valley, away from the woman's camp, and towards the hills of the Old Men and the red elder.

Auroch and Egret spent the afternoon climbing up the southern face of the sloping valley, mostly in silence, taking care not to move too far from the brook that carved its way through the landscape. Auroch noted some red paint on a tree trunk and pointed out to Egret they were leaving the hunting grounds.

"It's further south than I usually hunt," he added, hoping it would lead to a conversation about his exploits and he could impress with the details of animals he had done battle with. Egret met him with stony silence once again. Auroch wasn't sure exactly what he had done to irritate her, but he could only assume it was due to her having to help him with the red elder.

"What makes Morning Mist so sure the Old Men of the hills are dead?" Auroch pondered out loud, attempting to stimulate conversation. Egret stopped. Had it worked?

She turned to him. Her face lit up with fury, and she spat her words with a venom that surprised Auroch. "Before the northeastern plains, before the Summer Valley, all you could see was ice. The Old Men of the hills lived in a world of ice!"

It was only a simple question! "Did Morning Mist tell you of the world of ice?" he asked, knowing that he was poking the bear.

"She didn't tell me. She showed me!" Auroch realised she wasn't angry at him, but he had become a vessel for her discontent with Morning Mist. "She forced me to see it. When I lose control of my body and thrash around, she whispers to me, and her words melt into reality. The Old Men of the hills perished in their frozen land. They are dead."

Auroch was confused by the ringing emotion in her voice. It was unusual for the daughter of the tribal leader to be picked as Spirit-Maiden, but as a young girl, she had fallen to the ground unconscious and spasming. Morning Mist took it as a connection with the next world that the spirits of the dead would visit her as she thrashed around, unconscious.

Her voice trembled, "I saw the world of ice return! Across the Great Plains, along the ancient river that leads us there! Right here in the valley!" She stopped for a second and drew breath. "Do not poke and prod me about the Old Men of the hills. What meant death for them will mean death for you, Calf. For all of us."

Auroch wasn't quite sure what to say after Egret's outburst. They continued on awhile, stopping only to drink from the fast-flowing stream that guided them up the valley. The sun began to set, and the evening chorus of birds began in earnest.

"We have a little light left," Egret noted as Auroch scooped a handful of water to his mouth. She pushed on, not waiting for her companion's response.

"Stop!" Auroch shouted after her. She slowed and turned to face him. "Look up," Auroch motioned upwards, hoping Egret would see the large bird's nest above.

"Do we go up for them? Or continue? If we go for them, we will have to stay here for the night," Egret said, peering at the top of the tree through the rapidly fading light.

After a few moments of debate, the two decided that climbing the tree was the best course of action. Auroch hadn't had eggs in a while, and his stomach began to rumble at the thought of perhaps splitting them and cooking them on hot rocks. He volunteered to climb the tree, but Egret had insisted she scale it after him. Auroch presumed she was worried he would eat the eggs runny and raw at the top of the tree without her there to stop him. Rather than protest, he simply nodded and began to climb.

After removing her footwraps, Egret followed him, carefully noting the branches he used, which ones were solid, and which ones had bowed under his weight. The tree was taller than Auroch had expected, and the sap stuck to his hands and gave them an unpleasant texture. Higher and higher, they climbed. The nest was only a few branches away now. Auroch emerged from the canopy at eye level with the bird's nest but refrained from reaching into the cradle, instead waiting for his companion. Egret carefully tested the strength of the branch Auroch was standing on by giving it an almighty tug and then pulled herself up so that she was standing level with him. She, too, froze in place.

The pair could see all the way down the valley. The wooded sides gave way to the comparatively clear valley floor, and they could make out the various small camps of the settlements at the bottom. The fires had been lit, and the various points of light were dotted around the cleared grassy areas. In the time they had been climbing, it had become darker rapidly, and now the heavens revealed themselves. Thousands of brilliant, bright dots now appeared above them, as they did every evening. Right across the middle of the sky, they seemed to merge into a pinkish, purple furrow that ran from one edge of the horizon to another. The Great River. They had both seen it every night of their lives, but with the settlement directly beneath it, it seemed as if they were seeing it again for the first time. Auroch shook himself from his trance and looked over at Egret, still transfixed by the twilight scene.

"My feet touch the earth, and my fingers touch the heavens," she said quietly, reaching up with her hands as if to grasp the stars, maintaining her balance with her bare feet.

There were five eggs in the nest. The pair carefully retrieved them and used a piece of fabric to cushion them before placing them in Auroch's bag. They descended the tree, now in complete darkness. At the base of the tree, Auroch used his precious lump of pyrite to start a small fire by striking it against flint while Egret searched around for flat stones. They placed the flat rocks over the fire, enjoying the heat that was now beating at the stone. Auroch watched the flames briefly illuminate the individual lower branches of the canopy above them as they flickered and danced. Carefully testing the heat of the stones with her palm, Egret cracked two eggs, one each, over the flat surface. Auroch eyed it hungrily as the runny goo turned white. They quickly ate the meal, Auroch bedding down immediately afterward, where he fell into a deep, dreamy sleep. Egret sat for a while, watching the fire burn down.

Auroch woke just before dawn. Egret was already awake, cooking another egg each. Auroch devoured this one too, making sure he scooped up all the runny yolk with his hands. They then set off, marching up the slope towards the top of the valley. As they continued to climb, they could sense the walls of the valley narrowing. The trees were pushed tighter and tighter together, and the ground became steeper and steeper. Egret began to talk more freely. There were flowers that only grew at the top of the valley, and she seemed to know them all.

"Bell heather," she pointed to one purplish bud protruding from the ground.

Auroch was glad she was in a better mood than yesterday. Humouring her, he would ask the various names of plants, even the ones he already knew. He longed for an opening so he could talk about his hunts, but Egret didn't give him one.

It was midday by the time they reached the top of the valley. Auroch had been so focussed on making an impression on Egret that he hadn't realised how close they were to completing the first leg of their journey. The pair scrambled up the final mess of heather and brambles and arrived on the flat top, near the stream's source. The sun was directly above them in the sky now, and the pair started across the ridge on the second part of their trek. The great mountain range sat directly in front of them, dwarfing the pair. Titanic ancient rocks, like snow-covered giants, had been dropped from the heavens when the world was new, cracking the earth and creating the rivers and streams that characterised the foothills.

"The second peak," Auroch repeated Morning Mist's words.

"Look," Egret pointed to a gorge that sat on the southerly side of the ridge. What Auroch saw troubled him. Water did not move freely through the gorge but had stopped an age ago, and now a murky swamp awaited them.

"Is there a way around?" Egret pondered, "Perhaps we can follow the top and descend when the floor of the gorge is more solid?"

Auroch dismissed her in words he only realised sounded arrogant after they had left his mouth. "It may get steeper further on, and then we would have to backtrack," he said, descending the steep incline.

Egret set off after him. A revolting smell hit Auroch's nostrils almost immediately, and he spied its source, a dead elk, from a distance. Its huge antlers, easily bigger than father length to length, protruded from the mud and slime. The elk's body had deteriorated over time despite the mud, and Auroch could see its ribs poking through its side. The two reached the bottom of the gorge, only a few strides away now from the gigantic beast.

Auroch and Egret took off their footwraps. Better to walk with bare feet for a couple of hours than soaked muddy footwraps for days. The path through the gorge was narrow, and it was hard to see where the mud ended, and the firm ground began.

The two set off without a word. Auroch walked in front, squelching through the water. The walls of the gorge closed in on them, and the sun, moving slowly westwards, meant that the shadows thrown by the steep incline on either side made it difficult to make out where they should be stepping. Auroch became numb to the smell, but clearly Egret was finding it unpleasant. She muttered under her breath as she pulled hard to unstick herself when she put a foot wrong. Every big squelch was accompanied by a gasp of annoyance. Auroch noticed that her angry outbursts were becoming less and less audible. He turned to find her a reasonable distance behind him.

He started towards her, but she waved her arms and shouted, "Keep going. I need to pass water." She squelched a little way off to the side of the gorge and squatted down. Auroch turned, pulled his feet from the muck, and continued.

He was a few more muddy strides further down when he decided to turn around once again. The sound of Egret's feet in the sludge had not resumed.

She was no longer standing by the side of the gorge. He scanned up the sharp bank to no avail. It was as if the girl had disappeared. He had been striding ahead for mere moments. Where could she have gone? Had she used some kind of magic granted to her as Spirit-Maiden? An arm flung itself into the air, protruding from the mud and ooze below the bog water at the bottom of the gorge. She was on her back, just under the surface! Auroch ripped his legs from the muddy water and scrambled up the slippery rocks and grass that lined the sides of the depression. He could see her, but it was impossible to make out her features as the sludge covered her face, obstructing her breathing.

She was flailing around recklessly now, arms and legs thrashing at the thick black slit that covered most of her body. Auroch had seen it before. She was being visited by the dead. Her eyes would become vacant, and she would collapse, violently flailing her arms back and forth until she went still. She would then wake, confused and exhausted. Except now she was doing it under a layer of disgusting bog water.

Egret continued to swing her limbs around, every movement creating more of a vacuum in the mud to pull her down. Auroch moved as fast as he could, but he realised she was further away than he had anticipated. He scrambled back down the slope towards her, but his leg became stuck as he made contact with the bottom of the gorge. He would have to carefully wriggle it free, costing himself precious moments. The great elk that the two had passed earlier intruded his thoughts. Is this what it was like for the elk? Was it with a herd or even just one other elk? Did one have to helplessly watch as the other drowned?

His father's deep voice came to him. "Calm, boy!" echoing from a memory of one of his first hunts. His father helped him steady his hand and fling the spear with precision, accuracy, and grace. "Breathe. Never let the situation overcome you. Harden your heart to panic."

He yanked his leg from the mud and paced ahead. She had disappeared beneath the surface, and the swampy gorge was suddenly silent. Auroch was still several strides away. He couldn't believe it. Not only had he lost Egret, but he wouldn't be able to find the red elder! No! He threw himself at the area where she had disappeared below the surface. The mud that had taken Egret grabbed at him too; he did his best to remember the years of hunting beside his father. Calm and slow. Precise and powerful. He pulled himself through the bog. He glanced at something solid. Could it be? He felt the object. Fleshy and soft, and realised it was Egret's torso. He bent down, found her waist, and firmly put his arm around it. Grasping at the silt with his other hand, he began to pull, straining every muscle in his body, fighting the thick mud. It was impossible to tell if she was still breathing. Auroch gave one final, almighty pull and felt her head emerge from the bog. His own face was now covered in mud, sticking his hair to his forehead, obscuring his vision. He used his strength to propel Egret onto the solid ground at the side of the gorge.

As soon as her head emerged, she began to writhe and throw her arms about madly again. He wiped the silt from her face and held her for a moment as she continued to kick and throw her arms around. Then, without warning, she became limp and heavy for a few moments before returning to life once again, wriggling out of his grasp. She pulled herself onto the wet grassy rim of the bog and vomited. Food, water, and mud came out in equal measure. She pulled at the remaining mud on her face and snorted it out of her nose, coughing and choking and retching on the bank. Auroch was in a similar state. Despite his best efforts, he had swallowed a large amount of the disgusting water. He felt himself vomit. Mud still caked his face, and he snatched at it as if he wouldn't believe they were really out until he could see the sky. Finally, he cleared his face to see that Egret had done the same. Her hair was a disgusting mess, and her skin was caked in mud. Vomit was down her front. She was the most beautiful thing he had ever seen.

The two lay on their backs for a while. They said nothing, but neither felt the need. Auroch wondered what she had seen when the spirits had visited her. Why had they chosen to do it in such a dangerous location? Had they tried to kill her? Regardless, what a joy to be alive! Auroch listened to birdsong. After a time, the chirps changed, and the two became aware they should get moving. The adrenaline began to wear off, and Auroch realised how wet and cold he was. The filth had seeped into every part of his clothes, and suddenly, he felt vulnerable. Without warning, Egret sat bolt upright, a panicked look spreading across her face.

"What is it?" Auroch asked. His voice sounded weaker than he anticipated.

Egret turned and looked at him, her eyes wide with panic. "I think I just saw someone at the top of the gorge. Watching us."

Chapter 3

It took them the afternoon to work the rest of their way through the gorge. They were more careful this time, Auroch following behind Egret, who, despite her ordeal, seemed more confident.

"Perhaps I didn't see anything on the ridge," she said as she dislodged her foot from another deceptively muddy hole. "It could have been another elk! I was exhausted! Morning Mist talks about seeing things that aren't there."

Auroch was not convinced and suspected that Egret wasn't either. The ground became firmer and easier to walk on. They had lost a lot of time to the swamp, and Auroch noticed Egret shivering as they marched single file through the gorge. They needed to get warm and dry soon.

True to Morning Mist's word, the canyon narrowed into a point, and at the end of that point lay a cave opening below a steep rock face. The angle of the sun precluded the two from getting a good look into its gaping mouth.

"It's going to be dark in there, no matter if it's before or after nightfall. Let's make a fire now in the entrance and start working our way through when we are dry," Egret insisted.

Auroch was in no mood to argue. Egret immediately began searching the sides of the gorge for dry sticks they could use as kindling. Auroch joined her, and together they collected a small bundle. Auroch used around a quarter of his preprepared fungus and struck his lighting rock until the sparks jumped to them and began to smoulder. The pair sat shivering around the tiny fire in the entrance as the kindling began to catch. Egret let out a hysterical laugh. It echoed around the cave.

"Are you feeling warmer?" Auroch asked.

He was unsure how to speak to Egret now. She seemed more talkative after being hauled from the mud, although not in a better mood.

"This is my last summer in the valley." Egret laughed again bitterly. "Rather than savouring every moment, I have almost drowned looking after some mewling calf."

Her words cut into Auroch. He began to experience a very unpleasant feeling in his chest. His insides felt tight.

"Morning Mist has sent me here as a test. Do I have what it takes to gallop after some child who reckons himself a Master Huntsman? Can I hold my tongue and watch this boy blunder his way to the red elder? If I can, then I am ready to be sent off to be a Spirit-Mother. I won't annoy or lose favour with whatever man I am pared with when the tribes meet on the great plains."

Auroch turned his back to the fire. His chest had become tighter and tighter, and he felt tears sting his eyes. He mustn't cry. Crying was for infants.

"I rescued you from the bog," he said feebly. His voice had a booming quality in his head that failed to live up to expectations. His back was to Egret and the fire, and he watched as the shadows danced on the walls.

"And why were we slogging through some swamp?" Egret laughed bitterly. "Because you decided it was better than taking our time at the top of the gorge. All to save a baby that has no chance even if we do retrieve the red elder."

This final statement felt like a knife piercing his heart. The pressure on his chest was incredible now. Egret hated him, his brother would die, and his mother would have a weight added to her soul. The elation and pride he had felt at his earlier rescue now deserted him. He was wet, cold, and miserable. Egret laughed again, and his chest tightened further.

It was near sunset before the two felt warm and dry enough to get moving. The break had allowed them to construct several torches each. Egret had brought a small carved bark container full of pine resin that had survived the encounter with the swamp without bog water and mud contaminating it. After finding suitable branches, the two doused them in the resin before lighting them in the fire. The torches would burn down quickly, and each carried spares in their bag, ready to be swapped out. Auroch blew embers from the fire into a small clump of fungus that he knew would smoulder for hours and placed it in the small leather pouch attached to his belt.

He had said little since Egret's outburst but put aside his hurt and spoke in his most authoritative voice. "If you lose your flame or become lost, shout immediately," he instructed Egret.

She nodded. Despite the earlier disaster in the swamp, this was perhaps the most dangerous part of the journey. It took little effort to get lost in caverns like these. He thought back to Egret's sighting of unfamiliar men in the canyon and shivered. Did she really see them? Who were they? If they had hostile intent, they could easily trap them in the network of caves. Auroch took a second to focus his mind and then led the way into the dark.

The pair's every footstep echoed through the dimly lit caverns. Occasionally, they would come across small pools of stagnant water separated from the larger torrent that ran through the inside of the mountain. Egret suggested they follow the stream. Unlike in the gorge, Auroch was inclined to agree. The water cut a handy path through the natual chambers and halls, running downward towards the opening where Auroch and Egret had entered the cave network. It only stood to reason that it would flow in from the other side. The journey was surprisingly easygoing. The ancient waters had sliced a simple-to-follow groove through the hill, and for the most part, the pair could remain upright as they moved, only occasionally having to get down on all fours to scramble up an incline or pass through the small gap from one chamber to the next. Auroch began to feel confident again, gliding gracefully through the caverns. Perhaps this was the easiest part? Suddenly, almost as if the mountain was playing a joke on him, the passageway began to narrow horizontally rather than vertically.

Auroch slid his body lengthways as the walls pressed down on him. The pair edged through the passage, the walls constricting their movement further and further. Auroch thought back to the pain in his chest he had felt by the cave entrance and almost wished for it back.

This was getting more and more uncomfortable by the moment, and he could feel a quiver of panic at the back of his throat. He turned his head, knocking his chin on the wall in front of him, causing his teeth to clack together painfully. Egret was pushing her way through behind him. If she was as panicked as he, she certainly wasn't showing it. The walls constricting them pressed tighter and tighter until Auroch came to an abrupt halt. He couldn't move. He tried to wiggle himself free but to no avail.

"I cannot go any further."

He noticed that the passageway began to widen just a stride or so ahead of him. He couldn't believe his bad luck. His head, his ears parallel to the wall, couldn't be turned to look behind him.

"Breathe in," Egret instructed. Auroch detected a quake in her voice and realised she was more shaken than he had initially thought. She was hiding her fear on his behalf. "My bag is slung around the side facing you. Use your arm to reach into it. I'm holding the torch in my nearest hand."

Auroch followed her instructions and found the canvas flap. "You are looking for a lump of tallow wrapped in deerskin."

Auroch was happy to hear she had a solid lump of animal fat in her bag. After blindly examining a few different items via touch, he found the rectangular block he was looking for and removed it from the bag, bracing the tallow against the wall. Carefully unwrapping the bundle, he dug into the substance with his fingernails.

"Deer tallow?" he asked.

"Yes," Egret confirmed. "Take a big scoop and try and get as much on your chest and shoulders as possible."

Auroch used his limited movement to spread some of the fat around the upper half of his body. It was hard work, and in order to free his right hand, he threw his torch into the darkness before him.

"Hold still," Egret moved her torch closer to him.

He could feel the heat from its flame. It was too hot, making him want to shout or jump away, but the walls prevented him. He could feel the solid tallow melting, working its way down his arms and between the tiny cavities in between his chest and the wall.

"Now, loosen yourself!" Egret said calmly.

He attempted to relax his body, but he was having a hard time controlling his impulse to stiffen. Suddenly, he felt a powerful blow on his back. And another. He budged a little. Egret's torch flew through the air and landed in the chamber in front of him. She was using her full body weight to dislodge him, muttering a prayer to White Owl, the first woman and Maiden of Wisdom under her breath. A final push and Auroch and Egret lurched forward, clearing the narrow passage and stumbling a few strides into the cave. Auroch tumbled to the floor. He could feel the grazes and cuts the walls had given him, but the euphoria of escape drowned out any pain.

Auroch picked up Egret's torch and used it to light another from his bag. He still had around half of the resin smothered sticks that he had entered with. The chamber was large and deep enough that the torchlight couldn't penetrate the back of the cave.

"Thank you." Auroch turned to Egret, who was quietly catching her breath.

"Do you want some balm for your wounds?" She smiled at him for the first time, evidently pleased with her efforts to get them through the passage.

Her expression changed, and her eyes suddenly looked straight through him. She moved towards him and past him, squinting at the cave wall. Auroch's eyes followed her. The walls were covered in etchings. There were shapes and animals adorning every part of the cavern.

They both examined the work in amazement. There was something subtly different about it. It had been made long ago, but Auroch could recognise the spirits that guided men through the river of stars to eternal rest. He noted the familiar shapes of horses from the plains, the red deer, but more impressively gigantic mammoth and rhinoceroses. They had been scratched into the rock rather than painted and were colourless and drab compared to the red ochre art he was accustomed to. The shadows from their torches seemed to accentuate where ancient hands had chipped away to form the beasts, and his eyes followed the subtle grooves upwards towards the roof of the chamber. Across the ceiling, brought to life by the flickering torches, was a gigantic bear, its maw screaming at them. This was a secret place. A sacred place. Unlike the rest, a single handprint adorned the wall, painted with ochre. Egret placed hers up to it—its fingers and thumbs were considerably thicker than hers. Men would only go this deep when they needed to. This art wasn't meant to be gazed upon by anyone.

The two continued on. Auroch felt strangely disturbed as if he had seen something time had forgotten. Who had painted it? The Old Men of the hills? Perhaps they were all still here, waiting for them in the next chamber, ready to pounce? No! That was foolish—the Old

Men of the hills had died long ago, before the moon rose in the night sky and before the ancient chief, First Eagle, had blown light into the sun.

The passageways became broader, and the air warmer. Were they getting closer? Was it close to morning? It was difficult to determine how long the pair had been moving through the various passages. Egret walked in ahead of him confidently, maintaining a thoughtful silence. Auroch wondered if the paintings had bothered her as much as they had bothered him.

She stopped in her tracks, and Auroch almost singed her hair with his torch. He was about to open his mouth when he saw a mound of muscle and hair sitting at the opposite end of the cave, thirty paces or so from them. The mound moved up and down rhythmically, snorting as it inhaled and exhaled. A bear! Auroch had seen one killed before. But that was with a group of twenty or so and led by Bloodied Thistle. The pair stood little chance.

Auroch, despite his fatigue, felt adrenaline electrify him. They needed to get past the animal. They had poor eyesight but would undoubtedly smell the pair if awoken. It could potentially smell them already. Auroch suddenly became all too aware that he had smothered himself in animal fat earlier. Egret made a hand signal at him, using her fingers to imitate legs, walking very carefully on her palm. Auroch nodded in agreement. They were going to have to sneak past the bear. Slowly, they moved towards the beast, taking care not to make any noise.

The bigger problem, Auroch surmised, was if the heat or light of their torches would wake the sleeping bear. Using the thick leather hide of his bag, he smothered the dwindling flame and motioned for Egret to do the same. The bear, Egret, and the cave disappeared, replaced by an inky blackness. Auroch hoped his eyes would soon adjust to the darkness. He pressed himself to the wall. Egret grabbed his hand and gave it a reassuring squeeze. His heartbeat quickened. Pushing himself forward, he slowly moved against the wall toward the next chamber. Slowly, slowly, no noise. His foot stuck a small rock, which flew off with a crack, presumably skimming across the ground. Auroch winced, and Egret squeezed his hand tighter. The heavy breathing continued, and the pair strained their ears for the sound of movement. Nothing.

They moved through the cavern at an achingly slow pace, every footstep careful and quiet. The breathing became louder and louder, and Auroch realised the pair was maybe ten strides away from the sleeping giant. Still nothing. If it moved now, it could tear them in half before they could react. The sound receded as they slid past the animal. Had they done it? Egret seemed to move more quickly, but Auroch stayed the same pace. No mistakes now, not when they were so close. The bear's lair gave way to another chamber, and gradually, the darkness became less intimidating. A beam of moonlight penetrated the cave and illumined the centre of the cavern. Auroch looked up to see the stars through a tiny gap in the cave ceiling. They were almost out. He squeezed Egret's hand this time, and she responded in kind. The pair began to walk at a normal pace before breaking into a run. The geography of the cave became more comprehensible, and Auroch could smell the air, sweet, unlike the stale underground atmosphere of the last few hours. Without warning, they were out. Panting, they fell into the grass, happy to see the stars.

Chapter 4

The grass felt cool and wet against Auroch's skin. Dawn was breaking now, and he reluctantly rose with the morning chorus. The pair had decided to sleep a little after emerging from the cave network. They were tired after the previous day's dangers; they hadn't bothered to light a fire, eating the remaining eggs raw, gulping down the thick liquid inside before bedding down under the stars. Auroch shook off the morning dew that clung to him and took in his surroundings.

They were in a large meadow, hemmed in by wooded hills on either side. Tall grass stretched across the meadow where it met the treeline that covered the steep mountain slope. Huge peaks stood in front of the pair. This was further into the mountains than Auroch had ever been permitted to travel before, and he marvelled at how he now seemed to be standing directly underneath them in this mountain meadow. The only movement came from the long grass swaying in the morning breeze and the buzz of insects, biting and nipping at his legs. He was annoyed that they had supped at his blood while he dosed in the grass. He looked to where Egret had been lying next to him. She was gone. He called out her name, and his voice travelled through the wet, heavy air.

She appeared at the edge of the meadow, purposely sauntering towards him. It seemed to take an age, but he realised she was carrying something as she came closer. Mushrooms!

"Something more to eat!" she called across the meadow. Auroch started towards her, and the pair met halfway. "Raw eggs are good, but I prefer these." She handed him a handful of the fungi, and the pair ate them hungrily.

"I must apologise," Egret said without looking up.

"Why?" Auroch replied, guessing the reason but probing anyway.

"My outburst in the cave. I said many things I know not to be true." She continued to chew on her food. "You did well to get past that bear."

"You did well to help me through that passage."

The pair continued to eat, neither daring to look at one another. Auroch felt considerably better now. After they finished, they sat for a moment, feeling the warmth of the morning sun on their skin. Finally, Egret stood up.

"Time to find the red elder."

Auroch felt guilty. He had been so wrapped up in the trek and the tension with Egret that his mind had partly slipped from the journey's purpose. Poor mother and her newborn! He suddenly felt uncomfortable with the time spent in the grass waiting for dawn and gorging on mushrooms.

"What is the red elder's tell?" Auroch said in his most authoritative voice. He raised himself and straightened his back, puffing out his chest. He saw Egret stifle a laugh and felt his cheeks redden.

"It's a light red, like cooked flesh on top, with dark leaves below. It may have some berries on it."

The pair set off in separate directions from the centre of the meadow, intending to cover more ground. Auroch noticed a large amount of foliage in the clearing, closer to the tree line. White buds and flowers were in full bloom, enjoying the twilight of their lives before their death and rebirth in the coming seasons. The insects buzzed around his head and crawled up his legs relentlessly. The biting was getting worse now. Auroch cursed himself for not getting some repellent mixture from Egret before they parted ways. He could see her foraging at the other side of the meadow. Perusing the flora, he found some kind of plant that he thought perhaps was right, and waved Egret over. She hurried across the meadow, only for her to tell him that he had got it wrong.

"Not the right colour. Too dark!" Auroch heard her huff as she returned to where she had been searching last.

He resumed his hunt, pushing through the tall grass. His nostrils twitched as a pleasant, familiar smell wafted into them. Cooking! He ascended into the wooded area carefully, Egret's report of angry eyes at the top of the valley on his mind. He could hear the crackle of fire now. Retrieving father's blade from his belt, he crept past the tree and laid eyes on an empty campfire with a hunk of meat roasting over hot stones. He didn't recognise what part of the animal it came from, but it smelt like boar. A white bone picked clean, protruded from behind a rock. He inched toward it, carefully peeking behind the boulder. He could see legbones, ribs, and then behind them, a human head, tongueless, its jaw agape and eyes plucked from their sockets. It dawned on him what kind of meat was roasting on the fire. The head had been deformed by several blows and messily detached from the rest of the body, which had been stripped for flesh. Auroch could see where the bones had been cracked, and the marrow scraped out. The smell clung to his nostrils, the odour instantly changing from an inviting hearth to one of deep evil. He felt sick.

Where was the dead man's assailant? Auroch gripped his blade tighter, feeling vulnerable. Only monsters ate the flesh of men. The Old Men of the hills and other half-men who roamed in forbidden places. He had to warn Egret! Quickly leaving the dense mess of trees, he spotted Egret on the far side of the meadow waving excitedly at him.

"I have it!" She shouted excitedly.

Auroch felt a moment of elation despite his panic. Had the cannibal heard her shouts? He couldn't be far away. Auroch's walk turned into a run, and he found himself pelting across the meadow. Egret had paused now, obviously sensing something was wrong. Just a little further!

Auroch blew into her, grabbed her by both arms and shouted for her to run. She looked at him, puzzled, before opening her bag to show him the flower. Auroch didn't care what it looked like, or if she had enough, or if they were prepared for the journey back. They needed to leave.

At that moment, a man melted out of the tree line. He was naked, apart from a headpiece crafted from deer antlers and a belt from which a thick flint blade dangled. He was about average size, and red ochre had been smeared all over his skin, except for his face, which had been whitened with some chalky mixture. White lines in the shape of spearheads adorned his chest. In his left hand, he held a sling and a rock in his right.

Auroch pushed Egret in the direction of the cave entrance. She sprinted, and Auroch went after her. He heard a crack, followed by a piercing pain at the base of his neck. He stumbled. Egret turned, and Auroch shouted for her to go. She kept running. Good. A second stone hit him, this time in the shoulder blade. His entire right arm went numb. He was on his knees now and turned to see the man flying across the field at him, a white-hot rage in his eyes. He was arming his sling with a third stone. Auroch pushed himself to his feet and awkwardly pulled Father's blade from his belt, his arm still numb. The man slowed and took aim with the third projectile, but Auroch was ready for it. He pivoted his body at the last available moment, and it flew by him, missing by a hair's breadth. Feeling was returning to his arm.

Auroch began to move in a semi-circle, slowly. He had never fought a man before, outside of boyhood scraps. Certainly not to the death. Father had told him of the time he had been set upon by two men on the plains. Father had dispatched them, but not before they had taken three of his fingers. Auroch wriggled his own fingers as he thought about this, not wishing to lose a digit or his life.

The man slowed and pulled the chunky blade from his belt. Auroch gripped his own tighter. He and the man circled each other for what seemed like an eternity before his opponent broke loose with a piercing, guttural scream. Auroch felt himself shrink. The painted man charged, running full tilt at Auroch, swinging wildly. Auroch jumped back, dodging the blade. Without thinking, he swung his weapon at the man, hitting him in the ribcage. He felt nauseous as his weapon cut through flesh, blood pouring onto Auroch's hand and forearm. The man screamed again, dropping his knife. He twisted and lurched away from the boy. Auroch's hand, now wet from the man's blood, slipped from Father's blade. The momentum of the twist pulled the sharpened flint from the wound, sending it spinning into the long grass.

Auroch stood facing the man. Blood was beginning to drip down his attacker's legs, rolling off his bare feet and soaking into the soft ground of the meadow. The man let out the same nightmarish scream as earlier and lunged again for Auroch. It caught him off guard; Auroch had been expecting him to collapse! Then he was on top of him, his hands around Auroch's throat. He was squeezing. Tighter! Tighter! Auroch was vaguely aware of the blood from the stab wound seeping into his deerskin tunic. He flailed, kicked and punched, but his attacks were tired and ineffective. He couldn't breathe. The man was strong. Stronger than Auroch. Large hands were crushing his throat. He could feel the insects biting his legs. His thoughts turned to his family. His sister, his brother, the babies. Mother. Father. He had failed. Perhaps Egret could get the red elder back to the valley? His inability to breathe had ceased to bother him. He just wanted to sleep.

The man's head exploded. The pressure on Auroch's throat lifted instantly as his attacker's head was split vertically across the centre in a great gash, exposing fragments of his skull and brain. Gore ran down the man's arms onto Auroch's neck and face. A second blow landed on his exposed cranium. Then, a third. Auroch looked the man in the eyes, sadness and shock visible under the bloody mush. Behind him stood Egret, a jagged, heavy rock in her hands. She hit their attacker again. She was shaking. One last blow bounced off his skull. The man slumped on top of Auroch, his heavy hands falling away from the boy's throat.

Auroch tried to talk, but pain shot up his gullet. His neck felt stiff and bruised, and every breath caused a ripple of agony across his throat. He tried to push the man off, but it was as if his arms had been drained of their vigour. Blood clung to his skin and clothes. Egret knelt beside him, and together, they hauled the corpse off him. Auroch rolled over, smearing blood and brains across the grass. He ripped a tick from his shin.

"Can you stand?" Egret asked, not waiting for an answer before helping him up, lifting him with the full weight of her still-shaking body.

"Thank...thank you," Auroch said. Every word induced agony.

Egret bent down and grabbed a clump of grass, using it to mop the contents of the man's head off Auroch's torso, neck, and face. After taking a moment to collect herself, she strolled calmly over to where Father's knife lay. She retrieved the weapon and used another clump of wet grass to wipe the blade clean. She picked up the stranger's knife and did the same before bending down to examine the man. The damage she had done to his head made it difficult to make out his features, and the headdress, replete with antlers, had been split by the weighty stone. Only threads held it together. Egret removed it, and the man's head disintegrated.

"Do you recognise it?" croaked Auroch. He had never felt pain like this. Sheepishly, he asked, "Is this…Is this one of the Old Men of the hills?"

Egret shook her head and laughed. It was the same cruel, hysterical laugh from the cave entrance. "No. Just a man. A man like you. It's hard to make out his face, but that is a normal skull shattered in the grass."

Auroch felt sick. He couldn't understand how anyone could find this funny. Auroch forced himself to look at the headdress. The antlers were ornately carved and patterned. Did the man do this? He seemed crazed, barely human. Auroch looked to the ground and found the stranger's sling. He wiped his bloody hands on the grass before retrieving and stashing it inside his bag.

From the tree line flew a flock of birds, disturbed by another terrible noise. It was the same screech as their attacker, but this time amplified by multiple mouths. Auroch watched as men emerged from the tree line, one by one. They walked calmly, in a disorganised fashion, across the open grass. The pair stood frozen, rooted to the ground as the band formed a line across the meadow. Auroch counted them. Seven strange men marched towards the pair. Some wore nothing, others fur across the waist, but they were all painted in the same red ochre and chalk pattern as the first assailant. The blood-curdling, inhuman scream once again pierced the air. This time, though, it felt more threatening, as if it was a statement of intent. Auroch and Egret simultaneously snapped out of their shocked state. Without exchanging as much as a word, the pair began to run. They only knew one way out of the meadow, through the caves. He risked a glance behind him and saw the men had started to sprint. Auroch was running at a full pace now. Egret was struggling to keep up with him. He grabbed her hand and began to pull her along with him. The long grass was slowing them down.

They were almost at the entrance.

"No Torch!" shouted Egret.

They had no choice but to brave the cave network. Auroch turned and took one last look at their pursuers, their shadows blotting out the light pouring through the entrance. Auroch had no idea how they had almost caught them. The closest man was carrying a spear, and Auroch noticed the flint head, in contrast to his own made of antler. Auroch pulled Egret into the darkness. The two flew through the first chamber, tripping and stumbling. Where the moonlight had shone through small gaps in the cave roof the previous night, tiny sunbeams now illuminated the floor. Auroch realised that they were getting close to where the bear had slept. He had planned on luring it away or sneaking past, but now there was no time. They were going to have to make a run for it. Scrambling down a slope, the pair found themselves swallowed up by the darkness.

There was nothing in the chamber. No heavy breathing. No bear. His moment of elation was short-lived. They were acting purely on touch and sound. He could hear the men behind them, making their way through the caves. The pair moved along the wall, feeling for the narrow passage where they had entered. The men weren't too far behind, and the lack of light could only hide them for so long. Surely the narrow passage was right ahead of them? Egret found her little store and began to rub tallow onto Auroch's shoulders. Good thinking. He hadn't become any smaller since they last passed through. A small, concentrated light came from the void behind them, followed by faces, contorted with rage.

Their pursuers slowed. They held small animal fat lamps, and Auroch could make out the details of their complexion now. The taller man, who, from the way he carried himself, Auroch assumed to be the leader, had only one eye. A scar ran down one side of his face through the vacant socket, disfiguring him. A cruel smile crept across his face. He twirled a wooden club in his hand.

"You can take the girl," he said to the other man. Auroch understood the tongue, although it was strangely accented.

The second man laughed. He was short and stout. The one-eyed man shouted to the men in the chambers behind and received a muffled response. They were on their way. If they tried to get through the narrow passage, the men would hack them to death as they slowed. There was no way out.

Then, from out of the darkness came a terrible noise. A grunting, snarling roar that echoed through the network of caverns. The stout man stopped laughing. Down the slope into their chamber flew the monster. The massive brown beast thudded onto the cave floor, sending vibrations through the ground and up into Auroch's bones. The bear casually swatted at the stout man, the powerful paws sending him tumbling into the cave wall. Egret pulled at Auroch. Now was their chance! The pair sprinted through the cave, past the ancient art, now hidden by the gloom. Auroch didn't dare to look behind him. He hoped the one-eyed man had been dispatched but couldn't hear the screams he assumed would accompany further violence.

Egret hit a wall but slid her hands around the rock until she found the opening. She entered first, taking the torch from Auroch, pushing and squeezing herself through the narrow gap. Auroch was next. He edged himself in, concentrating all his strength on getting through the tight space. He felt the rock ripping at the skin on his chest. His head was hemmed in now; he couldn't turn it. The air behind him rippled with warmth, and he could hear and feel breath on his neck. The bear was right behind him! Had it killed the one-eyed man? Auroch didn't wish to die but thought it more dignified to fall to the bear than the man's carved wooden club. A swoosh of air kissed his back. The bear was reaching into the crack and trying to claw at him! Auroch felt the air pressure change again. It almost had him. He gave one more heave, and the pressure on his chest relaxed as he moved past the narrowest point. The tallow had done its work, lubricating him just enough to remain out of reach of the animal. He could turn his head and look back just in time to see the beast give one almighty roar before slinking back into the darkness.

After taking a moment to relight one of their remaining torches with the embers in his fungus pouch, the pair made their way back through the winding passages at a relentless pace. In their hurry, they grazed themselves, bruising their skin from smashing against the walls at speed. The passageway widened, and they made their way back into a large, empty cavern.

"Shall we stop?" Auroch asked. It still hurt to talk. Breathing also caused his throat to burn, but he hadn't noticed the pain while running. Now the danger had passed, and his shaking was beginning to subside; he realised how battered and bruised he really was. He was suddenly worried about being able to make it back to the valley.

"No," Egret answered flatly. She carried on walking. Auroch limped after her.

"Did you recognise those men?" Auroch asked. She said nothing, but her silence spoke for her. She had knowledge of the men. "Who are they?" Auroch probed further. No Answer. They continued at pace.

By the time they emerged from the caves, it was getting dark. After a quick discussion, they decided to continue on as far as possible. Luckily, their route through the swamp had been partly preserved in their footprints, and they were able to push through it with little difficulty. Auroch went first, using torchlight to retrace their path, taking care to avoid any missteps. An incident in the dark like this could be a death sentence. They passed the spot where Egret had almost drowned. Auroch looked at her and saw her shiver a little despite the warm night. They came eventually to the great dead elk, its huge antlers undisturbed. Auroch was in real pain now. Every step felt like a feat of endurance. His throat was bruised and sore, and he made little effort to speak. They climbed the wet, mossy slope out of the bog and found themselves at the top of the valley.

"You need healing. But more immediately, rest," said Egret.

Auroch secretly concurred but decided to disagree anyway. "It's half a day's journey. I can walk well enough."

After a short argument, they agreed that they would at least rest for a short while. Egret took Auroch's blade and guarded the pair while he dozed under a tree. The woods were still, other than the evening song of the birds, bidding each other farewell until dawn. Auroch drifted into a disturbed sleep.

Chapter 5

Egret shook Auroch awake. It was still dark.

"Don't panic. There's nobody following us," she reassured him while helping him to his feet. He was still sore. He felt a kind of residual terror that had gripped him in a dream, but it was now beginning to wane. He couldn't remember what he had seen.

"Time to go?" He croaked.

She nodded. Together, they set off down the slope. They said very little to each other, but Auroch felt the gulf between this and the first leg of their journey. There was a genuine warmth radiating from Egret towards him now. Auroch's thoughts moved more directly to his brother. They had only been gone for a couple days, but he easily could have succumbed to illness in that time. Would the red elder work? He wasn't sure if Mother could bear to lose another infant, and her pain would be doubled by the death of a child without a name. They stopped briefly, and Egret washed Auroch's wounds using water from a bladder, retrieved from a stream while he had slept.

"You are lucky none of these are deeper. White Owl must be watching over you." She said before muttering a prayer under her breath.

Auroch was more concerned with his throat. It still hurt to speak, and occasionally he would have to suck in air in a great gasp before erupting into a fit of coughs and wheezes.

It was light by the time they reached the hunting marker. Auroch had never been so glad to see the red marking, a pair of deer's antlers painted on the bark of a birch tree. They carried on, passing the familiar brooks and branches of the valley. Auroch felt like he was reunited with an old friend. They soon found themselves on a small ridge overlooking the men's camp. Egret paused, looking at the figures, as small as insects to their eyes, scurrying from one point to another as they carried out their morning duties.

Auroch noticed tears beginning to well up in her eyes. One ran down her cheek before being quickly wiped away.

"You aren't glad to see the valley?" Auroch asked.

She said nothing for a while, walking several paces and finding a rock to sit on. Auroch found himself sitting next to her.

"I'm not going down there, Auroch," she said softly. Her hands were clenched in her lap. "If I go down there, I will resume my normal duties, my work with Morning Mist. I will finish my training, and summer will end. We will make the long journey back to the Great Plains to the east. Father will grant me to a young chieftain, and I will myself become a Spirit-Mother. I will never return here to the valley. I will never make another decision for myself again. I will be sworn to this young chieftain, to this clan to whom I know nothing and do not care for. I will take a new name. My life as Egret will end."

She overturned her right hand and opened her palm. In it was the red elder. She prized open Auroch's hand and transferred the red elder to his, using her fingers to slowly close Auroch's fist around it.

"Tell them I am dead. Tell them I was drowned in the bog. Or killed by the Bear. Or eaten by those men."

"I cannot lie to your father. Not to Old Heron. He is Chieftain. If he discovered the lie, he would have me exiled or worse."

"You must do whatever you think is right. But I hope you can think of me when you return to the camp."

The two sat for a while, watching the sunrise. Golden beams pushed through the trees and over the peak of the valley walls. Egret rested her head on his shoulder as she gazed down onto the camp, and Auroch sensed she was already in mourning for the life she had lived for sixteen summers. She took his unoccupied hand and squeezed it before standing with purpose. She breathed in and dared to gaze upon the camp at the valley's floor one last time, and then she was gone, disappearing back into the woods.

Auroch limped toward the camp, stashing the red elder in his bag. He didn't know what he was going to say. Could he really lie? She had asked that of him. He passed by the men's camp but saw no sign of Father. Bloodied Thistle, the master of the hunt, was there, however, stoking the remnants of the previous night's fire. Auroch raised a hand in greeting, and Bloodied Thistle responded with the same gesture. He had obviously noticed that Auroch was alone. A concerned frown spread across his face. He's going to ask after Egret! Instead, Bloodied Thistle turned on his heels and began walking towards Old Heron's deerskin tent. Auroch began to feel an anxious tug in his belly. He picked up his pace and walked towards the women's camp. People were looking at him now. He could see Little Wren running to him.

"Brother! Auroch!" she shouted. She gave him a tremendous hug.

"Is the baby still alive?" Every time he spoke, he was reminded how much his throat stung.

"Yes, you must hurry though. You look injured? Where is Egret?" He hushed her with a swift motion of his finger. He was limping faster now.

He entered the tent. Mother sat alongside Morning Mist, the sick babe at her breast. His infant brother was pale and unresponsive. Auroch thought he looked dead. Mother handed the child off to Morning Mist and flew at him, wrapping her hands tightly around his neck.

"You live!" Tears rolled down her cheeks. Auroch felt himself close to weeping but decided to maintain a stoic exterior.

The embrace was cut short by Morning Mist. "The red elder," she demanded. Auroch obediently handed her the flower. "No Egret?" Morning Mist's face darkened with the seriousness of the sky before a storm. She motioned to the door. "Leave now. Your mother and I must attend to your brother."

Auroch sat on the ground outside the tent, fidgeting nervously. He knew he couldn't see the old woman at work. He expected even Mother would have to turn her back or else face some kind of punishment. Only an ordained Spirit-Maiden could watch the Spirit-Mother at work. His limbs ached, and his anxiety over the child's fate made him nauseous. He saw three men approaching in the distance. Father! His usual scowl was replaced by a furrowed brow. Next to him was Bloodied Thistle and the third man, Old Heron. Egret's father, the man who could decide between life and death with a word.

Old Heron was tall and thin. An ungenerous observer unaware of his status might have dared to call him gaunt and uncoordinated. His wiry frame hid strength though, both physical and of the soul. Auroch had always found him an intimidating presence, and as Old Heron strolled towards Auroch at pace, he considered if he should run. Could he really do this? Could he lie for Egret?

He used the last of his strength to pull himself to his feet. Old Heron was in front of him now. He slowed to a stop, looking Auroch up and down.

"Where is my daughter, Auroch?" Old Heron's tone laid down an implicit threat.

Auroch said nothing. Perhaps he could say that the men they had fought had taken her? Or she had drowned in the bog? Or the bear had killed her? Would the chieftain accept these stories?

Without further warning, Old Heron lifted him up and slammed him against a tree. Father moved to stop him, but Bloodied Thistle held him back.

"Where is my daughter!" bellowed Old Heron.

"She ran. Just before we got back to camp! She didn't want to come back!"

Auroch heard the words leave his mouth, but he couldn't believe he had said them. Coward. Old Heron dropped him on the ground. Perhaps this was for the best? One could easily die alone in the woods and hills; their attackers were still out there.

"Thank you," Old Heron said with an uncommon softness.

"Bloodied Thistle, gather a few men and take to the hills. She can't have gone far." He turned again to Auroch. "I suspected she might do this, given the chance. Morning Mist shouldn't have sent her with you."

Father helped Auroch to his feet, and the pair watched as Old Heron and Bloodied Thistle disappeared toward the men's camp, ready to hunt for the young girl.

They waited outside the tent for the rest of the day. Little Wren and Boar, the toddler, played on the ground before them while Auroch recounted his quest for the red elder to Father. He told him of the man in the meadow and their flight from their attackers through the caves. He realised upon revisiting the memory his hands were beginning to shake.

Father sat in silence for a while. "Describe again what they wore?"

"Red ochre, with white markings. A white chalked face and deer antlers on their temple."

"You are sure of this? There is no way you could have been mistaken?"

"No, Father. If Old Heron recaptures Egret, I am sure she will say the same."

Father continued to ponder in silence as Auroch recounted their journey back to the valley and Egret's goodbye.

"You did the right thing, telling Old Heron." He said after Auroch had finished. "I understand how easy it is to be charmed as a young man, but it would have created much discord if she hadn't been able to travel with us back to the Great Plains."

Auroch nodded. A lapse in relations with other tribes was

extremely undesirable. The skins, tools, and jewellery the larger groups brought each other at the winter solstice and gifted brides helped hold a constant peace for the different groups of plainsmen. Still, she had asked him to help her.

Father explained that the healthy baby twin had undergone the naming ceremony while he had been gone. His Brother was called Burgeoning Yew. The sick twin had grown weaker and weaker, his life only hanging by a thread now.

"It would cause your mother great anguish were her son to die before naming," Father said mournfully. "It would cause us both great pain."

The pair resolved to stay in front of the tent. Auroch could hear the muffled chants of Morning Mist from inside. Camp life went on all around them as it would any other day. He had hoped to avoid any exertion for the afternoon but was nabbed by a girl his own age known as Sparrowhawk, who made him sit with her and twist dried nettles into cord and then plait them into a strong rope. His body ached, but he secretly enjoyed the monotony of the work.

Soon, the afternoon gave way to evening, and Auroch found his eyelids drooping. Father poked around the fringe of the clearing for kindling before lighting a small fire in a pit in front of the tent.

"Are we able to sleep here, in the woman's camp?" Auroch asked.

"We will be fine," Father reassured him.

Auroch didn't hear the reply. He had already fallen into a deep, noiseless sleep. The exhaustion of the last few days left his body and, like the tips of the flames before him, drifted into the heavens above.

The sound of crying awoke Auroch. The wail of an infant. The normally distressing sound electrified him. The baby was alive! It was still dark, and the fire was little more than glowing embers, but adrenaline coursed through Auroch. His brother lived! He had done it! He had retrieved the red elder and saved him. Pride welled in his chest, pushing out the feelings of guilt over giving away Egret's flight from the valley. Father was awake too, and the pair stood at the entrance to the dwelling. The distinctive, toothless splutter of Morning Mist's voice pierced the air.

"Enter!"

Father pulled back the deerskin curtain covering the doorway, stepping into the smoky tent. Auroch followed. In the dim firelight, Auroch could see Mother, sweaty and tired, sitting on the floor. Before her lay the baby, wrapped in a light hide swaddling cloth, crying as hard as his little lungs could muster.

"He will live," proclaimed Morning Mist. A globule of spit was ejected from her mouth as she spoke and hit Auroch square in the chest. "Well done, my boy!" Her eyes, despite their blindness, seemed to narrow on him. "And the girl, Hmm? Where is she? Perished? No, No, No. Had you let her die, I don't think you would be back here so eagerly."

"She lives…she didn't want to become like you. She fled before we returned to camp."

Morning Mist laughed; more spittle was sent flying through the air. "Don't worry, Calf, yes, she will be back with us soon enough." She laughed again. She seemed to sense Father was also present. "Take me back to my tent!" She directed her bony finger at Mother now. "Call for me if the child's heat increases again!"

Father knelt to look at the infant, his hard exterior softening slightly, at least to Auroch's eyes. He rested his forehead against Mother's for a moment, before taking Morning Mist arm in arm and leading her out of the tent. Auroch sat beside Mother. She began to sing. She sang of the ice that had covered the world long ago, before First Eagle and his bride, White Owl, had created men of the various tribes from wet peat. She sang of the terrible, deformed Old Men of the hills who had once roamed the land only to be defeated by First Eagle. The baby slowly closed its eyes. Mother looked at Auroch as only a mother could look at her son. She mouthed words of thanks. He had given her a precious gift today. Her soul was to be saved, along with her son.

Chapter 6

Auroch spent the next few days resting and healing. He had tried to accompany Bloodied Thistle on a hunt but had been flatly refused. While he was limping around, he was to stay in camp. Auroch spent much of his day with Mother, watching over the twin infants. The named child, Burgeoning Yew, had been cared for by an older woman who could no longer bear children, and now the unnamed child was on the mend he had been returned to Mother.

Auroch felt listless. On his restless fourth day of sitting in camp, he left Burgeoning Yew with Little Wren and went to find some work. He considered helping Old Heron find Egret. Several men, led by Egret's father, were combing the valley day and night for the runaway girl. After a day spent stalking red deer, Bloodied Thistle and his huntsmen would ascend into the wooded hillside to help Old Heron well into the evening. Auroch shook off the notion of helping them. He had no idea what he would say if he did run into the young Spirit-Maiden.

He found himself idling by a pool of water, where the natural stream that ran through the valley widened. Sat on a large boulder, he began throwing pebbles at the glistening tarn, disrupting the first few yellowed leaves of the year that lay floating on the surface. He had asked Father and Mother about the men who had attacked them to no avail. He threw another rock. And another. Harder and harder. A familiar voice disrupted his aggressive game.

"Young Calf!" It was Morning Mist.

She had a long stick with her, which she used to prod the ground just ahead of her as she carefully navigated the forest. She walked uneasily over to Auroch.

"Careful, the stream is just there." Auroch pointed, before recoiling in embarrassment, realising he had attempted to gesticulate to a blind woman.

"I know where it is, stupid Calf. I have walked this valley since I was a young woman," Morning Mist grumbled. "Help me now as an old crone!"

Auroch rose from the boulder and grabbed Morning Mist by the arm, guiding her to the seat. She sat down and moved her stick around in the dirt by her feet until it eventually glanced off a pebble.

"Aha!" she exclaimed, picking up the small rock. She threw it into the pool with great effort, where it made a satisfying splash. Her toothless grimace turned into a smile, and she let out a cackle.

"What is the point of throwing it if you cannot see where it lands?" Auroch asked.

"It's not where it lands that's the fun part, idiot child! I enjoy throwing it!"

Auroch nodded, although he wasn't sure if he agreed. The pair sat throwing rocks for a while. Auroch began to find her cackle infectious and closed his eyes as he threw, trying to understand Morning Mist's dark world.

"I came to tell you something, boy. Bloodied Thistle just sent word. They've seen the girl up on the eastern side of the valley."

"Oh," said Auroch quietly, unsure of how to respond.

"She will be captured soon, Calf, don't you worry. Better this way than she is happened upon by accident, and you be found a liar. They would kill you. Or exile you if lucky."

"The men who attacked us, do you know who they were?" Auroch assumed someone had relayed the story of their journey to her by now. He had reluctantly told it a dozen times since to various inquisitive parties.

"I can guess." She replied, throwing another rock. "And I believe Egret could too. Interesting, she said nothing to you." She cackled again.

Her lack of trust stung him momentarily. He had guessed that Egret was withholding the truth from him, but the confirmation from Morning Mist hurt. He wondered how she was now. Was she injured? Had Old Heron's men caught up to her yet? His thoughts moved back to their attackers in the meadow.

"Will you tell me who they are?" Auroch asked.

The old woman laughed again and threw another stone. "They were once men who met for darkest winter on the plains, or at least their leader was. There was a schism...when I was young. After violence at the height of midwinter, we saw neither hide nor hair of that man… of the Skull Eaters. The following year, nothing. There were rumours of sightings in the west where the sun goes to die. That a pact had been made with a great beast, of a transformation into a gigantic mad stag, foaming at the mouth."

"The Skull Eaters?"

"That's what we began to call them. The sightings, the rumours coming from those who ventured away from the well-worn trails. We heard of bodies found, the skull crushed, and the juices inside consumed."

Auroch shivered. They seemed like men to Auroch, and the antlers worn on their forehead seemed to be little more than decoration. But he remembered the smell of the man roasting on the fire. Monsters from the west! Like all men, he knew it was the land of the dead. In winter, when the sun's life was at its shortest, the Valleyfolk would move east, only returning after the solstice ceremony was performed alongside the other tribes. He wondered what had caused such schism that would drive men even further west or south than the Summer Valley but dared not ask. He could tell that Morning Mist would not elaborate. They sat for a while longer before Auroch heard the words he had been waiting for his entire life.

"It is time for your father to give up his name. You will be the only Auroch. It is time for you to become a man." Morning Mist said flatly.

Auroch sat in stunned silence. He had known the moment was coming, but he still felt it's weight. He would be father's boy no more. Father would take a new name, and Auroch would become head of the family. His hands began to tremble, the feeling of responsibility overwhelming him.

"In two nights' time, when the moon is at its largest." She stood up and, without retrieving her stick, walked back towards the camp.

Auroch's throat pain had been reduced to a tickle by the day of the ceremony. A good thing too, as it was his duty to do a fearsome shout along with his dance. Old Heron had once again returned empty-handed during his daily hunt for Egret, as had Bloodied Thistle. The chances of finding her were becoming slim now and talk around the camp was that Old Heron was close to giving up. Auroch had smeared himself with red ochre for the ceremony, the red mixture, akin to blood, helping him be reborn in the womb of the forest. His thoughts took him back to the men in the hills. He didn't think he looked as fearsome as them. His father had given him a ceremonial loincloth with shiny coastal shells, traded for at midwinter, sewn into the seams. He had, as per custom, had his hair cut. He scratched the now bare scalp. He had usually cut the hair on his head only once every winter and never down to the skin. Now, he was completely bald. The girls in the camp had giggled as they did it.

Bloodied Thistle, when not searching for Egret, taught him the dance that he needed to perform. It was complex, and although confident at stomping and hollering, Auroch struggled at the more graceful moments. He tried to channel the light-footedness he was accustomed to when stalking prey but had little luck. Bloodied Thistle was becoming increasingly frustrated with him. The pair had always worked well on the hunt, silently communicating and adjusting to the quick changes in herd direction or their prey becoming startled. This was different, however. There was no improvisation.

"Use your toes!" Shouted the Master Huntsman. "Reach! You will do this dance only once! Do you wish to embarrass your father? Do you wish to humiliate yourself?"

Auroch had decided he had no aptitude for this and silently resented its inclusion in the ceremony. He went back to the first position and began again. Children were not permitted to see the ceremony, so Auroch had never had a chance to witness the dance and learn it, as he had with most of the Men of the Summer Valley's various rituals.

"You become a man tonight! How can you learn more in this time!" Bloodied Thistle berated him further. Auroch suspected that he wasn't too far off where he needed to be, but Bloodied Thistle was there to motivate him, nonetheless.

The light began to fade, and Bloodied Thistle decided to end the practice. "Good enough," he grumbled. "I will see you there. Do not shame me." He looked Auroch up and down, embraced him gruffly, and sloped off into the trees.

Auroch sat alone in the clearing. This was a big moment. Not just for him but for Father, too. After he was sure that Bloodied Thistle would have made his way back to camp, he lit a torch for himself using his secured embers before heading to the large fire in the men's camp. He knew Father and the others he would be waiting, ready to see his last moments as a boy. Was he ready to be a man? To take on the responsibility of his family? The stars were out now, and he took a moment to absorb the great stream of tightly packed white and purple that cut the night sky in two overhead. The child's naming ceremony would also soon be upon them, and he smiled to himself, knowing his success with the red elder had meant Mother wouldn't have the mark against her soul that the death an unnamed child would bring. Auroch had known of several women in the tribe whose infants had died before naming. The only way for a mother to wipe the mark from her soul was to spend winter alone in penance and prayer near the land of the dead. Auroch remembered the eyes of a woman they left in the valley when they migrated east in the autumn. He had never seen anyone so scared. She wasn't there when they returned in the spring, and they never found her. He shuddered, glad he had avoided this fate for Mother.

Auroch could see the light from the bonfire in the clearing from quite a distance, and a tsunami of heat followed, crashing over him and causing his skin to prick. He could hear the various shouts and singing clearly now. There were around forty people in the clearing, the whole tribe, excluding the children. Father, Old Heron, and Morning Mist stood by the fire, singing a sad, slow song. An ode to White Owl. Coupled with the rhythm, the terrible heat felt intoxicating, leaving him slow and lethargic. As instructed, he walked up to the trio and knelt before them. Old Heron took a chalky powder and threw a handful of the mixture over Auroch's head, the flakes settling on his scalp and shoulders. The singing stopped. Old Heron took a couple of steps backward as Morning Mist shuffled forward.

"Oh Sky Mother! White Owl!" she began. "This one has survived the perils of infancy and has grown into a man! His spear flies true, he has killed and provided for us! Let him take on the mantle of man. Let him become the only Auroch until he seeds his firstborn."

Two of his fellow huntsmen brought out a deer fawn, alive. Auroch imagined he had been captured earlier that day. Its legs were bound together, and it squirmed helplessly, fighting the strong hands that held it. The fawn was placed before Auroch. Taking his knee, Auroch lay on its windpipe. After a few short moments, the animal suffocated. Auroch took his knife and slit its throat before cupping his hands around the wound and taking a deep drink. Old Heron followed him, then Morning Mist, and lastly Father. Morning Mist took another handful of blood to trace two semicircles on Father's forehead, before turning to Auroch to do the same.

"Auroch," She addressed Father, "You will now lose your name to your son. Are you ready?" Father nodded.

"Auroch." This time she addressed the boy. "Are you ready to lead your family? To take on the responsibilities of manhood?" The boy nodded.

She turned back to Father. "You will now be known as Old Ox."

Now she addressed the son. "You are the sole Auroch until your firstborn son. When we next return the valley, you will have taken a woman to bear this child."

Auroch nodded again. Morning Mist produced a small birchwood bowl, made waterproof using pine resin. The bowl contained a strange black liquid.

"Drink."

Auroch drank deeply, the foul liquid displacing the taste of the fawn's blood. He felt ill. It was time for the dance.

He began to move slowly at first, throwing his hands in the air and pirouetting in front of the fire. A line was forming behind the dead fawn, and each member of the tribe drank hungrily from its neck. He saw Mother take a long gulp of the warm, red liquid. He was stomping now, making his body squat and low before leaping up through the air. They were now singing of First Eagle and how he made the world. Auroch jumped, and the ground beneath his feet began to melt away. Morning Mist's black liquid consumed him.

He found himself making his way through the trees towards a small cave entrance, just big enough to crawl through. Father was by his side, holding a small animal fat lamp. The world span around Auroch, and any attempt to raise his head and look at the treetops sent a spike of nausea slicing through his person. He blinked, and they were in the cave, crawling through the tunnels, the only light emanating from the tiny flame in Father's hand. They climbed down through narrow gaps, squeezing through passage after passage. Time seemed to stand still underground as if seasons were passing above their heads while they crawled down here in the gloom. Father, without whispering a word so as to not disturb the spirits that dwelt in the belly of the earth, held up a hand, indicating for Auroch to stop. The world twisted and Auroch gulped back some vomit, his throat burning. They had arrived.

It was unclear how long their task took them. Perhaps only a few moments, or perhaps generations lived and died above them as they worked. Father watched patiently as Auroch painted, holding the lamp to the flat surface to help him guide his hand. He was sure he didn't need it. Here now, in this tiny cavern, his mind was focussed, the sickness caused by the drink melting away. All that mattered was the image. He didn't remember bringing it, but he had a chalky mixture to his hand that he applied liberally, attacking the wall, his art seemingly crafting itself, his hand controlled by some outside force. His namesake, the great oxen, stood before him as a frieze on the wall, a living being who had been given a soul by his hand. Father stepped forward and did the same. Another great ox, this one older, its lines saggier, less defined. The two men admired their work for a moment. They held their hands to the wall, Father's slightly higher than Aurochs. With the other hand, each put the liquid paint to their mouths and rolled it around the inside of their cheeks with their tongue before spitting it at each other's hand. Two hand outlines now adorned the wall. The boy became a man, leaving his indelible mark here, deep inside the earth. My name is Auroch, he thought. I existed. I lived.

Chapter 7

Auroch awoke to birdsong. He was lying on his own in a clearing, the odour of vomit stinging his nostrils. He opened his eyes, but harsh light forced them closed again. He tried to move his body, but his muscles refused to listen. His head throbbed, the dull thud increasing in volume whenever he moved. He decided the best course of action would be to lie in the clearing for a while.

Auroch fell asleep again for a short time. He awoke again, this time thirsty, and crawled to the stream, now realising it lay only a few strides away from him. Slurping the cool water, he felt life returning to his body. He hauled himself from the ground and shook off the dew that clung to his arms and legs. Auroch took a few moments to orient himself before noticing a rotting tree trunk daubed with the sign of the hare, marking an area that was good for hunting. He knew where he was but didn't understand how he had got so far. He began to walk back to the men's camp. He felt dreadful and hoped that he hadn't done anything odd under the influence of Morning Mist's concoction. He had seen terrible behaviour from men who had drunk the black liquid. A living body could behave strangely when the soul became untethered from its fleshy vessel.

Angry shouts disrupted the morning chorus as he neared the camp. Had he destroyed something? Attacked someone? The Skull Eaters! He began to sprint, his head still pounding. He vaulted over a log and stumbled. He ran out of the woods to see Bloodied Thistle and Old Heron dragging a kicking and thrashing mass behind them. It was a woman covered in dirt and mud. Her hair was tangled and ratty, her legs battered and bruised. Egret. Auroch noticed her hands were bound, as were her feet. Her back was dragging along the ground, and Old Heron and Bloodied Thistle held a leg each, hauling her towards the camp. Auroch stopped in his tracks.

"Auroch!" shouted Bloodied Thistle, laughing, "How are you this morning? How was your journey into the caves? We caught the vixen!" Old Heron shot Bloodied Thistle a disapproving look, wiping the smile from the Master Huntsman's face.

"A man now, eh?" Old Heron dropped the pretence of disapproval and laughed. "Look my beautiful daughter has come back to us!"

Auroch looked at the injured, dirty girl they dragged behind them. Her head turned, and her wide, hazel eyes looked straight at him. She knew! She knew Auroch had told them she had ran away! Auroch could see tears welling up in her eyes, not of sadness but hate, spite, and frustration. Auroch tried to say something, but his mouth opened and closed impotently.

The pair continued pulling Egret towards the men's camp. Auroch sat on a rise and watched them as they treated her as if she were a deer carcass, tossing her painfully to the ground. He replayed his betrayal over and over in his mind, disgusted by his cowardice. He began to feel a twinge of hatred towards the men below. He watched as Bloodied Thistle found a tree and began to wind the same heavy rope Auroch had made days earlier around it before securing Egret's foot tightly to the tree using the same line. Old Heron unbound Egret's hands, and she flew at him. Her father easily grabbed her flailing wrists and held her. He pushed her face first into the ground, pulling her arms behind her before retying them behind her back. Her legs, still unbound at the ankles, were still tightly secured by the rope to the tree trunk. Auroch had seen this before. The prisoner could move a few paces by standing and walking but couldn't free their hands or feet. It was common punishment for minor transgressions in the valley to be tied like this and left without food for several days. Egret squirmed angrily on the ground, spitting and cursing the tribe's patriarch.

Old Heron laughed, "There you will stay, child, until the long walk back to the great plains. You will be fed, watered, and cared for. But I will not allow you to gamble away the Men of the Summer Valley's prosperity." Auroch watched from the rise as Old Heron sat with his daughter, laughing through her screams and protestations.

Bloodied Thistle made his way up the hill towards Auroch.

"We finally caught her!" He laughed before noticing the concern on Auroch's face. "You may be a man now, but you still have the stupidity of a boy! Don't let her pretty face charm you! If we are to survive the winter, we will need to trade with the other tribes on the plains. Many would have starved if she hadn't been recaptured by the end of summer. She will live the life of a great Spirit-Mother, married into another tribe!"

Auroch said nothing, fearing that if he opened his mouth, he would be unable to prevent himself bursting into a torrent of tears. Bloodied Thistle was right, of course. He had done what was expected of him. If they hadn't been able to present her to another young chieftain, then alliances may have been broken, and it would have been a difficult winter.

Bloodied Thistle ordered Auroch to follow him. They gathered two other men from camp, as well as Father. Upon seeing him approach, Father embraced him.

"Well done, Auroch," Father beamed at him. "I remember when I became a man! A pleasure and honour to share the depths of the earth with you!"

The previous night's elation had given away to the more tangible pain of watching Egret broken and bound, tethered to a tree. Auroch didn't let it show, joining in with the jokes and laughter. They retrieved their hunting dogs and made their way into the dense tree line, looking for something to eat. The dogs quickly picked up a scent, and the hunters chased them through the woods, jumping over obstacles and ducking below branches. They had smelled a fawn, which Bloodied Thistle managed to grab and hold without killing the animal. Auroch watched Bloodied Thistle grab the small deer's legs and bend them back, causing it to shriek in pain and fright for its mother. The men waited, but no parent appeared. Angry that his lure hadn't worked for the larger animal, Bloodied Thistle suffocated the fawn so the deer would lose no blood. It had been a disappointing morning.

Auroch spotted bees humming and buzzing around the trunk of an oak. He pointed it out to the others, and they urged him to climb the branches and retrieve the honeycomb. This was unexpected, as the first person to taste the honeycomb was usually Bloodied Thistle, Father, or one of the more senior hunters. Things had changed. He was a man now. He easily scaled the branches and made his way to the top of the tree. The violent kamikaze stings of the bees did little to stop him as he reached into the nest and broke off a piece of the comb. He took a bite, feeling the sweet honey and the juicy grubs sliding down his throat. Ripping off piece after piece, he threw them down below, where the men collected them in woven reed baskets or ate them on the spot. After he had endured about as many stings as he could handle, he made his way back down. Fresh red lumps covered his body, but he knew he would feel better after some balm that Mother could prepare. Bloodied Thistle was unsatisfied with the day's hunting, but the honeycomb put him somewhat at ease.

The men trudged back to the camp to find that another small hunting band had been far more successful. They found two young doe separated from the herd and butchered them. The deer were moving further and further away from the camp now, indicating the end of the season. Auroch found himself bieng congratulated by everyone he passed as he walked through the women's camp to deliver the honeycomb. He handed out the sticky, sweet substance and, in return, was given a mix of hazelnuts, berries, and tubers gathered earlier that day.

He entered Mother's tent to see her nursing the two babes. She audibly exhaled when she saw his stings.

"Did they make you climb the tree?" She asked angrily.

Auroch nodded. "It's my duty."

She placed the infants down on a worn deerskin mat and aggressively applied a balm to Auroch's shoulders and arms.

"They caught Egret, you know! I expect you have seen her already. Poor girl. She looks miserable up there. I hope they free her before the summer's end! I could use some more help with these two little ferrets!" She gestured to the two tiny pink humans lying on the ground.

Mother talked to him for a while about the various goings on in the women's camp. Auroch got the impression she wasn't telling him these things to inform him of anything but rather to expel her own thoughts. He listened for a while longer than he needed to before embracing her.

"You will help me with the unnamed child's ceremony? It was a pity we could not name the two children at the same time." Mother said.

Auroch nodded. The two embraced again, and then he departed.

There were no more shouts or angry outbursts from Egret as Auroch approached. He had bought a piece of the honeycomb with him but regretted it as the sticky texture was beginning to make his hands feel a little uncomfortable. He longed to wash them in the stream. He saw Egret lying on her side below the boughs of the tree. Her dark hair covered her face, and he couldn't make out her features, even if she were awake. He sat beside her, not daring to initiate conversation until she was ready.

"Leave." Her voice was muffled behind her hair.

Did she know it was him? Or did she think it was one of Old Heron's men who had come to check on her?

"It's me, Auroch. I have brought you something to eat."

"I have been offered no shortage of things to eat." She said sharply, no notes of affection on her tongue.

"Are you hurt?" Auroch asked, not sure if there were anything he could say that wouldn't sound apologetic and weak.

"Only my soul," she spat. "I thought you would help me. Or at least give me some time. But you told my father immediately. Hunters were looking for me constantly. I could barely find enough food to eat or move for fear of being spotted."

Auroch opened his mouth to apologise, but no sound left his lips. There were no words that could make this right.

"You did the right thing for the tribe." She laughed. "But I had hoped you would do the right thing for me."

Egret rolled over, showing her back to him. Auroch listened for sobs but heard none. He thought about taking his flint knife, cutting her bindings, and freeing her. Perhaps he could run with her; they could hide until the tribe left in the early autumn and survive on their own. It was wishful thinking. Deep down, he knew he couldn't do it. He couldn't take the chance of discord with the other tribes when they migrated back to the plains. Mother, Father, and his siblings could starve. He despised himself for it but couldn't grant Egret the freedom she craved. Getting up, he descended the slope towards the men's camp without looking back. He joined the roaring fire and the men roasting meat and laughing around it. Despite his new role in the tribe, he felt less a man than he had ever been.

Chapter 8

Although he wouldn't play a significant role in the naming ceremony, as the new head of his family unit, Auroch was to bear responsibly and participate in the celebration of new life. He had avoided Egret since they spoke, only glancing to see her pacing around or sitting forlorn in the dirt. Auroch had spent the intervening days hunting hares with some success. This particular morning, he had managed to skewer a few freshwater fish from the shallow river that ran through the valley with a harpoon carved from a sharpened antler. Father helped him gut the fish, and although he needed no instruction, let Auroch guide the process and dictate the pace of the preparation. They smiled as they worked, and Auroch felt as if he had regained some confidence that had been knocked out of him due to Egret's capture. The sun was beginning to dip behind the horizon. It was almost time.

The two men rubbed themselves with ochre before heading to the large bonfire by which Auroch had undergone his own transformation only recently. The whole tribe wouldn't be present for the naming; children were born frequently enough and bestowed with a moniker within the season of their birth, so the ceremony was reasonably common. Auroch didn't dare guess what name Morning Mist would give the child. She always knew the right name to choose. He wondered if this was something she had taught to Egret. When she became Spirit-Mother of her new tribe, perhaps she would always know the correct name to be chosen too. Auroch's mind drifted back to the defeated young woman on the hill, and he suppressed a pang of guilt. He stood behind Morning Mist, his back to the bonfire. It was dark now; as before, he could feel the familiar itching of heat on his skin.

Mother emerged from the darkness, carrying the child. She quickly passed him to Morning Mist, who began to recite an incantation, speaking in rhyme of the child's soul, which would be fully formed when named. She smeared a foul-smelling paste on the infant's forehead. Auroch's nostrils flared, and it made him gag. The baby started crying. Despite the odour he breathed a sigh of relief. The ceremony was almost at a close. Morning Mist Placed the baby on the ground gently and declared, "Child, born of the earth, you shall be tethered to this life with your name. You shall grow to be strong, swift, or cunning. You shall partake in great triumphs but will also suffer many defeats. But fear not. You soul shall be protected, through the name that will be granted to you. Your name is—"

A shout, followed by screams cut her off mid-sentence. Out of the darkness ran a woman Auroch knew as Young Glebe. She addressed Father first, rather improperly, as Auroch was now head of the family.

"The trees have gone up in flames!" She cried, hunched over, breathless.

Auroch forgot himself and looked at Father, expecting some command or another. Father simply looked back at him.

Auroch was in charge now. He needed to take action. "Father, take the family to the clearing by the river." It sounded like someone else was speaking, but his own lips were moving. "I will go to the fire and try to help Bloodied Thistle and the others put it out."

Father nodded. Mother picked the baby up from the floor. Father took Morning Mist by the arm, and they disappeared into the darkness.

Auroch ran in the direction of the men's camp. As he left the bonfire behind, it became easier to see the red haze snaking high above the treeline. He realised it must be close to the rise at the edge of the men's camp. Egret was there, tethered to her tree! He sped up, hoping that the dry trees on the edge of the clearing hadn't caught fire. The red glow was everywhere now, and thick black smoke wafted into his nostrils. The fire was out of control already. A deer flew past him, bleating, clearly terrified.

He reached the clearing that contained the men's camp. A wall of flame stood in front of him. The inferno had already engulfed the treeline, throwing a harsh, unnatural light on various figures scurrying below. Auroch spotted Bloodied Thistle amongst the men and sprinted over to him.

"Auroch!" Shouted the Master Huntsman! "Grab everything you can, and then make your way to the women's camp!"

An old man, known to Auroch as Mouse, clung to Bloodied Thistle's arm, terrified. He could barely walk, and his weight slowed the Master Huntsman down.

"We need to leave the valley now!" Auroch shouted back. Bloodied Thistle nodded. This wasn't the first fire that the men had dealt with. Their only option now was escape.

Auroch began gathering tools and food, working out the maximum weight he could carry. Where was his bag? He looked up to see Egret in the distance on her feet, clearly still tied to the tree. Auroch realised that in the panic nobody had untied her.

"Bloodied Thistle!" he called through the chaos and smoke. "I'm going to grab Egret!"

Bloodied Thistle turned, and the old man turned with him. Without warning, a flint-tipped spear flew through the air, hitting old Mouse between his shoulder blades. The fear in his eyes morphed into surprise and, a second later, into peace as his ancient frame hit the ground. Another spear narrowly missed Auroch's feet. A third flew and hit the torso of another man. He slumped over, the belongings he had desperately been collecting toppled to the floor. Horrified, Auroch saw familiar deer antlers emerging through the smoke, with white painted faces behind them. There were dozens of them! Skull Eaters! A barrage of rocks and spears whizzed through the air. Several stones bounced off Auroch's torso and body, but miraculously, the spears fell short.

The intense pain of the stones hitting him made him stagger, and he turned back toward Bloodied Thistle. The Master Huntsman was knelt over Mouse. His front and hands were covered in blood. Auroch wasn't sure if it belonged to the old man or his mentor. He seemed to snap out of the shock at the same moment as Auroch.

"Run!" he screamed.

Auroch turned back towards the advancing Skull Eaters just in time to see an injured fellow hunter, Green Frog, have his head smashed in by a carved wooden club. Auroch recognised the assailant as the one-eyed man from the cave. His single pupil locked onto Auroch, and he laughed before shouting something unintelligible through the roar of the fire. Auroch scrambled away from him. Egret! He saw Bloodied Thistle stagger into the wooded path towards the woman's camp. He knew the one-eyed man was on his tail, but Auroch struggled to his feet and ran as fast as he could, half crawling, half running up the rise.

Egret sat on the floor with her back to him. She had a small, unsharpened stone in her hand, which she was desperately using to try and cut her bound hands. She flinched when she heard Auroch's footsteps behind her, spinning on the spot defensively. Auroch saw a look of relief fall momentarily over her face before morphing into a look of horror as he approached.

"Auroch!" she screamed, and he turned to see the one-eyed man barrelling towards them. Auroch fumbled for his blade, but the man was mere paces away. Out of the smoke and darkness, a figure launched himself into the one-eyed man. Auroch could make out the gaunt face of Old Heron. He was unarmed but threw himself at the man with an admirable fury. The two men grappled on the ground.

"Free her!" shouted Old Heron, who managed to pin his opponent.

Auroch turned to Egret, finding her wrists. He cut through one coil of rope with ease, and the rest unravelled. Turning his head, he saw the two men still struggling. It was unclear who was winning the bout. Auroch bent down and quickly examined the rope by Egret's feet. Finding the most vulnerable point, he hacked at it, cutting her bonds. She jumped and yelped in pain. He had caught her skin with his flint.

Auroch turned back to the fight to help the chieftain, only to watch in horror as the one-eyed man, now on top, brought his club down onto Old Heron's skull. He went limp. The strong, wiry muscles that had been fighting only a moment earlier fell still in an instant. He couldn't see the extent of the damage, but he knew the Old Heron was dead. Egret screamed. The one-eyed man looked at the pair, a terrible smile once again crept across his face. Then Egret was gone, flying into the woods at pace. Auroch followed, sprinting as hard as he could.

He was barrelling through the forest blind, the smoke stinging his lungs, and fire's roar in his ears. He could hear the scared cries of animals. He shouted for Egret but heard nothing in response. He glanced behind him, but he couldn't see the one-eyed man. He saw a hunting marker on a tree through the smoke, allowing him to get his bearings. All he had to do was head downstream, and he would be where Father had taken the family. The fire was getting worse. The heat, noise, and smoke were becoming unbearable. Auroch fell several times, his hands becoming blistered and bloody. He winced as he picked himself up. He was almost there. Just a bit further! He thought about how scared his younger siblings must be. Hopefully, other survivors from the camp had managed to escape the Skull Eaters. Through the trees, he had glanced at the woman's camp. It too, was now aflame.

Auroch slipped out of the trees into the small clearing. The thick smoke was causing him to choke, but as his eyes swept across the scene that greeted him, he inhaled sharply. On the ground in front of him lay several bodies. The first one he recognised as Mother. She was splayed out on the floor, motionless, a dark liquid seeping from her head into the soil. Next to her lay Boar, his brother, only three summers old. He was on his back, and Auroch had a clear view of the terrible wound on the rear of the child's head. Vomit began to work its way up his throat. A tiny, inert arm stuck out from beneath Mother's frame. One of the twins. Auroch dry heaved. Was this real? How could this possibly be real? That's when he saw Father. He was slumped, his legs lying in the stream, his eyes wide open, and a large red patch on his chest. He was looking straight up as if gazing at the stars one last time. But there were no stars, only a thick smoke that obscured the night sky. In his arms, he held Little Wren. Auroch turned away. He couldn't look at her. He vomited. They were all dead. This was impossible. He slumped to the ground next to Mother's feet, feeling drowsy. He was coughing and spluttering, but he just wanted to sleep. Auroch put a hand tenderly on her leg. He could still feel her warmth.

He heard coughing that wasn't his own. Mother? Was she alive? He pulled himself to his feet, but Mother's body was as still as it had been previously. A lump towards the tree line moved. Auroch edged towards the shape, still in a state of unreality. He found himself over the mass, and kneeling, he turned it over. Morning Mist.

"Calf…" she spat the words "help me…"

Auroch picked the tiny old woman up in his arms. He found

himself carrying her away from the scene. It was like he was watching someone else perform his actions. Was he still undergoing part of the ritual? Had he drunk one of Morning Mist's elixirs? Surely Father couldn't be dead? He was bigger and stronger than any man Auroch knew. But his eyes! He stumbled out of the woods back into the large clearing. In the distance, he could see the women's camp in flames. He saw figures engaged in tired, futile fights with Skull Eaters or, even worse, being subjected to violent indignity by their attackers.

He laid the old woman down on the grass, noticing his hands were covered in her blood. She lay there, breathing heavily. Auroch looked up, and despite the flames ripping through the woodland all around him, he could just about make out the sky.

"I am sorry," Morning Mist wheezed. "So sorry".

Auroch wasn't sure if she was talking to him or what she was sorry for. He watched as the old woman died beneath the stars. Auroch felt the life leave her body, her useless eyes rolling backwards into her head.

Auroch sat with her body for a long time. He felt strong arms grab him from behind and bind his hands. He felt them shove him, urging him to walk. He didn't care. This wasn't real. This couldn't happen. It didn't matter where they took him.

Autumn

Chapter 9

Auroch sat on his backside, tied up in the mud at the river's edge. His hands were bound behind his back, and a short rope connected his ankles, forcing him to walk only in small strides. The Skull Eaters towered over him, their sharpened, flint tipped spears ready to strike. It had been days since the massacre, and still, Auroch was struggling to comprehend the fate of the Valleyfolk. Three men sat bound next to him. Bloodied Thistle, his face swollen and beaten, and two other hunters, Black Aldar and Yarrow. Black Aldar was one of the older hunters in the group. His face was turned to the ground, presumably in mourning for his young child. Auroch assumed the infant must be dead, along with his bride. Yarrow was a similar age to Auroch, but the two had never got on as children and spent as little time together as possible. Like the others, he seemed broken and forlorn. He had no child or woman, but his parents would have been counted among the dead. It was still unclear to Auroch how many of the inhabitants of the Summer Valley had escaped and how many had been killed or captured. As far as he could see, the four of them were guarded by only three Skull Eaters.

He had been in a daze for the first few days since his capture. With his wrists bound, he hadn't needed any prompting to be shuffled from place to place at speartip. The Skull Eaters shouted at him as he sloped past the bodies of men and women he had known his entire life, strewn lifelessly on the ground. The one-eyed man had barked orders at their guards, and Auroch had been marched to a clearing where his defeated, broken travelling companions had joined them. Then, flint points pressed into their backs, they had been urged forwards, marching through the still smouldering forest. The heavens had opened, and thick, cool rain had extinguished the growing fire and turned the soil into a quagmire. Each of the prisoners had slipped and fallen several times, and the guards had screamed at them to get up.

In his catatonic state, Auroch had lost track of the exact route into the mountains. They had been pushed south, far into the hills. He was marched up wooded slopes that soon became unfamiliar, the wind growing colder and harsher the higher they climbed. It wasn't the route he had taken with Egret, and he couldn't see any obvious landmarks. All he knew was that they were heading southwest. Between the fire, the forced march, the rain, and his general state of mind, he had lost track of how long they had been moving. None of his fellow prisoners said a word; each man wore a pained, grieving expression on his face.

Auroch guessed it had been maybe six or seven days walking from dawn till dusk. They had been fed some deer meat, likely taken from the raided camp, but exhaustion was now slowing them down. It was the first time Auroch had climbed all the way through the mountains to the south of the Summer Valley. None of his people were permitted to climb into the heavens lest they disturb First Eagle's slumber. He gasped as he sat down to rest one evening, only to be confronted by a view that seemingly went on forever. He could see beyond his decimated home easily and, with his eyes, could follow the river that ran from the valley floor as it turned into a raging torrent and cut a path through the distant plains. He wondered, if on a clear day, it was possible to see all the way to the great rock where the tribes met for the winter solstice. Despite his distress, he marvelled at the view above the clouds.

As quickly as they had ascended the mountains, they descended them again, crossing through barren chasms and craggy passes. Eventually, the naked slopes began to resemble the wooded foothills on the other side of the mountain range. Their captors seemed to have agreed that they could rest for longer than usual and had allowed them to squat or sit in the mud of a mountain stream clogged with dead branches. The violence of the attack on his tribe and the deaths of his family had begun to take a more digestible form in Auroch's mind. He was now quite certain that what he had experienced was real, that Mother, Father, and his siblings were all dead. He would have to find a way to escape. Or he could perhaps kill himself, given the opportunity. The second thought had shocked Auroch when it first entered his head, but the more and more he thought about it, the more feasible it became. There was a horrible ache in his chest, a searing pain that grew every time he pictured his parent's bodies in the clearing. If he could kill himself, that feeling may go away, and he could meet them in the next life. The Child! The new baby was never named! Mother's soul! A new pain hit him. Even if he ended his own life, she wouldn't be there waiting.

Bloodied Thistle was the first man to speak. "They're taking us in the opposite direction to the great plains, towards the dying sun." He said, his voice hushed.

Bloodied Thistle was perhaps the luckiest of the four. He and a woman named Blue Feather had been expecting a child two summers past, but both mother and infant had perished during childbirth. His parents had died of sickness around five or six summers ago. Bloodied Thistle had retreated into himself, showing only enthusiasm for the hunt and mentoring Auroch. In the two years since he hadn't found another woman on their trips to the great plains nor in the Summer Valley. Perhaps it was better this way? Auroch decided there was a difference between losing a loved one through natural misfortune rather than violence. He wasn't unfamiliar with the death, but this felt different. Below the ache, he felt a bubbling anger.

Bloodied Thistle stood up in the riverbed, his legs caked in mud. The guards stood on the bank, menacing him with their spears, but the Master Huntsman didn't move.

"None have walked this far west beyond the valley for an age. Only eastwards on our autumnal journey." He proclaimed. "And now we know why we do not head beyond the mountains. Only monsters dwell here, in the place where the winter sun dies."

Much to his own annoyance, Auroch had paid little attention to the landscape of the foothills but rather drowned himself in a grief-stricken haze. He assumed they had marched an almost straight path southwest through the mountains but had not studied the passes with his usual care. Auroch felt a kind of collected calm fall over him. He understood what Bloodied Thistle was suggesting now; they had to wait until the time was right.

The men shouted orders, and the prisoners got to their feet. Auroch wished that Bloodied Thistle hadn't risen as he had clearly aroused suspicion in the guards. They positioned themselves as instructed by their captors. A guard walked in front of Yarrow, with Auroch and Black Aldar before him. In front of the pair, another guard walked. All of them were behind Bloodied Thistle, who had made the journey with a flint-tipped spear pressed to his back. Progress was laborious, seemingly taking the group forever to navigate the rough ground of the forest beyond the mountains. Bloodied Thistle led the pack, but the short rope behind his ankles made him cumbersome and prone to trips and falls. Auroch realised he and Black Aldar were in the middle as the Skull Eaters must have assessed them as the two men who had been most broken by the massacre. The least likely to fight back. As they continued walking through the woodland, Auroch carefully studied Black Aldar's movements. His head and shoulders were slumped, and he still showed little inclination to talk.

Auroch pushed thoughts of the last few nights away, focusing on placing one step in front of another. He was starving despite the scraps they had been fed. The group walked until the evening sun blinded Auroch, stinging his eyes as he walked directly towards it, the mountains on his right all but hidden by the trees. Good, he thought. Easy to remember. The group emerged from the tree line to the mouth of a river.

Above the river he could see a series of caves, and in front of them on the bank, scattered tents, presumably above the point to which the river could swell. Figures hurried to and fro, carrying out a day's work familiar to Auroch. He could smell meat cooking, and his mouth began to water. The thought of the butchered man he had come across roasting in the meadow silenced these thoughts, making him feel suddenly grateful to have eaten scraps stolen from his own camp. He saw a figure run down the bank. It was a young girl, perhaps no more than seven summers old. The Skull Eater in the middle of the pack broke formation and ran towards the child, scooping her up in his arms. The child giggled, and her father laughed along with her. Auroch couldn't help but be reminded of Little Wren, how she had run to him upon returning from the meadow, or how Father would pick her up and hold her after days away on a lengthy hunt.

He considered that if he got the chance, he might kill this child. He surprised himself with the depth of his anger. He would kill this and every other Skull Eater child if it could bring even a fraction of the pain he had been dealt to these men. The young girl was sent scurrying back to the cave, and the group headed downriver into a broad canyon.

The water was shallow and cold and lapped at their thighs as they waded through it. Walking with his legs tied close together and his hands bound was hard enough even before they were in the water. There were several stumbles from each of the men. Yarrow fell on his front, necessitating one of the guards to reach in and hoist him to his feet.

Shortly, they came upon another large cave that was clearly inhabited. Outside stood five men equipped with the same flint spears as their captors. The prisoners hung back while words were exchanged between their guards and the Skull Eaters in front of the cave.

"Too many…not long now… Great Tusk." Auroch strained his ears to hear what the men were saying in their strange accents.

He had the impression that those waiting at the cave were upset that they had been brought there. One of the guards must have said something that broke the tension as suddenly all the men were laughing and slapping each other on the back.

The prisoners were led past the entrance to the cave, and once inside, Auroch's eyes began to adjust to the darkness. In the cave sat about five other men. Three looked around twenty summers, but there was one very elderly man and a young boy who couldn't have seen more than ten summers. Four of them formed a group in the middle and, in hushed tones, presumably began discussing the new arrivals. The old man sat alone in the corner. He was naked apart from a dirty loin cloth and had a large, messy grey beard. His skin was smeared black from soot and grime. Auroch noticed all the men were dirty. He felt a sharp spear tip in his back and jumped forward into the cave with a yelp. A guard laughed.

"We are captives then?" He realised this was the first time he had spoken since the massacre.

Bloodied Thistle was squatted down by the men. "Can you understand me?" He said to the group. In the gloom, he could make out a large green tattoo on the back of one of the men. It was a hand. Observing the other men, he noticed they all had the same, excluding the young boy.

One of the prisoners, around the same age as Father turned and replied, "Of course! I would recognise that jewellery anywhere!" He pointed to the deer incisor necklace Bloodied Thistle wore around his neck. "You come from the Summer Valley!"

"The Men of the Fen!" Exclaimed Yarrow excitedly, opening his mouth for the first time in days. They were another group who visited the plains to trade in midwinter. They often had interesting medicines made from plants and fish to trade, taken from the peat bogs they called home. Compared to the Skull Eaters, they were a friendly face.

Bloodied Thistle' frame immediately untensed. "You were taken too? Did they attack the fen?"

"No, a small group of us were captured south of the bogs, following the trail of oxen who wandered through our home."

The old man in the corner made a strange guttural coughing noise. He stopped, and his companions became as quiet as dead men.

"They're going to make you dig." The old man spoke awkwardly as if he had to think about every word. "The flint here is miraculous. I have never seen such a quality. What a sound it makes when you strike it!" He pulled himself from the floor slowly before walking towards the group of men. "Woodpecker," he pointed at himself. "My Name is Woodpecker."

Bloodied Thistle took the lead once again. "These men follow you?" He asked.

"Yes. I was on my last hunt before my body was returned to the bog. Until we return to the fen, I am responsible for these men." He paused and thought for a moment, "What became of Old Heron? I much valued his friendship."

Auroch was unsurprised to hear late chief's name. Old Heron had been one of five Grand Chief from the larger tribes who oversaw the meeting at the winter solstice. Part of his role, along with the Morning Mist, was to make connections between people as they welcomed the return of longer days. Auroch wondered if Egret had also been trained to act as a friend to all, maintaining and encouraging relations between the different groups.

Auroch stepped in. "They've brought us here to dig for flint?"

"Yes. It's hard work. They have given us very little to eat." Woodpecker looked more comfortable now, as if he had decided he could trust the new arrivals.

The old man joined them in the centre of the cave, and Auroch learned that the group of men had been there for at least two moons. On Woodpecker's final hunt, the men had been set upon during the night by a group of Skull Eaters. Auroch felt some envy that the men hadn't undergone a raid on their camp. There had been two more men, but they had died from a combination of exhaustion or malnourishment. They were sent out every day to dig for flint, watched over by the guards. Given very little food, they often fell over in the shallow river outside the cave when led to work just to get some more water to drink. The men became more comfortable, and a few nervous laughs were shared. In a strange way, Auroch almost felt at ease. The air was now full of discussion, of stories, mainly of tragedy. Auroch glanced over his shoulder to see Black Aldar sitting in the corner alone. He still hadn't spoken. The pain in Auroch's chest had not subsided, but he had decided to make room for it.

Chapter 10

The group awoke the next morning to the angry shouts of their captors. Auroch was prodded by a large, sharpened spear, its tip carved from the fine flint he supposed he would be digging. He found himself marched to the cave entrance before he had time to fully shake himself awake. Organised in line with guards between every man or so, the group was ordered up the river. The Men of the Fen slipped and fell several times in the river, taking big gulps of water when they fell. The guards behind them, exasperated, would then poke at them with their spears, resulting in a howl of pain and sometimes a drop of crimson in the clear water. After a short walk, they reached the smattering of small caves in the cliff above the bank they had seen the previous evening. Men in the same paint and headdresses watched as they passed, along with women, their faces also caked in the now familiar chalky makeup. A group of young children abruptly stopped whatever game they were playing to watch the prisoners pass. A small woman with a baby suckling at her breast sauntered down the bank so that she intercepted them on their route. Gargling for a second, she spat viciously, the large globule hitting the old man, Woodpecker, on the cheek. Laughter broke out amongst the onlookers.

The group continued upstream, walls rising on both sides until the small canyon hemmed them in. They reached a bank and were forced up it towards another cliff face. One of the guards slung a bag from around his shoulder and pulled out several large flakes of flint, the end of each knapped into a point. The guard barked another order, and the Men of the Fen obediently walked over to the limestone wall. Auroch and his companions followed their lead, pressing their front to the limestone. He felt his wrist bindings loosen as the guard undid them, and then the flint was in his hand. He had a weapon. Examining it, he realised it would struggle break skin, let alone kill a man. The prisoners began to chip away at the limestone. Another shout in his ear, and he was attacking the rockface, too.

They worked for most of the morning. The flint was next to useless, but he persevered. Around midday, they stopped, and the men were allowed to scoop some water into their mouths from the river. A handful of hazelnuts was given to each man from a sack, and Auroch ate them greedily, hunger pangs gnawing at him all the while. Then, back to work, hammering and chipping at the rock. Eventually, he heard a shout from Yarrow, and two guards went to where he had been beating at the limestone. Suddenly, he was being cajoled and pushed towards where the boy stood. He could see a jutting edge of a round, smooth grey rock amongst the limestone. A module of flint.

The module was large and weighty, around the same size as a man curled in a foetal position. The group recovered it from the limestone and laid it on the bank of the river. The guards once again moved to shouting orders, poking at the men with spears. Auroch, Bloodied Thistle, and another man lifted the flint module and began to walk it back down the river. They reached the bank by the caves the families lived in, and the guards motioned them to put the module on the ground. Forcing the three men to sit in front of the flint module, he produced an already worked piece of flint from his bag and laid it next to the larger module. Next to it, he put a large round stone. It was obvious what his instructions were. Taking the stone, Bloodied Thistle hit the large flint module, cracking it open. He placed his cracked stone between his knees and began hammering smaller chunks of the stone. Auroch took a large pebble from the river and followed his lead. The three men smashed the stone until they had several smaller pieces. Then they were each given a hammer made from antler that Auroch recognised as looted from his own camp. The prisoners began to drive flakes across the top of the smaller lumps of flint, creating a flat platform across its top. Auroch was astonished by the quality of the rock when knapped. He examined the black, shiny surface, appreciating how easily he had created a platform for knapping. Flakes could readily be struck from the side, making excellent bladelets to be used as barbs in a harpoon, spear tip, or knife, not to mention as burins or scrapers. When one was done, they started on another.

Auroch worked the flint until twilight. He was seriously impressed by the quality of the stone, far higher than anything he had seen in the valley or at the meeting on the plains. The guard, yawning, motioned for them to drop what they were doing, and they were marched once again past the Skull Eater women and children and back down the shallow river to the cave. The guard produced foul-smelling meat from his bag before passing it to the men. Auroch tentatively tried it before tearing at it hungrily once he ascertained it was deer. The rumbling of his stomach disguised its rancid taste. Their hands were bound once again, and they were pushed inside the cave entrance for a second time. After a little wait, the rest of the men returned, their faces white from chalk and their hands blistered. Woodpecker explained that sometimes they would dig, and other times they would do jobs like carving spear shafts from wood or creating beads and jewellery. Auroch was puzzled. He estimated that there were perhaps fifty people in the tribe. He had seen around twenty men overall, not counting the one-eyed man whom he hadn't seen since arriving at the Skull Eater camp. Why would they need to produce blade core after blade core? Surely, they wouldn't go through the effort of transporting, guarding, and feeding them for this? A twinge of pain hit Auroch as he remembered Father teaching him to strike flint precisely with a piece of antler when he was around six summers old.

It was cold in the cave. The men slept in a huddle, hoping their collective body heat would help them make the night more bearable. A noticeable chill was in the air, and when the men marched out of the cave in the morning, Auroch noticed yellowing leaves floating downstream. Autumn had arrived.

He imagined a different world where the attack had never happened. He was walking with Mother on his arm, Father striding ahead, little Boar on his shoulders. Little Wren walked beside them, asking incessant questions. How far was it to the great plain? How many tribes would be there? When do we eat? They had a long journey ahead, but the promise of warmth, laughter, and food when they eventually reached the plains kept them going.

Auroch was jerked back to reality by their arrival at the same limestone cliff as the previous day. Much like yesterday, they hacked away at the stone until they found a workable chunk of flint. This time, Yarrow, Black Aldar, and one of the Fen men begin to knap the module into blade cores. Auroch continued to attack the rock, making progress until the sun was only peeking over the horizon. Hungry and tired, he stumbled back to the guarded cave and, despite the cold wind that howled through the entrance at night, fell into a deep, haunted sleep. The next day was much the same. And the day after that.

Sometimes, the men would be put to work on knapping scrapers, burins, and blades. Often, they would knap the flint into spearheads that would be attached to long pieces of birchwood. Every day, Auroch admired how much of the limestone had been cleared out. The quantity of flint removed from the river was enormous. Day after day spent making blade cores and tools must be generating a huge number of items. What were they going to do with them? Most unusually, they were also put to work making jewellery, just as Woodpecker has said. Bones were hollowed out and painted with dye. The days began to slide together. Bloodied Thistle noted that they were being given just enough food to subsist, and Auroch watched as the great hunter's thick frame became thinner day by day. He could see the men's ribs in the cave now, their faces becoming progressively gaunter.

The men guarding them changed regularly. Auroch and Bloodied Thistle memorised their faces. They seemed to do about two days of guard duty, then swap with another six men. Auroch remembered some of them as the men who had attacked him and Egret in the meadow. They made a point of counting the members of the tribes as they passed the cave network by the stream. Bloodied Thistle, like Auroch, reckoned men and women numbered around fifty, with about fifteen children on top of that. Auroch had also now seen the one-eyed man again from a distance, standing on the hill, watching them as they walked past on their daily journey.

He learned the names and roles of his companions. The three men were Anemone, Buckbean, and Yellow Toad. All were brothers, Auroch had been surprised to learn. The young boy was their nephew, Pine Martin. All three men seemed grateful that they had been spared the catastrophe that had befallen the Summer Valley. Yarrow was trying to make the best of it, cracking jokes and discussing possible escape methods. Auroch and Bloodied Thistle joined in, knowing that as a dependable group, they had a better chance of finding a way out of this. Black Aldar was silent still. He mourned day and night quietly, barely saying a word. There was murder in his eyes, and his hand, he clutched beads that had been given to him by the mother of his child. There would be time for revenge, Auroch thought, but much like the man stalking a stag in the long grass, patience was the key. Auroch wondered how much time they had left to escape.

Chapter 11

Auroch could see his breath when he awoke on the morning of the escape attempt. The chill seemed to penetrate his body and echo through his frame. He felt weak. Slowly, quietly, the group had planned their escape. Made from material discarded while breaking the large modules open, Bloodied Thistle and Auroch had each knapped a heavy, flat stone that could be held in the palm of the hand by its blunt edge, with two sharp edges leading up to a point opposite. Using their feet, the pair had gracefully kicked them down the slope while they worked. They lay on the stream's bed, hopefully undisturbed from the previous day. The children had begun to play a game where they would hurl small stones at the men while they passed the caves every morning, coming within a couple of strides of the prisoners to inflict maximum pain. Bloodied Thistle and Auroch were to feign a fall, landing in the water where the flint was hopefully waiting. They would then pick up the heavy, sharpened lumps with their hands, presently bound around their front. Then, they would grab two of the children and negotiate their escape. Auroch thought it was a terrible plan, but it was all they had. The men hadn't discussed if they would be prepared to inflict violence on the children. Auroch thought back to the sight of his family, dead by the creek. Could he do that to a mother? He hoped not to find out.

The men obediently left the cave in single file, each with a guard watching their back. They marched up the river, the spectre of potential failure hanging over the group. None of them had much confidence in the plan, although no man had said it. Auroch could see the caves, the small birchwood and skin tents where the families slept. The gang of cruel children was already there, brandishing sticks and stones to attack the men with as they passed. They were standing in the right place! Auroch saw the white stone on the bank that he and Bloodied Thistle had placed parallel to where their weapons lay. Were they still there? Had they been taken by the slow current or picked up by a Skull Eater wading across the river? Bloodied Thistle, walking several paces ahead of him, feigned a fall as had been discussed. It looked unconvincing, but the guards were used to the prisoner's attempts to quench their thirst. Auroch watched as he splashed around in the water. A spearpoint was in his back, and the guard was pushing him along. Had Bloodied Thistle found it?

Auroch glanced down to see one of the weapons at his feet. It must have moved with the current! One more step, and he would be too far to retrieve it. He fell flat on his face into the stream, smashing his nose on a rock on the bottom. Pain shot through his skull as the water became cloudy with blood. The flint was by his ankles. He twisted, finding the curved edge with his still-bound hands. A strong hand grabbed him from behind and pulled him to his feet. He had done it! The sharp, heavy piece of flint was in his hand! He had mere moments before the guards noticed.

In front of him, on his right, the children stood on the bank. Today, they had acquired animal dung and were hurling it mercilessly at the Fenfolk. Auroch was so close. A boy, no more than seven summers old, hands full of the muck, threw it directly at Bloodied Thistle's face. He did nothing, walking on by without acknowledging the child. This meant he had failed to retrieve the flint. Auroch, only several steps away from the boy, flipped his weapon in his bound palms, the razor-sharp triangular edge cutting into his fingers. It was now or never. Before his guard could react, he threw himself at the child, throwing his bound hands around the boy's neck. He brought his bindings and flint up to the child's throat, turning him so that Auroch's frame was pressed into his back. The guard menaced him with a spear but quickly withdrew at the sight of the sharpened point under the boy's chin.

"Stand Back! I will tear his gullet open!" Auroch roared.

He pulled himself and the boy onto the bank, facing the men in the river. The guards had clearly come to their senses and had grabbed a man each. Bloodied Thistle pushed his guard, deftly avoiding the spear thrust he earned in response before scrambling up the bank towards Auroch.

The two men stood on the rise, looking down on the men in the river. The child began to cry loudly. Spectators began to emerge from the tents, watching in horror at the scene unfolding on the riverbank below. Auroch spied the one-eyed man in the gathering crowd. Unlike the others, he watched the standoff calmly, an expression spreading across his face that Auroch could only describe as amusement. It was the same cruel smile that Auroch had seen after he killed Old Heron.

"He will kill the boy!" Bloodied Thistle motioned towards the men in the river to come to him and then pointed at the boy before mimicking the action of a slit throat. "Let the rest of the bound men come to us, and we will release him."

The guards did not move. The child was bawling uncontrollably now; Auroch could feel the boy shaking with fear as he used his strength to hold him at the point of his blade. Nothing was happening. Auroch drew his arms tighter, the sharp point pressing lightly into the child's throat.

Black Aldar's guard must have relaxed his grip for a second because he was suddenly thrown into the stream, Black Aldar on top of him. The water, normally so clear, exploded in a bloom of scarlet as Black Aldar hauled himself up. He was holding the flint meant for Bloodied Thistle! He must have seen it at his feet! Black Aldar threw himself recklessly at a second guard holding Woodpecker, stabbing and slashing at the man before he had time to react. Woodpecker cried out in pain as he tripped and fell awkwardly onto the stones that lined the riverbed.

"Black Aldar! Come here!" Screamed Auroch, seeing his and Bloodied Thistle's guards advancing on him.

It was too late. They stabbed Black Aldar in the back and thigh in a coordinated motion. Black Aldar fell forward, and the men stabbed at him again and again until he lay motionless in the bloody water. Woodpecker tried to pick himself up, but the two guards thrust their spears into his shoulder and neck. He collapsed back into the river, his eyes fixed on Auroch. This hadn't been how this was meant to go.

Woodpecker lay in the stream, twitching and writhing. The two guards didn't even look at the old man, turning their attention immediately back to Auroch. He could see Woodpecker's guard gasping and splashing about, clearly grievously injured. Three corpses were in the stream, and at least one more was soon to follow. Auroch and Bloodied Thistle were shouting at the guards, and the guards were shouting at them. Nobody could understand each other in the chaos, and it wasn't clear if anyone was attempting to.

"Do it!" shouted Bloodied Thistle to Auroch. "Kill the child!"

This wasn't part of the plan.

"Not yet!" responded Auroch weakly.

Could he do it? Kill this mewling Skull Eater child? He thought of his siblings lying dead. Father's limp frame on the ground. Mother's corpse, still warm. He pressed the bladed edge closer to the boy's throat.

A voice cut through the shouts. It was the one-eyed man.

"Enough!"

He made his way down the bank from the caves, screaming orders at the guards in the river. The men holding the remaining prisoners backed off, retreating around the bend in the stream and out of sight with the slaves. It was just Auroch, Bloodied Thistle, the crying child on one side, and the one-eyed man on the other. The injured guard had stopped struggling and sank below the shallow surface. Four corpses. Once again, Auroch pulled the flint closer to the boy's throat, and his captive squealed. He had drawn blood. The one-eyed man fixed his solitary pupil dead on Auroch and shrugged.

"Do it!" shouted Bloodied Thistle.

The boy squirmed. Auroch increased the pressure on his throat. Any more, and he would slice cleanly into the boy's windpipe. He thought of the hunt he had participated in just before this had all started, before his brother was ill, before the red elder. He remembered the deer's frantic, panicked movements as it bled to death. Bloodied Thistle was still shouting at him to kill the boy. He loosened his grip. The boy struggled out of his grasp and ran down to the river, to the one-eyed man, and threw himself behind his legs, peeking out at the hostage taker.

Auroch fell to his knees. He looked to his side where Bloodied Thistle was previously, but he was gone, running into the trees. He was unlikely to get far, with his legs still bound by the short rope. One of the spearmen from the caves was on him, chasing after him. The one-eyed man jumped into the river and strode up the slope before grabbing Auroch. He pulled a knife, a beautiful blade crafted from obsidian, and held it to Auroch's throat. It was over.

He was lifted to his feet, the knife now at his back. The one-eyed man walked him down the slope and through the sanguine river. As he waded through the water, Auroch noticed one of the guards flipping the body of Black Aldar over in the water. As he turned, he spasmed and seemed to gasp for air. He was alive!

"Do not spare yourself from weeping. This man will be dead soon." The one-eyed man said, kicking Auroch in the back of his legs, "Many tears will be shed tonight because of your foolishness."

This was it. He was going to die. A sense of calm fell over him. They had one chance, and he had failed. What could he have done differently? Killed the child? Was it Black Aldar's fault? Whatever the reason, it didn't matter now. The one-eyed man had called his bluff, and now he would be killed in the forest, just as his family had been.

They walked for a while longer before descending into the undergrowth. Stumbling and tripping, he was led down a small hill before they arrived at a clearing. Auroch could see the remains of a hearth and bits of furs on the ground, evidentially used for sleeping. The opening of a cave swelled out of the ground on one end of the secluded glade, the arches of its entrance decorated with moss. A spooled rope was produced by the one-eyed man, who used it to tightly secure Auroch's ankles to a tree. He cut the bindings on Auroch's wrists, before tying them once again behind his back. He kicked Auroch again, this time hard in the back of the shin, causing him to crumple to the floor. The man laughed. Auroch wondered if this was how he had laughed as he had butchered his family. He prepared himself, tapping into a stoic energy within him. This was the end. Then, quite surprisingly, the man turned on his heel and left.

Auroch was alone, lying in the clearing. He was alive, unharmed, and unguarded. He struggled, wriggling his way over to a low-lying branch and rubbing his hands on the sharp, protruding bits of wood. No Luck. The one-eyed man had bound his hands tight. Still, he pressed on, knowing his bindings would not budge. He continued, lying on his front first on the ground, his cheek turned to the earth, moving his hands up and down the branch, hoping it would somehow unpack the strong chords that made the rope. With half his face pressed to the floor, he could see a puddle directly in front of him at eye level, created in the mud by the feet of some beast. Unusually, he didn't recognise it, but it occupied only a fraction of his attention. The deep footprint was half-filled with water. The ground itself was soaking. Auroch had become used to the river water constantly splashing around his calves, but this was different. The rain had penetrated the ground, meaning that every time he moved or jolted, water rose from the earth, seeping into his mouth and nose. It was useless. He wasn't getting the bindings off his hands. Auroch slumped forward. Should he accept his fate?

The water in a shallow puddle began to move. Slowly at first, as if a single drop of water had hit it. Then, quicker and more violently. Auroch could feel the vibrations, the earth-shaking rhythmically. He could hear something making its way through the trees and undergrowth. He could hear birch creaking and cracking and the shouts of men, laughing and talking. He pulled himself onto his knees, and struggled to his feet. Through the forest came the monster, its massive frame pushing aside low-lying branches and leaving enormous footprints on the wet ground. The beast was only several strides from him now, and Auroch found himself frozen in fear. It was twice the size of him and stood on four thick legs. It was covered in matted brown fur and two huge tusks protruded from its maw. They curved down and then back up, reaching almost back up to the animal's head in height. A long, hairy, prehensile tusk that moved as if it was searching for something sat about the creature's mouth, snaking through the air. It was escorted by four guards, including the one-eyed man. Astride it sat another monster, wearing the same antler headdress and white makeup.

Auroch had heard of this animal. He had seen its bones. He had seen the paintings crafted by those who had hunted them. They were rare now, often only in the east and in fewer and fewer numbers every winter. In the age of the First Eagle, they had been numerous hunted regularly for their meat. This was the first he had heard of a solitary one. One controlled by a man. A mammoth!

The man riding the beast looked ancient. His clothing seemed vaguely familiar, and marvellous, strange tattoos covered his chest and arms. Swirling bright patterns, intricate. The headdress, too; dyed with greens and reds. How could he command this thing? How could it be controlled? The great beast lowered itself to its knees as if on command, and the old man dismounted.

Auroch was astonished. He controlled it like it were a hound. The old man bent over and kissed the mammoth on its thick brown fur, and it rose again. Its trunk touched and prodded at the old man affectionately, and Auroch noticed the patterns painted onto the ivory of its tusks. The Old man was speaking softly to it under his breath. Auroch couldn't make out the words, but they were warm and gentle. This continued for a few moments longer before the ancient man turned and fixed his eyes on Auroch. He walked surprisingly fast for his age, striding over to Auroch in several purposeful steps.

"You are the child that has caused so much trouble?" The Old man said.

Auroch said nothing. He had guessed that this was the Skull Eater chieftain. Auroch was going to kill him.

"Two of my men lie dead," the old man said bluntly. "One of your men is dead, and the other will not survive the night." He spoke quickly and forcefully. As with his stride, his speech had a youthful air that didn't match his appearance. "I suggest that we now agree to no more violence. We have drawn even lots. I have been told you are excellent with our flint. I wouldn't want to lose that skill."

A pang of guilt travelled through him like a twanged nerve. Black Aldar was on the verge of death! The poor old man, Woodpecker, had been killed without a second thought, just like his family. He resolved to be as uncooperative as possible towards this man. Auroch's throat was dry, but he summoned all the moisture from the back of his mouth and let fly the largest, most aggressive globule of spit he could muster from his lips. It landed pathetically at the old man's feet. The chieftain didn't even look at it. The man sighed and then lowered himself to the floor. He groaned as he adjusted his legs to sit cross-legged opposite Auroch, exposing his frailty. Auroch had a chance to study him now. He had a large grey beard, and Auroch could see the dark stains on his face where tattoos had faded, and new ones, in bright colours had replaced them in different patterns and permutations. He looked calm and pensive.

"I'm sure you have many, many questions. About myself, about your fate, about why I ordered such a terrible tragedy to be inflicted upon your people." He paused and looked Auroch dead in the eyes. "I will answer, in time. But not now. Now, we will eat." He signalled to the one-eyed man.

One-eye seemed delighted upon receiving the strict instruction and almost skipped through the undergrowth back towards the river camp. The old man laughed, "Red Fox is very excited."

The old man got up and caressed the mammoth's thick fir. The animal playfully reciprocated, brushing up against him with his trunk. Auroch watched the strange scene for what seemed like an age. The beast hoovered up some water with his truck and sprayed it at the old man, who laughed in response.

Curiosity got the better of Auroch, and he dropped his stoic defiance. "How did you tame this animal?"

The old man, still playing with the mammoth, looked up and smiled; his eyes twinkled.

"Many years ago, when I was a young man, I found myself wondering alone. I was thirsty, hungry, and injured. I was on the verge of death when I discovered Great-Tusk here." He motioned to the mammoth, who was obliviously stripping leaves from a branch. "Great-Tusk was stuck in a swamp. I thought of killing him, of feasting on his flesh. But he was only small, an abandoned infant. He cried, much like a human babe cries when he's separated from his mother's bosom. He's smart, my Great-Tusk. I offered a branch to him, and with the last of my strength, I helped him steady himself as he wiggled and squirmed. And then he was free. I was dying, but I couldn't drink the foul swamp water. He led me out of that swamp and to a lakebed, where I could scoop water from the earth." He looked again at Great-Tusk, smiling, exposing his blackened and missing teeth. "He travelled with me. Often times were tough, and I was very hungry. My stomach hurt! My insides longed for meat. But never Great-Tusk! And he grew! He grew bigger and stronger, and as summers passed, I could sit astride him! Men feared him. They feared me!"

He stroked Great-Tusk's coat lovingly before gently guiding him forward so that he was within arm's length of Auroch. The long trunk made its way towards the boy, reaching forward, poking and prodding him. Auroch was frozen. The size of the animal! It could gore him with one thrust of its tusks or rear and stomp on him, crushing his frame into the mud. Auroch flinched and shivered at the beast's touch.

"Calm," urged the old man, his tone commanding. "Let him see you."

The trunk ran itself up Auroch's chest and onto his upper back. Auroch forced himself to look up from the floor and into the great mouth of the animal. He understood why this strange old man led such a ruthless group. He understood why the Skull Eaters, who were capable of such terrible cruelty, followed this wizened, eccentric ruler. He understood why he had been able to destroy Auroch's entire world in a single evening. He controlled this beast; he was able to shape it to his will. It was one thing to kill an animal, another to wield its force and savagery. He stood alone, above men like Auroch, who merely battled with beasts. The long trunk made its way over Auroch's hair.

"He likes you!" Laughed the old man.

Chapter 12

The old man and his prisoner sat in the clearing for a while longer, waiting for Red Fox to return. Great-Tusk continued to strip branches with his trunk, and the old man moved away from Auroch, talking and laughing with his guards. Auroch's momentary curiosity and awe had quickly given way to fear. What was going to happen now? They weren't going to kill him; that much was certain. But he was unlikely to be released back to his fellow workers without punishment. He was so hungry. He had eaten so little, and the sight of the mammoth munching on the leaves and shoots did little to abate his hunger. What he wouldn't do for a lovely hare! Or perhaps a deer's hind quarters. He wished to carry it back to camp with Father, for Mother to cook the meat in a broth made from various herbs and fungi collected whilst scouring the valley. He wished to be sat around the hearth with his family, with Bloodied Thistle, with Egret and all the other people who had made up the portion of his life that had been so swiftly and violently ended.

He was lost in his daydream when the sounds of the returning men talking and joking drifted through the woods towards him.

Several of the Skull Eater men he recognised made their way down the slope into the clearing. They were led by the one-eyed man, Red Fox. Two men carried between them the grievously wounded Black Aldar. Behind them walked Bloodied Thistle, his face sullen and swollen, pockmarked by new cuts and bruises. He was followed by a guard. Easily recaptured, Auroch mused despondently. Clearly, the Skull Eaters had shown little restraint, and Auroch could see that he now walked with a limp.

The men reached the group in the clearing. They dropped Black Aldar on the ground with a thud. He was now in a death trance, too close to his ancestors to understand what was happening. He moaned in pain. Despite his injuries, he was clinging to life. Auroch reassured himself that he would soon die, crossing the great river to meet his family. He thought of his own mother, stuck on one bank of the ethereal deluge, unable to cross due to the unnamed child's death. Tears welled up in his eyes. Bloodied Thistle, his hands bound, was pushed to the ground next to him, and through his swollen face, saw the big droplets of water begin to push themselves out of the corner of Auroch's eyes. A look of pure disdain swept across Bloodied Thistle's damaged complexion. Why didn't you kill the boy? His glare said it all.

Despite the mammoth's size and presence, Bloodied Thistle's eyes continued to fix unswervingly on Auroch. Black Aldar was still twitching and groaning on the ground. Several of the men made their way into the woods before returning a short while later with kindling. Auroch and Bloodied Thistle watched as the men built a fire, heaping the wood on a small flame in a pit. Across the pit, they lay stones.

Auroch watched fearfully as they heated them.

Two men approached Black Aldar and picked him up, dragging him to the low cave entrance at the edge of the clearing. A trail of blood marked his path, and the two bound men watched mournfully as he was manhandled. There was little doubt in Auroch's mind what would happen next. The Old man followed to the cave entrance. Pulling a small leather pouch from his belt, he wiped his finger around the inside of the cloth before scooping some red powder and throwing it over the dying man's body. Getting to his knees, he whispered in the dying man's ear. The Old man waved his hands across Black Aldar's face before retrieving a stubby blade fashioned from the quality flint of the riverbank. He took Black Aldar's hand and used the point to cut across the palm. He placed his mouth on the wound and squeezed the appendage, drinking the liquid that spewed out aggressively. After several large gulps, he dropped Black Aldar's hand, wiping the blood from his tangled mess of a beard.

The old man ducked out of the cave before muttering something to the men who stood outside. Producing their own blades, they got to work. Auroch couldn't look but didn't hear Black Aldar make a noise as he was butchered. He silently hoped the man had been too far gone to feel the men hack at his flesh. He looked up to see Bloodied Thistle still glaring at him. He didn't seem to react to the violence. The heavy thwack of flint on bone crawled into his ears, the sound of each hit seemingly vibrating through him. A feeling of sickness began to rise in his stomach as if something unpleasant was trying to force its way up his oesophagus. The noise continued until Auroch felt numb to it. The sun was beginning to set, and the light from the fire in the pit caused shadows to dance across the ground where Auroch had focussed his gaze, avoiding Bloodied Thistle on one side and the Black Aldar on the other. The sound of butchery stopped as darkness descended on the scene.

The sounds of sizzling meat and the smell accompanying it hung over the clearing. The tightness in Aurochs's chest was unbearable. He maintained his focus on the point in front of him, trying to pretend the odour of cooking meat was instead coming from slices of a deer's thigh or a hare, freshly caught today. He was so hungry, and the images of Mother cooking meat on stones over a fire made his mouth water. He felt guilty and ashamed. Bloodied Thistle had stopped looking at him now and was focussed on the same point on the ground. Perhaps if the pair stared enough, the earth would open up and swallow them. Auroch carefully counted the number of droplets that ran down a blade of grass. Six. The sounds of laughter between friends over the fire. The muffled sounds of someone talking with a full mouth. The men were eating now. More people were entering the clearing. Auroch heard the shrill voices of children and the soft laughs of women. The whole tribe was here for the feast. The hubbub of voices suddenly fell silent. Out of the corner of his eye, he saw Bloodied Thistle raise his head to look at the scene. Should he? He had to. He glanced up. Luckily, the butchered corpse of Black Aldar was concealed by the legs of a group of children, their hands and mouths full of his comrade. Bloody juices ran down their chins, and mothers fussed around them, wiping it away with their hands.

The silent crowd gave way to the old man, dancing through his people with a spring in his step. He held a shiny white human skull in his hand, the white bone buffed and cleaned. Its top was hollowed out, and Auroch watched as he bent over the fire, scooping up a chunk of Black Aldar's flesh into the ghastly receptacle. He bounded over to the two men, making sure to give Great-Tusk the mammoth a stroke on his way over. Kneeling in front of them, he pulled a small bladder from his belt and added a brown liquid to the mixture in the skull before using his finger to stir it.

"In order for one to learn, it is important to eat the flesh of men." He seemed to take delight in the horrified look on Auroch's face. "This man was your friend and was a fine fighter. He managed to kill my men. Don't let him be forgotten. Absorb his soul. Eat from his flesh."

Auroch said nothing, fearing the consequences of refusal or acceptance. It was wrong to eat human flesh. First Eagle had decried it as evil, and the soul of the consumed dead wouldn't be able to cross the river. Auroch wasn't sure if even Morning Mist would be able to lift a curse like that.

The Old man eyed up Auroch before deciding to offer it to Bloodied Thistle first. Bloodied Thistle hesitated, glancing at Auroch. No! Auroch pleaded with his eyes, but Bloodied Thistle no longer wished to listen. Bloodied Thistle didn't want to die here in this clearing. He wanted to live. He allowed the old man to bring the bowl to his lips and opened it wide, allowing the wet meat to slither down his gullet. The Old man turned to Auroch. This was it. Auroch wasn't going to eat the flesh of poor Black Aldar. These people had destroyed the only life he had ever known. He wasn't going to give them the satisfaction. The Old man put the bowl to Auroch's lips.

Auroch didn't move. Rough hands grabbed his head from behind and jerked it back so he was looking up at the canopy of the trees above him. A second pair of hands grabbed his nose and smothered his face, causing him to gasp for air. His mouth opened for a second, and the deathly receptacle was at his lips. The tender and juicy meat was in his mouth, along with the blood it had been marinating in. The hands clamped his jaws shut, and he began to choke. Almost instinctively, he gulped, and the sanguine meal was down his throat, forcing its way towards his stomach. The hands released him, and he fell forward, retching. He wanted to vomit, but his bound hands prevented him from forcing it back up with his fingers.

He fell on his side, laughter echoing all around him. The Skull Eater men, women, and children had found his revulsion funny. The humour turned to hostility, and the crowd began to hurl cruel words and taunts toward him. A bony, ancient hand grabbed his hair and yanked his head up so his face was forced to eye level with the old clan chief. A beard stained with blood brushed his chin. The red clashed with the charcoal rubbed into the old man's skin to form his tattoos.

He laughed, a long, heartless, toothy laugh. "My name is Grey Stag of the two tusks, leader of these people. I killed your family. I killed your tribe. But I'm not going to kill you. You will embrace us or toil here for the rest of your days."

He turned to the crowd and repeated it to the braying mob, who in turn laughed, shouted, and stomped. Auroch crumpled to the floor. Figures danced and jumped around the fire, throwing their shadows, dark reflections of demons, onto the trees. Auroch closed his eyes. He wanted this over. The pain was so intense in his chest now. He longed for the eternal night.

Chapter 13

The dancing subsided before dawn, and the men and women returned to the river camp. Auroch hadn't slept, but the cool morning dew of the grass pressed to his face soothed him. His head was pounding. He lifted his face from the wet ground to see a familiar elongated furry snout snaking its way towards him. It brushed him gently, and Auroch felt compelled to lift himself to his feet. Grey Stag, the clan chief, was nowhere to be seen. A yawning guard sat across from them, obviously instructed to watch them. Auroch turned to see a circle of men sleeping peacefully in the cave entrance. Great-Tusk gently poked and prodded at him with his trunk. He moved as close as the rope around his ankle would permit him, tugging cautiously, hoping the secure rope would suddenly loosen and he would be free. It held, and he found himself examining the gigantic tusk that jutted from the animal's mouth. The ivory had been purposefully stained with ornate patterns, and Auroch recognised the outlines of the animals painted there. A great bison, a bear, and a rhinoceros, its shaggy fur rendered by a careful smudging of colour on the tusk. The mammoth moved closer and pressed its large frame into him. There was comfort in the warmth of the fur. Great-Tusk lay down, and Auroch followed. He felt his eyes close, and in a moment, he was sleeping gently, cushioned by the mass of fur and flesh.

He was woken by the tip of a spear poking him softly in the ribs. The guard pulled him away from Great-Tusk, and the great beast stirred, then rose, before wandering over to a tree to strip its bark clean. Two women were waiting. Auroch recognised their faces from the riverbank. The younger of the two, with soft, mousey features, went to Bloodied Thistle and began to wash him, wiping him down with a wet cloth woven from plant fibre. The older of the two women began to do the same to Auroch, wiping the layers of dirt from his hands and chest. The older woman didn't show any emotion, scrubbing hard as if she was trying to wash Auroch out of existence. Auroch glanced at Bloodied Thistle and saw the young woman giggling, embarrassed by the hunter's manhood. In contrast, the old woman's hands clawed and scratched at him.

When the pair had been sufficiently cleaned, the two women left them, and the guards backed off, leaving them alone. The tension between them was palpable. Why did Bloodied Thistle drink the mixture from the skull? Auroch braved a look back at where Black Aldar had been roasted. Something was lying at the small cave's entrance, but it was unrecognisable. Auroch could scarcely believe it had been a man. He had become almost acclimatised to the smell that had embedded itself into the roots and the trees, but every now and again, the stench of cooked human meat caught him by surprise, and the knot in his stomach tightened.

One of the spearmen cut the ropes around their feet, and the guards led them back through the woodland. Auroch walked behind Bloodied Thistle. The man's posture seemed to have recovered, and there was purpose in his stride now. He was meaner, taller than the man who had sat solemnly in the cave waiting to be worked to death with the other prisoners. Auroch wondered if Black Aldar's flesh, which had tasted like poison to him, had awoken something in Bloodied Thistle. Was Grey Stag right? Had he absorbed some of the man's power?

They wound their way through the forest. Auroch was unsure if they were to be put straight back to work. The sound of water focussed his thoughts. They were almost back at the shallow river where he had spent many days working. Through the trees he spied the limestone cliffs, and below it the prisoners, hacking away at the rockface. The guards gestured for them to walk down the slope. Auroch and Bloodied Thistle obeyed, awkwardly throwing themselves down the bank. Auroch's bound hands made it hard for him to steady himself, and he fell forward, splashing into the water. The noise alerted the prisoners, who stopped digging and looked back. Auroch gasped and coughed as his head broke the surface to find astonished eyes gazing at him. Auroch realised they must have assumed he had been killed. A rough arm looped below his and pulled him out of the water. They marched down downriver before the familiar sight of the cave openings and tents on the riverbank greeted them.

Instead of the usual route back to the cave where they slept, Auroch and Bloodied Thistle were directed up the riverbank towards one of the smaller cave openings. Auroch was closer to the Skull Eater's living space than he had ever been. A small fire lit the inside of the cave, and the illuminated walls displayed dazzling, intricate art. The two men were roughly ordered into the cave and then to sit. Auroch sat and examined the walls. Figures depicted faced from left to right, and the same deer-headed man was depicted multiple times. Chalk had been used to smudge and redraw the lines around figures and animals. The shadows cast by the flickering flame made the images come alive. A herd of horses galloping through a field! The stag-headed man as a lone figure, wandering. The Mammoth, Great-Tusk!

He was so transfixed by the artwork Auroch hadn't noticed the figure approaching the cave entrance. The elderly muse, whose life was depicted with so much reverence, entered, followed by a child. Auroch recognised him as the boy whom he had taken hostage yesterday.

"Beautiful work, don't you think?" Grey Stag asked. "My sons are overflowing with talent."

Auroch said nothing, but Bloodied Thistle responded by grunting positively in affirmation. Grey Stag smiled.

"What is your name? I don't remember your face from my time spent with the Valleyfolk."

"Bloodied Thistle. You knew our people?"

"It's been a long time, but yes, I knew them."

Auroch decided to chime in, "The Skull Eaters were once like us! You met on the plains for midwinter! But you were cast out!"

A dark look thundered across the old man's face! "Skull Eaters! Nonsense! Invention! More lies, there are no Skull Eaters. True—many here are the children or grandchildren of plainsmen who were denigrated and ejected from that pit of snakes. But not one tribe, no! The mewling cretins who fatten themselves every winter on the reindeer caught by others, who clothe themselves in the furs of beasts slain while they sleep, who make trades for womenfolk could never be so bold as to do battle. So, they pick the threads at the edge of the cloth. They eject a man here and there who could cause trouble."

Surprised by this new information, Auroch pressed further, "And why were you banished?" Auroch tried to deepen his voice but saw a smirk across Grey Stag's Mouth.

"A tale for another time perhaps, Calf." Grey Stag laughed, his voice dripping with condescension.

A fire was rekindled inside Auroch's chest. How dare he! This monster had decimated his people. Women had been taken, then slain. His family lay dead. He steeled himself and then looked the old man in the eye.

"I will kill you. You killed Mother. You killed Father. You killed my siblings. You killed the clan chief, Old Heron. You killed the medicine woman, Morning Mist." He saw Grey Stag's face contorted into genuine pain for the first time. Morning Mist.

"Say that name again, boy…" Grey Stag stammered. It was if the wind had been knocked out of him.

"Morning Mist. Our Spirit-Mother. As ancient as the valley itself and as wise as the birds who watch over it. I held her as she died."

Grey Stag stood up; his old, hunched shoulders tightened, and his bony arms tensed as he balled his fists. Auroch could see the faint outline of the strong man he must have been in his youth. He threw himself at Auroch, his emaciated fists smashing into his upper chest.

Despite the relative weakness of the old man, the rage in his punches threw Auroch off balance, and he found himself on the floor yet again. The blows reigned down until Grey Stag stood over him, panting and sweating. The child fled, scrambling over rocks and out of the cave. Auroch found himself largely unharmed. The wizened old man, who commanded so many and rode a terrifying beast, who had destroyed his life, could do little more than give him a few welts. He glanced at Bloodied Thistle, who was clearly thinking the same thing. They needed just a few moments alone and unbound with the old man to send him to the next life.

Grey Stag caught his breath before turning to the guards outside. He spoke quickly, barking orders. One of them descended the slope towards the river, and Grey Stag followed, muttering under his breath. Other than the guard at the entrance, the two men were left alone, unmolested. The sun was high, marking midday.

"Why did you drink Black Aldar's blood?" Auroch asked when they were alone.

He was afraid of Bloodied Thistle's response. That he might justify it and persuade Auroch that he should have held his nerve and gulped the viscera down to save his skin. Was there a way out of his predicament? Bloodied Thistle looked up, meeting Auroch's gaze.

"For the same reason I would have slain that child, Auroch. I wish to live." He sighed. "Why weren't we killed in the camp with the rest of the tribe? Grey Stag values utility. Why have we been making tools and jewellery day and night? He wishes to trade his way back into the winter gathering."

"Why would they let us live?" he felt young, childish. Bloodied

Thistle had seen something in Grey Stag's eyes he had failed to notice. His voice cracked, and he was suddenly a mere boy, unworthy of Father's name.

"If we were to make ourselves loyal…indulge in their rituals, be useful, be less threatening, then we may have a chance." Bloodied Thistle said, his eyes scanning the various depictions of Grey Stag on the walls. "Think about what he said. They aren't a tribe, these Skull Eaters! They are the banished! He's collected these men and women from the rivers, the forests, the plains. He sees something in this wild band of outcasts!"

Bloodied Thistle seemed to have all the answers. "Why…why would he attack the Men of the Summer Valley?" Auroch asked cautiously.

Bloodied thistle threw his head back in a spiteful laugh. "Because of you." He seemed angrier with Auroch than the men who had destroyed their lives. "You and Egret, you stumbled on them feasting on the flesh of men. You know as well as I do that it's forbidden. If he wishes to make peace with the leaders of the plainsmen, to trade his goods at the winter solstice, then they can never know."

"So, we gain his favour? When we reach the great plains, we tell them?"

Bloodied Thistle didn't answer. Auroch felt helpless and stupid. Bloodied Thistle had figured this all out while he wallowed in his pit of misery. There was no plan. Auroch didn't know how to escape. Bloodied Thistle's only suggestion was that the pair grovel and indulge in cringing subservience, to participate in heinous acts until they reached a point where maybe, if they were lucky, they could somehow gain their freedom. Bloodied Thistle lay down on his side, his back to Auroch. The two men spoke no more.

Chapter 14

A flurry of activity engulfed the camp throughout the evening and into the night. Auroch wondered if the events of the previous day had expedited something. Were they leaving? What was to become of them? The fire burned down to embers, and the dramatic images of dancing and swaying on the cave wall became fainter and fainter until they disappeared, replaced by silver moonlight.

The pair were awoken at dawn. They were led by spearmen down the bank and to a mass of people gathered by the river. Men, women, and children waited, huddled, their possessions strapped to their backs. The banished must have been around sixty or seventy in number, including children.

Bloodied Thistle and Auroch were directed to a pair of sleds. The two women who had washed them previously were waiting and helped to place the rough plant fibre ropes around their waists and shoulders. Auroch peered through the crowd and could see a couple of his fellow prisoners, including Yarrow and a couple of the hardier slaves. Where were all the rest? He could only see about half their number. There was a sense of anticipation in the air. Auroch peered at the sledges they were going to pull, presumably to the meeting on the plains. It would take them at least two moons, perhaps more, to get there with this many people carrying so many sleds burdened with wares. They could make the plains by the winter solstice, but it would be hard.

The muttering and talking began to subside, and a hush fell over the crowd. It was about to begin. From behind the bend in the river, the huge, imposing frame of Great-Tusk emerged. Grey Stag sat atop him, moving up and down rhythmically in time with the stride of the beast. The Skull Eaters stood in complete silence. Great-Tusk and Grey Stag made their way toward the crowd, the great splash of the water at the mammoth's ankles generating waves that broke on the shins of the men, women, and children who stood in the river. A baby, strapped to the back of a woman stood a few paces from Auroch began to cry. Great-Tusk made his way out of the stream onto the bank. The beast turned around at the head of the column of people, and various figures jumped back, fearing they could be crushed under Great-Tusk's massive feet.

A small flute, carved from the wing bones of a swan, was carefully retrieved from Grey Stag's belt. He raised it to his withered lips and blew. The dawn chorus paused; the safe routine of the forest was disrupted by a loud, sharp whistle. Then, the mass of people began to move, with Grey Stag on his war beast at the head of the snake. Auroch began to pull, and the weight of the sled caused his feet to sink into the wet mud of the riverbank. A hide covered the contents of the sled, tied down with rope, but beneath it, he could see the goods he had whittled from flint. He pulled again, and the sled dislodged itself from the mud.

After only a morning of pulling the sledge, Auroch decided that this was the most unpleasant activity he had ever engaged in. The route up the wooded hillside was unwieldy and awkward to account for Great-Tusk's size. Natural paths were few and far between, and despite the banished clearly finding a route ahead of time, branches often had to be cleared and alternate paths for the mammoth to be found. Both Auroch and Bloodied Thistle's sleds became stuck repeatedly, forcing them, still under threat of a jab from a spear, to walk back and pull them from the mud with their bound hands. Their captors had been kind enough to rebind them at the front and remove any restraints around their legs. Auroch gasped when he saw his wrists as they were retied. They had become raw from the rope. It itched and burned at his wrists, and he longed for respite. He wondered what the experience was like for the slaves at the back of the column. It was apparent now that he and Bloodied Thistle had been separated with purpose from the other men.

By nightfall on the first day, it was clear that progress was slower than planned. Auroch would have considered the distance covered a leisurely morning's walk, not a full day of hard pulling. They would be lucky to reach the edge of the great mesa by the first snow.

Fires were lit, and despite his ravenous hunger and his sapped strength, when a small clump of meat was offered to him, he refused it. Bloodied Thistle ate his noisily. Auroch spied a couple of mushrooms from his position, laying on the damp earth. Despite the fires being lit enough distance from him that he couldn't gain from their warmth, he recognised the fat, juicy, scarlet-capped mushrooms.

Quietly, without alerting the spearmen that sat only a few paces away, he shuffled over. Rather than pick them, he pulled his face close and bit into them, taking as much as he could with one bite. They were wet and had some kind of algae or slime on them that tasted unpleasant. He hoped that it was nothing that would cause illness. Auroch shuffled his body close to Bloodied Thistle, who was already asleep, or at least pretending to be, and curled up. It was getting colder night by night, and his teeth began their familiar chatter. The hard labour of the day made him feel as if his muscles had been turned to liquid.

The next several days proceeded much like the last. They would wake at dawn, Auroch's bones stiff from the night air that became harsher the further they ventured into the mountains. The chill would be knocked out of him almost immediately as they began to pull the sleds, only to feel the cold nipping at them again as they sat waiting for a path to be made safe for Grey Stag to ride Great-Tusk triumphantly at the head of the column. They were out of the trees now, and for the first time, Auroch could clearly count the number of banished in the procession. Perhaps seventy men and women and numerous children followed the great beast into the mountains.

Little progress was made each day, and it was clear the Skull Eaters who made up the band were becoming restless. Auroch wondered how they were going to provide enough food for the journey. He tried not to think about it. Luckily, the food offered to him on the following days largely consisted of nuts, so he felt safe to eat without the risk of ingesting human meat. As he settled down at night, he would scan the mountain grasses around his head for any insects. As if someone would steal them away from Auroch, he would quickly devour them, savouring additional meagre sustenance.

The cautious distance that the Skull Eaters kept from Auroch and Bloodied Thistle slowly evaporated as their journey dragged on. They would be given their food by the same pair of women who had washed them in the clearing. The younger of the two would walk beside them now during the day, even helping Bloodied Thistle when his sledge became snagged on rocks or tangled mountain shrubs. The old woman lagged behind, and Auroch found himself consciously slowing down when she walked beside him. Occasionally, the pair would disappear before returning with hazelnuts or berries. Most were shared with their guards or passed down the long line of weary travellers, but Auroch saw the younger woman pass some to Bloodied Thistle, blushing as the Master Huntsman thanked her.

Auroch still slept a distance from the fire, but he was awoken one night by movement as a third person joined them on the edge of the camp, away from the warmth of the hearth. Auroch feigned sleep, but he knew the younger woman now lay with Bloodied Thistle, away from prying eyes. She left again before dawn, and the day resumed as usual, Bloodied Thistle's new lover giggling as she walked beside him.

Despite the frothing hate that boiled in his chest, he was amazed by the sight of Grey Stag commanding his beast through the narrow mountain passageways. Every morning, scouts would work in pairs, running ahead of the column, before sending one man back to advise if the mountain ridges were passable with Great-Tusk. They were methodical and canny, and surprisingly, it seemed easier for the mammoth to navigate the slopes than it had been to move through the dense brush for the foothills.

Bloodied Thistle said little to Auroch, only addressing him when the two worked together to navigate an obstacle. Auroch felt a pang of anger as Bloodied Thistle flashed a smile to the girl that seemed so enamoured with him. He watched from a distance, seething, as the Master Huntsman let out a hearty laugh when she whispered in his ear. What was he doing? After what these people had done!

On the tenth day, Auroch was awakened by a routine kick before being hauled to his feet, along with Bloodied Thistle. Descending through the foothills the night before, it had been dark when they had finally camped down. Now in the dawn's first light, he recognised his surroundings. They were a morning's walk from the most southerly point of the valley. Auroch noticed an ochre handprint on the bark of a tree, marking out the area furthest from the river where deer grazed in number. He wondered which member of his former hunting band had made the mark, relishing the thrill of tracking his prey through the lush trees before daubing the bark. Likely dead now, slain by the men who now surrounded him. The trees were losing their leaves rapidly, gold and brown winning a war for the forest with the green. Bloodied Thistle and Auroch were led north, out of sight of the main caravan, following the stream. They still had a large distance to cover, thought Auroch. *They aren't going to kill us yet. Are they taking us to the back to the camp?*

From behind a tree stepped Grey Stag, his wiry bones threatening to poke holes in his thin skin. With him was the one-eyed man, Red Fox. His absence over the last few days had been noted by Auroch. As expected, he had clearly been sent ahead. His face lit up when he saw

Auroch, the cruelty he had shown so many times bubbling just below the surface.

"I have a task for you, Calf." Grey Stag directed his question to Auroch, not initially acknowledging Bloodied Thistle's presence. "Red Fox and I will escort you to what remains of your camp." He turned to Bloodied Thistle and smiled at the pair of them. "I will allow the pair of you to tend to your dead. And you will help me find the body of the woman named Morning Mist and help me perform the rites of the final journey."

Auroch was taken aback. He guessed that Grey Stag had spent some time with his tribe when he was youth, but the rite was intimate. It was only performed in the Summer Valley, and if an elder died on the plains in the winter, they would be dragged on a sled back to the valley to rest in the glade of the dead, nestled in the foothills.

"Do this for me," Grey Stag smiled, "and I can help you sew a new life from the hide of the old."

Two guards joined Red Fox and Grey Stag, walking behind the two prisoners, spears at the ready as they made their way up the well-worn path beside the river. A strange nostalgia fell over Auroch. Over there, he and Father had trapped his first hare when he was only six summers old. The handprints on the trees became more and more frequent. He noticed his own, placed on the oak at the beginning of summer just gone. The sap from the tree had seeped onto his fingers. He had washed them in the stream before spearing a fat trout, then carried it proudly back to camp. He was heading in the same direction, back to his family, only now he was beaten and tired, and his home contained no warm fires or smiling faces. It was difficult to tell how long he had been a prisoner, but he feared seeing the bodies of his family. The idea of laying them to rest had lit a fire in his chest. There was nothing he could do for Mother after the death of the unnamed child, but Father, Little Wren, Boar, and Burgeoning Yew could all make the journey across the river more easily with the proper preparation. Free from the sled, Auroch's shoulders relaxed. He felt stronger with every step. It was two men against four, but Grey Stag was old and frail. If they could just get some distance between himself and the three able-bodied men, they would be free.

Surprised at Grey Stag's pace, they made good progress, reaching the women's camp just before midday. The damage from the fire wasn't as bad as he remembered, most of the thick birch trees were untouched. The Skull Eaters had been deliberate and clever with their burn. Bodies were strewn on the ground. They had deteriorated significantly, and while some were recognisable, he struggled to identify once familiar faces due to the weather and scavengers. Auroch noted that most of the corpses were women and children. Most of the men must have been killed by the tree line. He recalled details of the night with simultaneous haziness and razor-sharp focus. He could remember specific details: the smell of the fire, the look in Old Heron's eyes as he died, the glint of the stars as he held Morning Mist.

"Please," Grey Stag said, "find her."

Auroch looked across the clearing to the bottom of the hill where he had held the old woman. He could see a lump of wet, brown leather that presumably was Morning Mist's clothing. How much of her had survived the elements? He walked over to her trepidatiously, unsure what he would find. Grey Stag followed closely behind.

Auroch could hear the old man's short, sharp breaths quicken as they reached the old woman's corpse. Animals had been at her, and the smell drifting from her body was intense. Auroch was sure that Grey Stag would not have been able to identify her without him.

"Here she is," Auroch said softly, motioning with his bound hands to the body.

Grey Stag let out a wild, anguished cry, throwing himself down beside her. He grabbed the clothes, attempting to cradle her in his arms. "They told me you died." he sobbed. "Many summers ago now. If I had known!"

He buried his head into the leather. The smell that had repulsed Auroch seemed to have no effect on Grey Stag as he smothered himself in the folds of the dirty, bloody clothes. Auroch stood watching and, despite his hate, felt a kernel of pity for the man. Had he really loved the unassailable old medicine woman? Auroch could see his shoulders shake as he wept silently. After a while, he stopped, and began to speak softly, whispering something to the old woman while tenderly caressing what remained of her hair.

He turned to Auroch. "Go to your kin. Bring them to the glade. We will ready them for their crossing."

Autumn leaves crunched beneath his feet as he made his way towards the bend of the river. Morning Mist's withered, deteriorated visage had forced a lump into his throat, and he wasn't sure how he would react upon seeing his parents. Only one guard escorted him. He didn't recognise the man from the night of the massacre and was unsure how he would have reacted if Red Fox's cruel smile had followed him to the site of his family's death. He held his breath as he walked the final steps towards the quiet patch where they lay.

It was as he feared. As with Morning Mist, Animals had attacked their bodies, leaving them in a terrible state. Mother's clothes torn open by some kind of scavenger had seen the worst of it. Poor Boar had also been decimated. One of the twins was there but had gone untouched. They had gone for the larger meal. Upsettingly, he couldn't find the second baby. He presumed that perhaps a vixen had taken him, perhaps to her cubs. After examining the swaddling clothes wrapped around the dead infant, he realised it was the unnamed of the two that had been carried away.

The worst was yet to come. Father and his sister, Little Wren, had been moved by the slow current of the river. When he found them thirty of forty paces downstream, creating a dam with their bodies at a natural narrowing of the stream, Auroch let out a silent cry. The water had bloated their bodies, damaging them to where they were almost unrecognisable. The young man that was his guard couldn't have been much older than Auroch. He had far kinder eyes than one would expect from a Skull Eater, and he didn't hesitate to help Auroch lift the corpses from the stream. Auroch wondered if he had been there that night, if he felt guilt now, looking at Auroch's familial dead.

One by one, the two men carried the bodies to the small glade that was a sanctuary for the dead. The glade was situated away from the river, equidistant between the men's camp and the women's camp. The grass grew long here, but Auroch knew that if he parted the strands that reached his waist, he would find the bones of his ancestors exposed on the ground.

Bloodied Thistle was waiting. He had reclaimed some furs and bits of clothing from the ruined camps and had set up a small area where he could begin washing and purifying the dead. By the time they brought the first body, that of his sister, Auroch could see that he had removed most of Morning Mist's half-eaten tunic and replaced it with something clean and fresh. Auroch could see dips and creases where parts of her were missing, scavenged by rodents or birds. Auroch and his guard laid the little girl down gently, and Bloodied Thistle began to perform the rites to the best of his ability. Auroch hoped she would look slightly more presentable by the time he returned. Father was in a terrible state, and the two men had to hold his soaked clothes extremely tightly to stop his waterlogged body from falling apart.

Now all the bodies were in the glade, Auroch had to find something that belonged to each of them that could be used to barter for passage across the river to the next life. For Boar, he found a painted rock, the same that his brother had been playing with on the day he had left with Egret to locate the red elder. He found a fishbone needle of his mothers, who had traded a skin for it at the winter meeting on the plains. Although doubtful she could cross, he took it just in case. He flexed it in his fingers, finding it tense and tough, like her. Little Wren had been wearing some jewellery when she died, and Auroch decided to use that as her token. The baby, Burgeoning Yew, was wrapped in a swaddling cloth. Mother had used some dyed fibre to embroider a red zig-zag pattern through its centre. It would do as his token. Mother had stitched a green zig-zag in contrast for the other twin, and it burnt at his conscience that he could not find the unnamed infant's body.

Father's blade had been presumably lost when Auroch had

discovered his family on the night of the massacre. After a bit searching, he found it squashed into the mud near the stump of a tree. He didn't remember dropping it but assumed he must have when he had carried Morning Mist out of the woods. His guard watched patiently as he washed it in the stream before carrying it back to the glade. He placed it in his father's hands, clasping them together with the precious objects as he had with the other corpses.

It was twilight when the Red Fox and Grey Stag made their way to the glade of the dead. Auroch again was impressed with their timing. Grey Stag knew their customs well. Bringing a handful of pebbles from the stream, he pushed one under the tongue of each of his family members. Grey Stag followed his lead, placing the small stone deep in Morning Mist's gullet. Grey Stag, Bloodied Thistle, and Auroch began to carry the bodies deeper and deeper into the long grass. Red Fox, his spear at the ready, held a torch. From its light, it was possible to observe the ancient images, created by Auroch's ancestors, daubed on large freestanding stones, brought there by the ice eons ago, that parted the sea of grass. Wild beasts and the images of First Eagle, who long had driven the Old Men of the hills from the Summer Valley. Mother had told Auroch he also lay here. The first body to be carried was Morning Mist. They brought her deep into the glade, where they were surrounded by dead. Every footstep collided with the bones of one ancestor or another. Auroch had seen many people carried here, but this was the first time he had ever made the journey into the furthest reaches of the glade. Then, out of the darkness, something unexpected. A body, dry and decayed but new, wrapped and prepared just as Bloodied Thistle had done, pushing aside the long grass. And on its face, despite the deterioration, a distinctive headdress of feathers. Old Heron, the chief. Someone had moved his body, prepared him, and placed him here. Auroch's heart began to beat faster. Egret was alive!

Chapter 15

It took them until late into the evening to complete the journey for all the members of Auroch's family. Grey Stag had asked Bloodied Thistle if there was anyone he wished to move into the glade, but he had simply shrugged and grunted no.

"There must have been some survivors," Grey Stag had said, almost cheerfully, as he had examined the chieftain's headdress. "They must have moved Old Heron here. He looked a fine man, much like his father." The elder Old Heron has died long before Auroch's birth, but he would have been a similar age to that of Morning Mist. Every new fact that Grey Stag provided him helped him work out a little bit more of his story. He imagined himself hacking away at a piece of obsidian or flint, sharpening it until it was the perfect shape. The more information he had, the closer he was to completing the imaginary blade. Then he could strike.

Mother was the last to be carried to her rest. Grey Stag stood over Morning Mist as if he was mourning a life never lived. Auroch looked at each of his family members one last time. He said a silent prayer to help guide their crossing. Then he turned around, knowing that if he ever returned, they would be nothing but bones and dust. The dead were dead, and there was nothing more he could do to help them with their forward journey. Time to focus on the living.

The four men made the journey by torchlight back toward the men's camp and the small fire the lit by the remaining guards. They were not pushed away from the campfire that night, as if there was now some understanding between captor and captive. They had travelled out of their way to give the old woman some peace, even according to the customs of her own people. Auroch lay with his back to the fire. Despite the relative gentleness of the men, they were still responsible. If he could, Auroch would still escape, to kill if possible. The discovery of Old Heron has set his mind ablaze. After the initial shock, he realised it didn't have to be Egret who had moved the dead chief. However, the lack of other bodies! Surely if it was someone else, their first instinct wouldn't be to bury Old Heron; there would have been at least one other body there to greet them in the glade. As he lay there, he felt a flicker of hope rising in his chest. He was going to escape, he was going to find Egret, and he was going to kill the old man and his one-eyed companion.

He awoke before all but one of his guards the next morning. Red Fox was there, his one cruel eye squinting at him as he blinked the sleep from his eyelids. Red Fox passed by him, and Auroch could hear Grey Stag stretching and groaning as he tried to stand.

Red Fox spoke to him softly. "Easy now! Careful, you are a young man no longer." He helped the clan chief to his feet.

Bloodied Thistle was risen too. He looked distant. Grey Stag was upright now and stood over him.

"My thanks for your help yesterday, Calf." Auroch could see a cloudiness in his eyes. Perhaps he was beginning to lose the ability to see, as many elderly people did. "Go now with Red Fox and relieve yourself. Then we will rejoin the others."

Red Fox, grabbing his spear, pulled Auroch to his feet. Bloodied Thistle followed voluntarily, and the two men marched toward the treeline. Squatting over a natural depression in the ground, Auroch, his hands still bound, struggled with his deerskin britches, pulling them below his waist. Red Fox was staring at him, making it difficult for him to defecate.

From behind them, Auroch sensed movement. Red Fox was suddenly alert. Auroch turned his head to see a giant elk, its huge horns at least the diameter of a fully grown man, lowered and pointed menacingly at the trio. Auroch recalled the corpse of the elk he had seen in the bog with Egret. Father had always advised him to stay clear. The elk lifted its head and shrieked a warning, ready to charge. Instinctively, Auroch tried to pull his britches up, but his bound hands made him clumsy, and he fell backward, rolling into the ditch intended for his excrement. Red Fox froze, his one eye trained on the elk. The creature began to stomp and paw at the ground. They all knew what was about to happen next. The creature charged, covering the distance between them with lightning speed. Red Fox threw his spear, the shaft spinning towards the elk. It missed.

A surprised, defeated look spread over Red Fox's face as the elk lept over the trench where Auroch lay and ran full tilt into the one-eyed man. Red Fox didn't make a sound as the elk's antlers drove themselves into him, nor did he as it lifted its head up high, tossing him skywards. He flew up at least double his own height, then landed with a thump on the ground, motionless. Auroch was still struggling to pull his britches up around his waist. The elk began to violently stab at Red Fox's body with his antlers before pulling him under his powerful legs, stomping and kicking at him. Bloodied Thistle and Auroch, lying in the trench, watched as he was thrown and pushed around by the animal.

Auroch wasn't sure what caused the elk to divert his attention from the bleeding and battered Red Fox. After a while, it seemed to hear something imperceptible to the two men, raising its head before running off into the woodland. The pair silently waited a moment before rising from the trench. The need to defecate had deserted Auroch. Red Fox was lying on his front, a pool of his blood seeping into the damp earth. He lay motionless, but when Bloodied Thistle turned him, a sharp, painful breath rattled through his chest. He was alive. Just.

"Let us depart." Auroch felt the words leave his mouth without thinking. They could run now while they still had a chance. They were in familiar terrain. Perhaps they could even beat the slow-moving column of men, women, and children to the meeting on the plains.

"He's going to die," said Bloodied Thistle with a twinge of sympathy. "Perhaps they have medicine to help him?"

"Curse him," Auroch gritted his teeth. What was Bloodied Thistle thinking? "Why bother helping this animal?"

"Everyone is dead." Bloodied Thistle announced solemnly. "Where to run to? What are we to do?"

"To the plains? We can tell the other tribes about the massacre.

About the consumption of men's flesh!"

Bloodied thistle looked at his feet, shame bubbling over into his face. "We ate it too. Not willingly, but we ate it."

Auroch realised what was going to happen now. "Please don't," he said weakly.

"They may give us a life, Auroch. A great evil has been done, but perhaps we can rekindle something of our former selves when we have gained their trust."

Auroch's heart was pounding. He couldn't believe that Bloodied Thistle was about to throw away this opportunity for escape. He swallowed, pulling himself together.

"I'm going to run," Auroch said calmly. "Please give me time."

"You have a little while," Bloodied Thistle said glumly. "But then I will shout for help."

Bloodied Thistle bent down, pulling a blade hanging from the tunic of the barely conscious Red Fox. He began to rub it on the bindings around Auroch's wrist, freeing the boy. Auroch shook off the rope, liberated for the first time in at least a moon. The rope had burned and cut into his flesh. Now he was free of it; the stinging he had pushed to the periphery of his mind began to incapacitate his thoughts. Regardless, he was free! He stood up and looked Bloodied Thistle in the eyes. He wasn't sure if he should hit him or embrace him. The two men nodded at each other before Auroch disappeared into the undergrowth.

He was still close enough to hear when Bloodied Thistle called for help. But he was far enough away where he could get away from the Skull Eaters. He would easily outrun the two spearmen and Grey Stag if he kept moving now. Using the morning sun as a guide, he headed east. He needed to get through the valley, walk the well-worn path through the great mesa, then follow the river down towards the Great Lake, and beyond, the meeting rock on the Great Plains. Auroch was getting excited now. It was Autumn; he knew that much, but he had to reach the plains before the winter solstice. He was sprinting now, madly, uncontrollably through the trees. On his left side, the dense treeline gave way to a river, a harsh, almost vertical bank leading down to cold water, thrashing and twisting below. It was unusually violent for the time of year, but Auroch knew this tributary would take him at least out of the valley, where he could begin to gather some food and perhaps cut a weapon for the long journey. He had nothing but the clothes on his back, but he felt confident. He had the knowledge that Father had taught him. He knew these lands, and he knew the trees and the animals that lived within them. He was going to survive.

At that exact moment, Auroch's foot caught a protruding branch. He fell forward, stopping himself with his hands before his face hit the wet earth. He picked himself up and tried to stand. As soon as he exerted pressure on his left foot, he fell again, landing back on the ground, the mud oozing between his fingers. He tried to stand for a second time, and a horrific shooting pain ran through his ankle. He had twisted his muscle or broken a bone. He was done for. After all that, he would be undone by a momentary error. He tried again but collapsed back into a shivering puddle. It was bad enough if someone had a severe injury in summer when food was plentiful and the nights were warm. But out here, now, alone, he was going to die.

The voices of the guards that had accompanied them to the valley began to echo through the trees. They were looking for him. The shouts were becoming louder and louder. There was no way he could outrun them now. Perhaps he could conceal himself by hanging vertically on the slope over the river? He pulled himself to his knees and began to crawl. The pain was terrible but at least bearable compared to his attempt to walk. He made his way to the side of the slope. The protruding root of a tree provided a neat handhold, and he grasped onto it firmly as he lowered himself over the side. There was little purchase on the slope, and as he was unable to put one foot down, he found himself dangling almost vertically over the river, his hands turning white as he gripped onto the exposed roots. He kicked at the dirt with his uninjured foot until he was able to bury his toes into the side. He wondered how long he could hang like this, the top of his head peering over the edge of the riverbank. He looked down briefly. The fall wasn't too bad, perhaps twice his height to drop until he hit the water rushing through the ravine below. The voices were louder now, and he could hear them above the sound of the water crashing against the rocks.

    They were right on top of him. He lowered his head below the bank, hoping his muddy hands wouldn't be seen, holding onto the root just above. From his hiding place, he listened. The men had slowed to a stop, obviously out of breath. His hands were slipping from the wet roots. Not much longer. They would leave soon, he told himself. The conversation continued, the men bickering worriedly. He needed to adjust his hand to get a better grip but didn't dare risk movement. The voices began to get quieter, and Auroch guessed they had started to move away. He had to risk it. He pulled himself up, his head bobbing above the riverbank. He could see the two men walking away from him through the undergrowth. Momentary elation turned to horror as one of the men casually glanced back, meeting Auroch's gaze. He shouted, and the other spearman turned. The two men bolted for him, covering the ground towards the cliff in mere moments. Auroch had no time to react. He couldn't allow himself to be captured again. He let go of the root and fell backward, silently, into the churning river below.

Waves of agony engulfed his body as he was thrown back and forth beneath the water. The pain in his ankle was just part of the general assault on his person by the bends of the river as he bounced off rocks and was smashed into the riverbed as the current took him under. He pushed against the force dragging him along, pulling himself above the water, only to be pulled under again. He tried to put his feet down to stop himself, but a jolt of pain passed through him. Water was pouring down his gullet. A sense of finality began to overcome him. Even if he managed not to drown and haul himself out of the river, he wouldn't be able to move until his leg was healed. He felt peaceful. There was no panic. And besides, he was so, so tired. He began to slip into a pleasant unconsciousness. Despite the rocks banging into him, the pain faded into a dull thump. He was jolted out of the calm respite by a shooting pain under his arm. Someone was gripping him. Someone strong. Another hand under his other arm. Someone was pulling him from the water. He found himself hauled out of the water and onto a bank. A figure towered over him. Auroch momentarily wondered who it was before passing out.

Chapter 16

It wasn't clear where he lay initially. He was moving, and snatches of consciousness revealed a flat landscape. He was close to the ground and being dragged along at a steady rate. A few seconds, then stop. A few more seconds, then he would stop again. He fell into oblivion once more before briefly awakening as cold snowflakes hit his face. When he opened his eyes again, the muddy ground had been covered in a thin sheet of white snow. It was coming down fast, and he was finding it harder and harder to fall back into tranquil darkness as the cold began working its way into his bones. He managed to open his eyes and move his stiff neck to see enough to see what was going on. He was on some kind of sled, secured to it, and covered in furs. A broad, muscular figure was pulling it. Next to him walked a dog, obediently patting through the white-speckled ground at his master's heels. Auroch felt fatigue and pain overcoming him, and he fell back into a deep sleep.

The next time he awoke, he was no longer moving. He was warmer now, and it was dark. He could see the outline of stalagmites above him, lit by a flame coming from another chamber. He was sweating and realised he was weighted down by a heavy pile of furs. He tried to move, but a cloak of soreness and pain enveloped him. It travelled through his muscles and almost caused him to cry out. He licked his lips. He was thirsty. How long had he been unconscious? A figure tottered into the entrance of the chamber. It was an older woman hunched over. She smiled, a kindly face below a web of grey facial tattoos. She shuffled over to where Auroch lay, producing a bowl of water. He held it to his lips, and he drank greedily. Producing herbs from a moleskin pouch, she began to grind them against a small flat rock with a round stone. She waddled back to the chamber with the fire and then back again, the crushed herbs having been converted into a bowl of greenish broth. Once again, she held it to his mouth, and he drank.

"Sleep. You can sleep now young man," she said. Her soothing voice had a strange lilt, but Auroch was pleased to hear that she could speak his tongue. Whatever was in the broth seemed to relax his muscles. Her eyes watched him as he drifted from the tangible and back into a realm of dreams.

He was with Father, walking across the tundra. Snow smattered the ground. An elk was on the horizon, the one that had attacked Red Fox. There was no hint of aggression in its demeanour. It didn't lower its head or stomp its feet. Father and son walked towards the animal slowly and calmly. The elk continued to watch them, unperturbed. When they were within charging distance, Auroch stopped.

"No Father, please," he pleaded, "please stop."

Father didn't listen. He continued towards the elk cautiously. He held out his hand, and the elk trotted towards him. Father laughed as the elk lay its snout in his outstretched hand. Auroch was too far away; Father and the elk seemed to stretch away from him. He ran towards them, but he couldn't get any closer. The elk's long face began to absorb Father's arm, and Father's whole body disappeared into the elk, melting away into the huge animal's frame. Auroch couldn't reach them.

When Auroch awoke again, he could see a different kind of light seeping into the chamber. The light was harsher, and a cold breeze blew through the cave, rattling through the thick furs that covered him. It was daytime, and whatever fire had been lit in the next chamber was extinguished now. He tried to move, but every movement betrayed how bruised and battered his body was. It was clear that these people meant him no harm in the short term. They had pulled him from the river downstream of where he had escaped, so it was unlikely they were with the Skull Eaters. They had fed and watered him, and seemingly left him alone in this cave. Maybe they had left? He wondered if he should get up and look for them outside. As he thought about his options, he watched the light entering the chamber grow dimmer and dimmer, the cool white light of the day giving way to the orange of sunset. He accepted he wasn't going to move. He heard voices, too far away to make out the words but close enough to recognise that there were three. The old woman he had seen the night before and presumably the man who had pulled him from the river. The third voice was lighter and more feminine. Auroch felt he if he recognised it, as if it were something from a half-forgotten dream.

The conversation trailed off as the three entered the cave and lit a fire in the chamber next to his. The old woman once again waddled into his chamber, and Auroch closed his eyes, feigning a deep sleep. Perhaps he could learn something while he lay here. The sound of her footsteps echoed around the chamber for a while, obviously checking to see if Auroch had awakened. After a while she turned back, mumbling something to the man, who grunted in agreement. Auroch chanced, opening his eyes. The glow from the fire was bouncing off the walls once again, creating a light show as flickering shadows fought and merged into each other. Auroch again tested himself to see if he could rise from his bedding. Perhaps tomorrow.

He was beginning to drift back into an easy and trouble-free sleep when another voice bounced through the cave. However, this wasn't a few mumbled words of hurried instruction but a wail. The sound was loud, angry, sad, and scared, but it was a sound that Auroch had heard a thousand times. The cry of an infant. The hairs on the back of his neck stood up. He knew the chances were slim, but for the first time in days, he felt a surge of strength pass through him. His aching bones obeyed him, and he cast off the thick furs that covered him. He stood, making sure not to put too much weight on his leg. It still hurt, but Auroch could tell he was on his way to recovery. He limped forward, making his way toward the occupied chamber. Beyond the baby's cry, he could hear hushed voices. He rounded the corner and took in the scene.

There were four sitting around the fire. There was the woman with her face tattoos, her gnarled complexion unable to hide the kindness below. There was the old man who had pulled him from the river, a lifetime of hardship making him strong and adept. Opposite to where Auroch stood sat a girl with dark braided hair, the grace and poise of a future Spirit-Mother and a knowing smile on her lips. Egret. As overjoyed as he was to see her, he couldn't take his eyes off the source of the noise. In Egret's arms was a baby, wrapped in a cloth with a green zig-zag pattern embroidered onto it. Mother's handiwork. The unnamed child, his brother. He lived.

Winter

Chapter 17

The cold grabbed at Auroch's exposed face as he made his way up the sharp slope. He was getting desperate, and beginning to wonder what exactly he had done this afternoon to upset the ancestors. Peering across the snowy landscape, he spotted the rock he had used to mark his next snare. He trudged through the thick snowdrift, careful not to put too much weight on his recovering ankle. The snare was empty. He sighed. There wasn't much sunlight left. He would have to get lucky soon if they were to eat tonight.

He continued, picking up the trail of distinctive pockmarks in the snow of hooves that he had spent the morning following. He sensed he was close and instinctively lowered himself to the ground. There was little cover on the Tundra. Auroch crawled through the snow to a remaining patch of yellowed long grass and hid himself as best he could. Across the bow of the small hill trotted thirty or so reindeer. He was downwind, and they hadn't seen him. Seeing the reindeer was a sharp reminder of how far behind the usual seasonal routine he was. The huge herds of reindeer would normally be intercepted on the plains, travelling south in late autumn. This small group had been separated from the others somehow, perhaps intentionally by hunters.

This was going to be difficult. If only he had convinced the old man to help him set more snares, then there would be less riding on a successful deer kill. His rescuer, also known as Weary Horse, had gone to the river to fish as he always did. He was a keen fisherman, and as Auroch was amateurish at spearing the silvery trout, he thought better to leave him to it. Auroch watched as the reindeer scraped away the snow with their hooves to get at the lichen below. If he was quick and quiet, he could still quite easily hit one whilst it was stationary. Grasping his spear tightly, he pulled himself up from the long grass and breathed in. The long, thin dart flew through the air, hitting a young buck square in the neck. It dropped to the ground immediately, bleating, and the rest of the herd scattered. He had it. He was ready.

Carrying the carcass back to the cave, he reflected on the time he had spent so far with Egret and the couple. He had guessed she had escaped when he had found the wrapped body of her father, but it was a relief to see her again in the flesh. She had explained to him that on the night of the massacre, she had made her way through the smoke and haze before finding her way to the river, where she had arrived just in time to see Auroch's family slaughtered by several of Grey Stag's men. She had hidden in the undergrowth, frozen by fear, until they had moved on. As she had begun to leave, she heard the baby crying amongst the bodies.

Grabbing the child, she fled into the thick forest on the walls of the valley. Egret had hidden with the infant for days, starved and scared before venturing down to the river a drink. She had one of her episodes at the river's edge, falling to the ground, convulsing and unconscious, choking on her own tongue.

Weary Horse, fishing for trout upriver, had seen the girl shaking and twitching on the river's bank and ran to her, rolling Egret on her side and holding her head still so she didn't bash it on the pebbles. After the spirits had passed through her, he had decided to take her in.

Weary Horse and his wife, known as Stoat, were clanless people. Auroch had encountered clanless before, folk who lived alone or in tiny groups of just two or three, eking out a harsh living without much contact with the larger groups. They weren't generally considered to be harmful. Although rare, sometimes they appeared on the plains over winter for trade, a few precious stones here and there in exchange for some antler tools or meat. Many of the clanless had once belonged to the tribes of the plains, and as such, most of them knew their customs. Egret explained how Weary Horse and Stoat had, as they lived in the vicinity of the valley, been in contact several times with the Valleyfolk and, as recently as ten summers ago, actually accompanied them to the plains for the winter solstice.

Taking in Egret and the baby, they had nursed the pair back to health. Stoat had been a willing carer to the infant. She had raised children of her own, but they were long since dead. The old couple lived just as a pair, fishing and scavenging food for two. Auroch couldn't imagine such a lonely life. But with the Men of the Summer Valley gone, wasn't he just as alone? He tried to push this thought to the back of his mind.

Egret explained how she had pleaded with the couple to let her return to the old camp to bury Old Heron and as many of the dead tribe as she could manage. They hadn't relented until one evening, as the winter's cold began to set in, Weary Horse had agreed. They set off back to the valley the next day, leaving the child with Stoat.

Reaching the valley, Egret identified her father and laid him to rest with the respect she felt he deserved. Her voice had quivered as she told Auroch this, and despite his cruelty to her just before his death, she seemed to have expunged him of his sins. Auroch wondered if she would do the same for him. As Egret and Weary Horse emerged from the glade, they had heard voices. Quickly ducking out of sight, they had witnessed Auroch and Bloodied Thistle arrive as captives alongside Grey Stag and his men to bury Morning Mist. Egret had looked at the floor as she told Auroch this part. They hadn't attempted some grand rescue. They had decided to leave, unable to help the two men. He had been lucky then, ending up in the river, swept to a point only a few strides from where Weary Horse and Egret were slowly trudging back to the cave that had become their winter home.

It took Auroch longer than expected to haul the deer carcass across the windswept landscape. The reindeer, slung over his back, caused him to sink in the heavier snowdrifts as he climbed across the barren hillocks back to the rocky outcrop where the old couple lived. The hide boots he had been given kept most of the cold and wet out, but the wind was sharp and hard and seemed to blow through him no matter what he was wearing. The sun was setting now, creating an orange glow across the horizon. Auroch had already reached the plains this time of year as far back as he could remember. There was something strange and slightly magical about seeing familiar places under winter's spell. He could see features that he recognised, partly obfuscated by mountains of fresh, thick white power and the ravages of winter on leaves and bark. He didn't see another set of large footprints leading back to the cave. Good. Weary Horse had not yet returned. He seemed like a decent old man, but Auroch wasn't terribly fond of him. He said very little and appeared to possess no kind of humour or levity. He had cared for Egret and the child and taken in Auroch when he was injured. However, Auroch felt as if the old man mistrusted him in some way, as if he had assumed responsibility for Egret and sensed that Auroch had previously hurt her. Perhaps she had told him of his earlier betrayal while he was unconscious? Auroch wished not to broach the subject.

He entered the cave to find Egret and Stoat sorting through an assortment of berries on the ground. He noticed their bright red colour and felt a small sigh of relief leave his lips. The winter fruits had come a little early this year. The child lay on the floor, unable to move due to the heavy cloth wrapped around him. Egret's eyes widened as she saw the reindeer carcass. An audible cheer came from little old Stoat, who began to instruct him.

"Put it in the other chamber. I will see to it, my dear. Quickly, warm yourself by the fire! Before the winter spirits get into your muscles!"

Auroch carefully placed the carcass in the other chamber that had been designated by Weary Horse for butchering meat. Stoat began to fuss and scurry around, making sure she had everything she needed to ready the animal for use. Auroch strode back to the fire and sat down opposite Egret.

"Thank you," she said quietly, without looking up from her task.

"Clearly as we approach the solstice, the huntsman spirit favours your arm."

Auroch thought for a second, unsure how to approach the difficult conversation he was about to have. "I'm ready. My ankle has healed, and I can feel the strength returning to my body." He spoke with a quiet confidence. Still, Egret didn't look up.

"You are going to leave?" She asked, her voice not betraying her feelings towards his proposition.

"The Skull Eaters…the banished. They are moving so slowly. I can beat them to the meeting on the plains. I can warn the other tribes. They won't stand for what they did. They have other prisoners; they can be freed." Auroch insisted.

"You have lost a lot of time, Calf." Egret replied, "It's a long, lonely road ahead."

"I know. That is why I want you to come with me."

Egret finally looked up incredulously. A pit formed in Auroch's stomach. This wasn't going to go to plan.

"Why would I go with you, Auroch? My life is worth even more in barter now as the last Spirit-Maiden of the Summer Valley. I would be taken and paired off even faster than before! What a curiosity, the last woman with knowledge of the medicines of the valley. The last who can perform their ceremonies, their rites."

"But what about what Grey Stag did? To my family! To your father! To Morning Mist!" as he mentioned Old Heron, he thought he saw a crack in her facade. He had hoped retribution would be a strong enough motivator. Egret dropped a handful of berries in the bowl by her side and looked him dead in the eyes.

"Auroch, when I left you in the valley that day after we had the red elder, what did I ask? I don't wish to participate in any vengeful hunt. I don't wish to carry on the wishes of my dead father or to be Spirit-Mother like Morning Mist. I am happy tribeless. My life is my own here in this little cave. I will look after the child here while you run headfirst into more conflict and misery. I do not wish to leave. Whatever thread connected us through the shared destiny of the Summer Valley has been severed. I am not going with you." She paused for a moment and sighed. "The Solstice is soon, the most important time of the year for any Spirit-Maiden, when I must renew my connection to White Owl and restate my vows. To walk away from this commitment would incur a punishment of death, yet I still may not do it. I wish to leave that life behind."

Auroch raised his hand to object, but as he brought his finger to an accusatory point, a shadow fell across the pair as Weary Horse's aged, bulky frame blocked the entrance. Under one arm, he carried an enormous trout. They would eat well tonight.

"Thank you, First Eagle, maker, for blessing us this day." Egret said, her words far away from the blasphemous intent she had muttered only moments ago.

Auroch sat up late that night. After a meal of reindeer meat, he had taken some ochre and begun to paint images on the cave walls. From memory, he drew Great-Tusk, the mammoth, imposing but gentle. He suspected the others hadn't believed him when he told them about the man who could command such a beast, but he hadn't expected them to. He had tried to broach the possibility with Weary Horse of all four of them and the baby making the trip to the plains, but the old man had cut him off sharply.

"We are too old," he said, angry at the impetuousness of youth. "We will die in these hills."

Of course, there was no discussion about what was to happen to Egret and the baby. The old couple hadn't thought that far ahead. Weary Horse, Stoat, Egret, and the baby had retired to the other chamber as the fire began to die down. As Auroch sat in the cave, he tried to focus on the colours and shapes he was creating, smearing the ochre into tangible, something real. He heard footsteps behind him and turned to see Egret emerge from the other chamber.

"Foul dreams pester me," she said bluntly, taking a seat beside the painting boy.

She watched him for a while, noticing how he smudged the colours together to create the illusion of fur on the lower body of the mammoth. Coupled with the fire's flickering and the rock's curvature, it looked as if the great beast was moving, trudging through whatever landscape they dared to imagine behind it.

"Would you like to join me?" Auroch asked earnestly.

Painting was a communal process just as often as it was a solitary one, with different people adding different animals to create a scene collaboratively. She shook her head.

"May I perform a rite for your journey?" she asked.

"Please do."

She pulled out a medicine bag, and from it, a pouch containing powdery rock scraped from a stalactite. She let a tiny dribble pour onto her palm and closed her fingers over it, using the tips to roll the grains into an ever-finer powder.

"Hold out your tongue," she commanded. Auroch opened his mouth and obeyed. She opened her palm and let the powder fall onto it. "Swallow." He did as instructed.

"Take this one, White Owl. Hold him tightly in your warm palm and carry him through the trials that lie ahead. Hold him fast against the crashing waves of fate and against the angry charge of death. Keep him close, White Owl, for his long journey through the canyon of the soul, as slings and spears reign down upon him. Keep him safe, White Owl."

She looked him in the eyes as she recited the rite of safe passage, and Auroch realised how long it had been since he had seen anything that had stirred anything but hate and misery in his heart. Her big green eyes, with the red ochre painting set behind her, were a beacon of technicolour in the drab white, grey, and brown landscape. He hadn't noticed her grab his hands as she had given him the powder to taste, but her warm, soft palms cupped his. He felt natural urges rise inside him, but he beat them back. He was leaving at first light.

"May I ask you a question, Spirit-Maiden?" He said, aware that this might be the last time in a while he would receive any kind of guidance. Egret nodded, not releasing his gaze. "Mother. She died without naming the child. Is there anything we can do to help her cross the river, to meet her ancestors?"

Egret released his hands and stood up. She turned, pacing back and forth. "We don't have long before the solstice." She said, deep in thought. "I would have to make the offering to renew my commitment under the winter sun."

"Less than a single moon," Auroch said, not enjoying her change in demeanour.

"Perhaps…" she turned and looked intensely at Auroch. "It can be done. We can name the child with the first buds of spring."

"And that will guarantee Mother's passage?" Auroch exclaimed excitedly.

"It should. But we can no longer do it in the valley. There is no birth there, only death, between charred trees and corpses."

"Then where?" Auroch asked, his heart beating faster and louder. Egret looked mournfully at the floor. She didn't want to say. Auroch guessed the next words before they left her mouth.

"On the plains, on the hilltop by the great cavern where tribes gather. The old oak stood lonely on the grasses. Under which the men of the world come to meet. We can perform the ceremony in spring, under its green boughs, when the tree is born anew."

"And you will help me? You will perform the ceremony?"

"I will."

Chapter 18

The pair left that same night without saying farewell. Egret made no noise as she retrieved the supplies they needed the long journey to the plains. Auroch suspected the old couple were awake, but they said nothing and didn't move as Egret pulled dried fruits, meats, and tools into a bag for Auroch to carry. He carefully slung the fox skin bag over his shoulders, gaging its weight for the long journey ahead. After wrapping the baby in thick layers of fur, Auroch placed him in a cradleboard before securing it to Egret's back. The child made the journey exponentially more difficult, but it was the sole reason he now had a travelling companion in Egret, and it meant more of a chance for salvation for his mother's soul.

They departed just before dawn, the fresh snow falling away from their thick deerskin boots as they walked with purpose upstream. They were headed northeast now, following along the bank of the great river as it cut a swath through the frozen landscape. Blocks of ice bobbed in the water as they moved along its bank. Despite the harshness of this time of year, there were plenty of animals to be seen as they followed the river. Hares, foxes, and other small mammals could be occasionally spotted sipping at the water's edge. Fishes, making their way downstream, could be seen through the churning mass of black water.

Auroch, grateful for Egret's sacrifice, spoke little as they trudged through the snow. They hadn't discussed what would happen when they reached the meeting of the tribes. The elders there would know her. She was right. With the Men of the Summer Valley dead, she would be viewed as an even more valuable commodity. Auroch hoped that more of his people had escaped the massacre and made their way to the plains. He pushed the thought to the back of his mind. It had been a miracle that Egret and the child had survived; he didn't wish to trick himself into thinking this event was likely repeatable. The silence became comfortable, only pierced when the child began to wail or cry. Taking this as a sign it was time to stop, the pair would briefly halt, taking the baby out of its pouch and cradling or feeding it some of the berries mashed into a fine paste by Egret's pestle and mortar. However, the child was largely quiet and content to either sleep or gurgle as they made their way along the riverbank.

In the mid-afternoon, it began to grow dark, and finding a rocky outcrop sheltered below a few barren trees, the pair collected kindling before starting a fire and settling in for the night. They slept together for warmth, pressed into one another as the fire burned down to embers. Auroch would shudder as he got up from the warmth of the furs and Egret's body to put some more dry wood on the fire. Occasionally, the wind managed to find its way through the trees and force its way into their shelter. The flame would bow down as if it was ready to go out before springing back to life.

The next few days progressed in much the same fashion. Auroch was able to snare a couple of unfortunate hares, and they ate them greedily at the end of each day's trek after roasting them. The river began to cut down through the ground as they followed its path and other tributaries joined it. They carefully made their way around the various confluences, occasionally having to risk a dangerous crossing on a downed log or having to backtrack in order to find a suitable place to cross. As the canyon began to rise on either side, shelters became more and more numerous, but there were fewer and fewer animals descending the steep walls to drink at the bottom. Still, they continued, stopping only to nurse the child, find food, and eat. The comfortable silence gave way to small talk and eventually the humdrum natter of travelling companions talking the hours away as they followed the river. Auroch joked that he had eaten better when he was kept as a slave, and Egret laughed, throwing her head back and flashing Auroch with her pretty smile.

They were perhaps five days into the journey when the canyon became impassable due to heavy snow and ice. A rockslide caused by heavy snowfall had destroyed the narrow path by the river, making it impossible for Auroch and Egret to carry on. Conferring quickly, the pair decided to retrace their steps, returning to a natural path out of the canyon they had passed earlier this morning.

"We can climb out and then walk across the mesa," Auroch said hopefully as they made their way up the steep path.

"How far until the tributaries converge?" Egret asked. She knew the answer, Auroch suspected, but was attempting to stimulate conversation.

"Perhaps two-days walk? We have never gone over the mesa before. The route through the canyon is usually clear in summer." He tried to sound confident, but there was little substance behind his words. He didn't know what was waiting for them up there, especially as he hadn't been up there at this time of year before.

They reached the top quicker than he expected. It had been a challenging climb, and Auroch wouldn't bring to Egret's attention that his ankle was still causing him some discomfort. As if she could read his mind, she began fussing over the infant, giving Auroch ample time to catch his breath and let the sharp pain settle into a dull thud. The pair could see far into the distance, across the plain, scarred by the deep, narrow canyon that cut through it. They began to walk, following as near enough to the top of the canyon walls as possible. The wind blew over the flat landscape ferociously, causing Auroch's hands to numb underneath his fur gloves. The child's cries intensified, but the only solution was to keep pressing on. They could perhaps reach a path back down into the canyon. Auroch could see hills stretching in front of him across the flats. Maybe they could make it there before nightfall? There would be shelter; they could warm the child and plot a new route. They couldn't just keep walking across the open like this.

The afternoon's walk became a slow trudge through the fresh snow. The meagre wildlife in the canyon had disappeared completely, and there was little to differentiate one part of the mesa from the next as all the natural features melted away underneath the blanket of white. The sunlight turned to gloom as clouds rolled in, and soon the sky became the same colour as the ground. Snowflakes began to fall thick and fast, and the child cried even louder. It was hard to tell the difference between the sky and the snow, but the pair kept marching, focussing on the grey of the partially covered rockface against a sea of white.

A flash of brown and red interrupted the monochrome of the landscape directly in front of them. A mass, some sort of huge animal, lay in front of them, partially buried by snowfall. Auroch approached it, the thick blanket that covered much of the beast obscuring its identity. It had been carved up, and much of the meat and organs had been removed. There was very little left, although it had clearly been butchered in a hurry, without the care and attention usually reserved for the largest of beasts. Auroch recognised the thick, mattered wool hanging limply off its frame and the long face devoid of its distinctive horn. A rhino. This was rare. They lived in small groups, some even living solitary lives, and there were very few. Auroch was a little surprised to see one so far west.

"They may have come through here," Auroch said bluntly, not wishing to commit to a hypothesis.

"The Skull Eaters? How long ago?" replied Egret, using the stop to attend to the child.

"The Banished, yes. The cold has preserved the meat. It's hard to tell. A moon? It's butchered clumsily, in a hurry, but they have removed much of the flesh and insides. Many hands worked here." Auroch said, shivering. The procession may be closer than he had anticipated. Perhaps there were scouts watching from the hills ahead, tracking them as they moved across the flats.

Auroch chopped away at any tendons or bone that looked usable and placed it in his bag. He felt unnerved, as if eyes could be watching him. It wasn't the solstice yet, and he had assumed that the group would have reached the plains before then. But there was still a great deal of the journey to go. It was an uncanny omen to see a woolly rhino here. He understood they had once been greater in number, but this was the first time the Valleyfolk had encountered one for perhaps twelve winters. Occasionally, individuals would make their way onto the plains, but it was rare and made for quite an event when one was spotted. The prized horns Auroch had seen had been larger than this, and he guessed this was a juvenile. The pair continued, the grey sky making it increasingly difficult to tell what time of day it was. The evening must be coming to a close, Auroch thought, yet those hills felt as far away as ever. They would have to keep walking after sundown. They could not sleep here in the open. He decided not to let Egret know his concern until it was necessary, although he suspected, as usual, she was thinking the same.

Then, out of the white and grey gloom came another colour, from the west. It was a shade of brown, lighter in some parts, darker in others, and moving toward them at pace. Another rhino. Egret saw it too, and the pair began to run through the thick snow away from the animal. Auroch knew the rhino could see very little but had a proficient sense of smell. He hoped that the snow might help cover their scent. He was acutely aware of how little more he knew, their sightings being a rarity, mostly reported by the eastern tribes. It was behind them now, following them, padding through the snow with far greater ease than was afforded to them. Every few strides, Egret glanced back. Auroch thought through the equipment he had. Thin spears tipped with deer antler, a flint knife, and scrapers. Not enough to kill the beast. He needed a group of hunters.

"I'm going to draw its attention," Auroch panted. "Keep moving towards the hills."

Egret nodded, barely slowing down. The precious cargo secured to her back was crying loudly now, the sound echoing around the empty plains. Auroch broke away from them, running right towards the canyon. He thought he could lower himself onto a ledge, throwing the beast off his trail when Egret was far away. He shouted and hollered, hoping the rhino would go for him.

Auroch glanced over his shoulder to see it barrelling towards him across the plain. Good. It was faster, but Auroch guessed like most animals, it couldn't maintain it's speed for as long as a man could run. He was sprinting as fast as he could now, the adrenaline helping his legs cut through the heavy snow and keeping his residual ankle pain at bay. He took another look behind him. It was still coming. A twang of agony shot up his leg as his foot collided with a rock buried beneath the snow. He stumbled, falling onto all fours before pulling himself to his feet. He gulped and imagined himself swallowing the pain, feeling it slide down his throat and into his stomach, where it became a distant ache. He scrambled to his feet and sprinted again, but the thick white sea surrounding his legs impeded him. He was stuck in it now, weight pushing him down with every step. He could hear the heavy crunch of the rhino, its breathing. He didn't dare look behind him, but he knew it was upon him. He dived to the left.

He felt the smooth keratin rub against his skin, grazing him, as the Rhino's horn penetrated his thick winter tunic just above his shoulder.

He was lifted instantaneously into the air, missing out on being impaled by a hair's breadth. The world spun violently as Auroch, whose clothing was now impaled on the rhino's horn, was picked up and thrown to and fro as the animal thrashed around. With a great rip, the stitching on his clothes came undone, and he was flying again through the air. The snow cushioned his landing, and the cold sent a shock through his body as it touched the now-exposed parts of his upper torso. His tunic was completely ripped. Auroch patted himself down instinctively, looking for a great wound where the horn might have torn into his flesh. Nothing. He was impossibly, miraculously unharmed. He could hear the animal snorting and battering the ground with its hooves only a few strides from him. Perhaps he should play dead? He had been told that it wouldn't fall for it, but he couldn't think of any alternatives.

He whispered a quick prayer to White Owl, the maiden of wisdom, hoping that inspiration would strike him. He had to get up to see the beast, to devise some kind of plan in the moments before the beast charged again. He stretched forward, putting his arm out to push himself up. There was nothing there. He realised he was at the edge of the mesa. Below him was the ravine he and Egret had been following, hoping they could find their way back down. A sheer drop. Had he been tossed any further and he would have fallen straight down to his death. His snow blindness had completely obscured it while fleeing from the rhino.

He pushed himself back from the edge and leaped to his feet, spinning as he did so to face the rhino. It snorted, tattered thread and animal skins hanging from its face. It stood about eight strides from him now, angrily bobbing its head around. Auroch watched its movement, meeting its small, black eyes with his own. They had terrible eyes, the men from the east had said. He moved his feet around, placing his foot down with force to test his ankle. His eyes watered in pain. But it was strong enough. He howled, hoping to rile the beast. Removing his mitten, he bent down and grabbed a lump of snow, balling it up with his exposed hand. He threw it squarely at the rhino's head, waiting to see its reaction. It charged.

Auroch was ready. He threw himself to the side, rolling out of the way of the heavy hooves smashing through the snow. He turned just in time to see the rhino wiggle its limbs helplessly in the air as it tumbled down the cliff face into the frozen river below.

Chapter 19

Auroch watched the river for a short while as if he was worried the beast would suddenly spring from its depths, alive and vengeful. The shaking that had been caused by the adrenaline of his encounter was gradually replaced by shivering, and quickly Auroch became aware of his tattered clothes. He was missing a mitten and spent a few moments searching for it before concluding it had gone over the cliff with his opponent. It was twilight now, and he scanned his surroundings. He could just about make out the outline of the rock face where he assumed Egret had fled with the baby. It was snowing harder every moment he stood by the ravine, and he knew shortly that he wouldn't be able to see anything. The clouds, pregnant with snow, obscured any trace of moonlight or the guiding instrument of the stars. His ankle pain worsened, the throbbing fighting through Auroch's mental defences. Turning to the hills, he began to walk, hoping his aggressive pace would keep him warm and that holding a steady direction would keep him on course. The weather was getting worse. It was pitch black now, and even the snowflakes bouncing off the exposed parts of his torso were invisible. A dark, swilling mass battered him, confounding him. Was he going the right way? He tripped and fell, finding himself disorientated.

His thoughts turned to Egret and the baby. Had they made it to the rocks in time to find shelter? He was cold. Really cold. He hoped they had found warmth. The baby couldn't survive in this. His shoulder had ceased to hurt from the winds and snow ripping into it and had taken on a kind of numbness that worked its way down through his arm and attacked his ungloved hand. He tripped again. He lay for a moment before pulling himself to his feet. Was he walking in the same direction as he had been previously? He was lost in an inky maelstrom. He tripped for a third time, falling to his knees. After all this, he was going to die alone, lost in a snowstorm. He couldn't feel his hands or feet at all now.

Then, out of the darkness, a tiny light appeared. It seemed to be a speck on the edge of his vision, but it grew steadily larger. Auroch fell on his side. He watched it as it moved around, zigzagging across the landscape. Suddenly, it was moving in a constant direction towards him. From behind it, he could see a round, soft face. Egret. She bent down next to him, examining his ripped clothing.

"Look away, Auroch. You are not permitted to see this." Her voice was barely audible above the sound of the wind.

Arouch obliged, tightly shutting his eyes. She began to whisper breathlessly. Auroch could only catch one word in ten but heard one clear above the cacophony of winds.

"Calm."

She helped him to his feet, and the two began to walk back in the direction she had appeared from. He wasn't sure how she knew where she was going in the dark, but he let her guide him, trusting her instincts. The wind against his skin seemed to soften, and the swirling flurry of snow in front of his face began to slow. They were walking, hand in hand, Egret confidently pulling his cold, battered body along behind her.

Then, out of nowhere, a cliff face appeared ahead of him. It was dark, but the torch, still lit against all expectations, revealed its contours and crevasses to them. Egret slowly worked her way around it with her hand, following the outline of the cliff wall until she found a narrow gap. She squeezed through it, pulling Auroch along after her. The darkness gave way to light, and Auroch found himself in a dimly lit hollow among the rocks, a small fire burning.

The child was there, cushioned under a mass of clothing, near the fire. Auroch wondered how long the infant had been left in Egret's attempt to find him. She sat him down by the small fire and grabbed some of the clothes covering the child, and placed them around Auroch's frozen shoulders. She carefully removed his mitten and boots before instructing him to place his extremities by the fire. He did so, noticing a waxy texture covering the left hand's two most outer fingers. Frostbite.

The cave wasn't perfect by any stretch of the imagination. There was an opening somewhere above them, and occasionally, a gust of wind blew through it, causing the small fire to flicker and almost die. The baby had begun to cry, and Egret tended to him, feeding the child some mashed winter berries she had been storing in her bag. She picked up the child and sang to him a sweet, soothing melody. Auroch watched her gently sway as she slowly paced the cave, the child in her arms before placing him back beneath the furs she used as bedding. The pair dared not say a word, worried he might wake again. Egret sat beside Auroch and rubbed his waxy hand with her own, trying to generate some heat in his fingers. It was no use, but he appreciated her trying. The pair sat and watched the fire until, one after another, they fell into a deep sleep.

Auroch's fingers were no better when he awoke. The waxy film had begun to blister and swell, and there was little Egret could do for it.

"I have nothing to treat them." She said bluntly. "Perhaps if we get to the plains."

Auroch knew the fingers wouldn't last that long if the damage was as bad as he believed. He suspected that Egret knew it also but was choosing to say nothing. The same storm from the previous night howled and smashed against the rocks outside the cave. Auroch made a half-hearted statement about leaving, but Egret put her foot down. They couldn't go out in this, the pair of them would struggle; never mind the baby. So instead, Auroch lay, curled up under as much fur as possible, attempting to keep warm. He desperately tried to ignore the unbearable throbbing as he watched Egret stitch as much of his clothes back together as was feasible with a fine bone needle. Auroch rose to help her prepare more mashed berries for the child, and then the pair slunk again below the furs. He hadn't realised how exhausted he was. His hand, his feet, and his back all caused him great pain. He knew they had to keep moving but was grateful for the chance to just lie there and listen to the wind howling outside.

It was dark again when the wind stopped. He had done little

today, and the silence that followed the storm caused a tiny bit of panic to rise in his throat. He wasn't sure if he was ready to leave, but he pulled himself from the bedding and pushed himself through the narrow entrance. It was almost dark, and he had to use his good hand to dig snow away from the entrance before painfully scrambling out. The landscape lay beneath another blanket of thick white snow, but the sky was clear, making it easier to make out their surroundings in the moonlight. Turning to his left he saw a natural path, created by water that must have flowed down through the cliff face long ago, urging him to climb a little higher. He obliged, pulling himself up the rockface and well above the cave in which they had sheltered. He took his time, careful to avoid knocking his damaged fingers. It was cold but fresh and without windchill, the way Auroch liked it in the winter. He was soon lying on an overhang about halfway up the rock face with a view across the mesa. It was twilight, but he could still make out distinct landmarks below. The mesa began to slope down before matching the elevation of the river with what he knew in warmer times would be grassland. The river flowed for what looked like around a day's walk before meeting a lake. And next to that lake, he could see several tiny points of light in the distance. Fire. Someone was just ahead of them.

He scrambled back down the rockface and back into the cave.

"There are fires down by the great lake," he relayed to Egret. "If we leave at first light, we may catch them."

"The Skull Eaters?" She replied fearfully.

"I know not, although there are too few fires, and I would expect them to be further along the river by now."

"And you wish to meet the men who lit these fires? It could be anyone!"

"We stalk them first." Auroch looked at his sore, waxy fingers and then the baby. "We need more food, some balms and skins. They could help us."

Egret turned away from him. She had let him make the decision here but was clearly worried about who these people could be. He privately shared her fears. Although most men cooperated, and almost all larger groups made their way to the plains for the winter solstice, there was still danger out there. Wild men and smaller groups preyed on travellers. They were especially vulnerable with the baby in tow. He wondered how many of these wild men had been co-opted into Grey Stag's band of rogues. An army of beasts, shunned from the winter congress, now on their way to buy their way back in.

Just before dawn, the pair left their temporary home and headed once again across the mesa, loudly crunching through the thick snow. The sky was bright and clear, the wind was calm, and while it was fresh, it wasn't as bitterly cold as it had been the previous two days. Auroch cheerfully commented on this, and Egret scolded him for tempting fate. It seemed they were in the clear however, as they were soon descending a slope that would bring them back to the same level as the river. It was hard work; the ground at points had hardened and frozen into ice, and there were few branches to grab onto.

Carefully, they made their way down, sliding on their rears when they could, careful not to fall with the child in hand. Egret had done the best job she could with his clothes. She had managed to skilfully stitch his tunic back together, so it covered the whole of his shoulder, although it had lost a lot of its thickness and warmth. It was suitable on a day like today when the winds were low and the air not too bitter, but he worried about how it would perform the next day or the day after that. They may not be as fortunate with the weather. The exertion of making his way down the slope helped keep him warm at least. He was being more careful, however, with his frostbitten fingers. They were sore, and he could feel them rubbing inside the glove. The pair stopped after one particularly challenging part of the slope, and he removed his mitten to examine his fingers. Blisters were breaking out now. He hoped something could be done.

It was mid-morning by the time they were walking along the river. It had widened, and not even the ice flows could stop the water as it rushed through the ancient route it had carved in the landscape. The well-worn path, created by the to and fro of feet beside the river every autumn, was nowhere to be seen as they pushed their way through the snow. The bare trees that stood to attention beside the river became fewer and fewer. By the time it was almost nightfall, only a few dotted at various points on the bank. The pair found a formation of rocks with an overhang that would be suitable as a home for the night. Auroch snapped some dry kindling off a nearby tree, and they began lighting the fire until a small flame warmed their bones.

"Im going to climb that tree to look for the fires you saw last night," Egret said abruptly.

"I can do it," Auroch objected. He began to rise, but Egret handed him the baby.

"You're weak. I can do it," she stated, before walking out into the dark and cold.

She was right. He looked at the child, its rosy cheeks glistening. It gurgled and swung its arms toward his face, exploring its contours with chubby fingers. Auroch realised he had been so focussed on the journey he hadn't thought of a suitable name for the baby. Or who was going to look after it? Perhaps he could? He had no doubt once winter was over, Egret would be taken by another tribal chief. A pang of guilt forced its way into his mind. Despite this, she had travelled with him to help name the baby and aid mothers crossing. Auroch had the selfish thought of abandoning her in the night with the child. He could go to the plains and leave her to live her life in the wilderness, clanless. But what about mother's soul? He couldn't do that. Egret was the only remaining repository for Morning Mist's knowledge; he couldn't perform the ceremony without her in accordance with the rites of the Valleyfolk. Could he disguise her? No, as Old Heron's daughter, she would be recognised almost immediately. If not by her face, then by the tattoos adorning her chin and neck, clearly marking her as such. It seemed that Egret had accepted her fate, which both horrified and impressed him. More so, she had helped him now when he had chosen to not lie on her behalf. The thoughts swimming inside his head dissipated as Egret reappeared at the entrance to the cave.

"Did you see them?" he asked earnestly.

"Three more fires, not far from here. I am not sure they have moved. We should reach them tomorrow." She sighed, "This is a wretched idea; they could be anyone."

"Likely clanless," Auroch said optimistically, notes of trepidation in his voice cutting through just enough to validate Egret's feelings. "What choice do we have?"

The pair fell into the usual watchful sleep, awakening every time a small animal scurried past or the wind caused a tree to creak. The baby was unusually quiet, causing neither pair to get up before dawn to gently rock it back to sleep. Auroch lay awake, contemplating reaching the group just ahead. He could be walking Egret and the child into mortal danger. It was dark early, and he found himself still conscious at least halfway to daylight. How long did he think it would take to reach them? Half a morning? If he moved quickly, he could be there by dawn.

Auroch rose silently, taking care to leave his bag, and some of his tools. That way Egret wouldn't suspect he was leaving the cave to do anything other than pass water. He slyly retrieved his spears, hoping that his travelling companion has passed back into a deep sleep. Turning to look back, he saw the dwindling flame of the fire illuminating the young woman's face, her eyes still tightly closed. She looked very beautiful.

Chapter 20

The midnight glare of the moon worked to light up both the heavens and the earth as Auroch left the cave. The lack of trees made it easy to see where he was going, and after scrambling halfway up the solitary pine Egret had climbed earlier, Auroch saw the fires lit at twilight still burned brightly. If they were sleeping out in the open, they would need to be tended. His dying fingers were a testimony to how quickly the weather could be one's undoing this time of year, far from the warm fires of the great plains camp. He took one look at the glowing dots in the distance and then set off down the slope, light from the celestial objects bouncing off the pitch-white snow and making it simple to navigate despite the dark of night. The air was still, and he wished he could be out here on a rare night hunt with Father and Bloodied Thistle rather than on his way to creep up on a camp. He missed the anticipation and the bonding that came before a successful hunt and the dancing and laughter that came after it. He had seen meagre times when there was an added seriousness to a herd of deer but never the solemnity of being alone in these freezing wastes, desperately trying to find a hare for Egret and the baby.

The river path wore on, and he realised he was almost at the lake he had seen from the trees. The throbbing and itching in his frostbitten fingers was close to unbearable, and he considered ripping off the glove and gnawing them down to two stumps on his left hand if only to be rid of the monotonous drumbeat of pain. The trees were thicker towards the lake, and the pine hadn't shed its leaves like the barren birch that had passed on their journey so far. He smelled smoke first; then, he saw light through the branches. Those tending the fire had to be close. He didn't go directly to the fire but circled the area, far enough to be undetectable, even walking at a normal pace. He found himself on the shore of the lake, a layer of thick ice lying across its surface. Auroch gingerly tested it with his foot. It was solid. He took two or three steps on it. There was a deep creak, but it held easily. Another direction he could escape in if he was discovered. The lake was vast, but he could see all the way across its surface, and in the centre sat a large island, completely covered in white. The island's evergreen pine, frosted with snow, caused it to loom out of the water next to the peaceful icy surface.

He began to walk the shore, crouching now, careful not to give himself away. The fires were lit a little way down the snow-covered beach. He couldn't hear any songs or voices. It was almost dawn, he reasoned, seeing a tinge of blue beginning to appear on the horizon. He had little time to complete his reconnaissance. The first fire was ahead. He crept up to it, looking for any hint of movement or noise. At the shoreline, he noticed three wooden dugout canoes, the square, angular vessels built from hollowed-out tree trunks. His heart began to race. This could get them down the river fast. He had seen them before, although they were uncommon and mainly used by the coastal tribes for floating around the inlets at the edge of the world. He wished to see the great water one day and often wondered what lay beyond the seemingly infinite size of the world lake, to which all the known land was just a little island. He had heard it had a violent, cruel current and that shellfish were plentiful, but terrifying monsters patrolled the depths, ready to take an unsuspecting fisherman.

In his heady youth, Father had taken the journey south from the plains with the coastal peoples one spring before Mother was with child. The people there wore a cap of shellfish, beaded together, on their heads and were expert fishermen, using sharp hooks on long lines to catch huge fish, bigger than anything that Auroch had ever seen in the river valleys of his childhood. Auroch had bemoaned that he had seen little of the world. Every year he had travelled back and forth from the river to the plain; he had wished and hoped to follow another tribe for a season or two. Auroch grimaced at the memory. What he wouldn't give now for his familial yearly routine to be intact.

He crept closer to the light. It was pouring out a thin makeshift skin tent hastily erected over a wooden frame. Slowly reaching the shelter, he pressed his face to a gap in the side where the tanned covers didn't quite stretch across the wooden construction. He could see figures on the ground inside. Two women, older. A little girl, no more than six or seven summers. A painful pang of regret passed through him as he thought of his own sister. There were four thick skins for sleeping in place by the fire. One was empty.

He felt the sharp flint blade slide across his throat, narrowly avoiding drawing blood. Someone had managed to creep up behind him. Rather than worried, he felt a keen sense of embarrassment fall over him. He had been stupid and careless. He could tell that the man was large, much taller than him. Warm breath tickled the top of his head. A low, calm voice emanated from behind him.

"Drop your spear."

Auroch did as instructed. The man pushed him forward, his thick hairy arms placed firmly on his shoulder, his knife at his throat. He manoeuvred Auroch through the loose flap that constituted the doorway. The three women lay around the fire began to stir, and the young girl let out a frightened yelp when she saw him. The man pulled the knife away from his throat and pushed him to the floor. Auroch fell limply on purpose, tensing his muscles only as he hit the ground, ready to bolt. The man was in his fortieth or so summer, strong and grizzled. He looked Auroch up and down.

"The Tattoos on your chin. You have come from the Summer Valley?" he said calmly.

Auroch nodded. The man spoke confidently and fluidly, and Auroch relaxed as he realised who had accosted him. Born of the current, the Riverfolk survived in the waterways, paddling to and fro, catching fish in the dugout canoes Auroch had seen earlier. They were a normal sight at the winter solstice, and Auroch was a little taken aback to see them this far west this time of year.

"The Men of the Summer Valley are dead. Killed by Grey Stag and his band of Skull Eaters." Auroch decided he would forgo caution and explain everything.

"I've seen them." The man replied solemnly, "Men, women and children. A large group. And with them a beast from the plains."

"When did they pass?" Auroch asked. Others were appearing from behind the trees behind the shelter. Auroch noticed women and children but no men.

"Pass?" The man laughed bitterly. "They did not pass. We spied them, feasting on a fallen man's flesh. Our scout didn't escape without being seen, and they followed him to the riverbank." He motioned at the cold, struggling campers. "Most of the women and children made it into canoes and out onto the island. We were blessed that the lake hadn't completely frozen over yet. But the rest…" He paused, "Massacred on the shore."

Auroch relayed what had happened to his own tribe. He explained he was travelling with Egret, and they hoped to beat Grey Stag to the plains. He realised it was the first time he had explained the situation out loud and felt an immediate kinship with the remaining members of the Riverfolk. The man introduced himself as Long Eel. He said nothing about why the Skull Eaters hadn't killed him on the beach, and Auroch did not pry. He was not a meek man and appeared skilled in violence. Auroch couldn't imagine he had fled. Auroch explained that Egret and the baby were a little walk away, and Long Eel suggested that they bring her to the camp. He had plenty of good, strong hides they could give to them, and in return, Auroch could help him catch some fish.

Auroch said his goodbyes and began the walk back to the cave. Although the encounter would hopefully make their journey easier, he wasn't looking forward to explaining his flight to Egret. Still, the air was crisp and clean, and he had a spring in his step for the first time in days. His fingers still ached, but he felt more hopeful and pushed his anxieties about their worsening condition to the back of his mind.

The walk was quiet and uneventful, and his footprints, made earlier in the dark, made the return journey easy. As he approached the rise that had sheltered them the previous night, he saw the outline of Egret, passing her water in the snow. It was obvious that she had also spotted him, and he watched as she drew herself up and then waited, arms folded, for him to make his way up the hill. He was expecting her to let loose on him, ask him why he was being so reckless, and shout or scream at him. But instead, she glared at him and said a single word.

"Well?"

"It's the Riverfolk. Many are dead at the hands of Grey Stag. Mainly women and children remain."

"Did you trade? Can they help us?"

"They are going to, in trade for my help with the ice fishing."

Egret snorted. "You think Riverfolk women don't know how to fish? There's another reason we are needed, Auroch."

Auroch once again felt very stupid. Why would anyone want the Men of the Summer Valley's help with fishing? They spent their days hunting deer. Even Riverfolk children were likely more adept than him.

"Should we go then? If there's another reason, they wish us to return?" Auroch asked quietly, knowing there was little to disguise his foolishness.

"Even if they have ulterior motives, they seem not to wish us any harm. Otherwise, I think it unlikely that they would have let you return here without a guard. We shall keep our wits about us, our hands close to our blades, and see what real reason they wish us to visit them on the shore."

Chapter 21

It was past midday when Auroch, Egret, and the baby entered the camp. Children ran around their legs, and old women swarmed them, pestering them for food. What little they could give was gone instantly, and Auroch began to feel concerned about the prospect of keeping the child fed. Long Eel was stood with three younger women, around twenty summers or so in age, who he introduced as his wives. He explained that he had inherited them from his brothers after the attack, as well as their children. Auroch tried not to gawp at this custom. When a man died in the Summer Valley, his woman was given on the plains to another tribe in return for another woman. The idea of keeping a brother's wife seemed like it might foster conflict, but Egret poked him in the small of the back, and he greeted the trio.

"You are a Spirit-Maiden?" Long Eel asked Egret, "I remember you with the old woman, Morning Mist. A fine Spirit-Mother, she was."

Egret stepped forward. "A pleasure to meet you, Long Eel," she said, holding the palms of her hands outstretched in the universal gesture of peace and cooperation. "You are the new leader of the

Riverfolk? Perhaps I can be of use? Are there many women with illnesses or with child? I will aid them as best I can."

"Our own Spirit-Mother, Silver Roach, was killed during the attack, along with the young girl who worked under her." Long Eel said solemnly. "We have many complaints of aches and fever, as well as boils and watery defecation. Please do what you can while Auroch helps me."

Egret nodded and showed her palms formally again before scurrying back to the throng of women, who by now had all developed some ailment or complaint that she could help with. She handed the child to another young woman, barely out of childhood herself, and those not seeking healing began to fawn and coo over the infant.

"Now, Auroch," Long Eel put a large, meaty hand on his shoulder. "We shall test your fishing skill."

Grabbing a foxskin bag and placing it on a sled, he began to walk out onto the ice, dragging it behind him. Auroch followed closely behind, taking care to walk carefully and slowly over the creaking, cracking ice sheet below their feet. He used his boot to scrape away the powdery snow covering the surface and noted that the water below the ice was a cool grey-blue. Long Eel powered on, walking across the surface of the huge lake with a kind of confidence that Auroch couldn't begin to emulate. Auroch was used to passing the lake on the yearly pilgrimage to the plains, but now it lay still under the ice; he was awed by its size. He turned to look at the shore and realised they had barely moved relative to the vastness of the lake.

In the centre stood the island, its surface dotted with snow-covered pine. He had seen Riverfolk boats before, gliding to and fro from it during the early autumn journey, and had asked about them. Father had known little.

The pair continued across the endless ice. In the distance, he began to make out a thin stick planted in the surface, its top with painted red lines making a point on the surface. It was bent over slightly as if some weight had been applied to it.

"Aha!" exclaimed Long Eel, who began to jog over to the pole.

The ice groaned, and Auroch began to panic a little. This was not something he would consider normally doing. Pulling out his flint blade, Long Eel began to chip away at the ice around the pole, revealing a large stone buried in the frozen water. The stone was wrapped in a chord woven from flax, and as Long Eel pulled it free, Auroch noticed that the line ran along the surface of the lake before disappearing beneath another circular hole. Auroch was instructed to place his hands on the chord and to stand with his feet apart. He tested the weight on the end of the line by tugging on it. Something heavy lay beneath the surface.

"Walk the line back, then return." Long Eel instructed.

Auroch, the line slung over his shoulder walked until he reached the sled, before winding the line around the sled's handle to secure it. Long Eel crouched at the hole, checking the line was coming back smoothly to prevent it from getting stuck as it was pulled from the ice. Auroch walked back and forth each time, the amount of chord attached to the sled growing with each pass. He was on his fourth trip to the sled when he heard a shout. He turned to look, but Long Eel scolded him.

"Keep Pulling!"

Auroch heaved as hard as his cold, tired muscles would allow. Something was thrashing on the line now, rather than the dead weight he had felt previously. He steeled himself and made one last trip to the sled. Wrapping the line once again around the handle, he turned in time to see Long Eel enthusiastically pulling a huge fish from the hole. The fish attempted to fight him, but the riverman threw it a little distance and let it die on the ice, noiselessly gasping, confused. Auroch watched as the fish impotently flopped around.

"We will make a fisherman of you yet, eh!" He beamed and slapped Auroch on the back.

Auroch let go of the rope and allowed the pain of his frostbitten fingers to overcome him. It was unbearable. The line cutting into them had caused the soreness that had dulled to throb to return with a vengeance. He removed the mitten to examine his hand. It was well blistered now, and the fingers had turned blue-black. Auroch knew what would happen to them, how they would blacken and die. He pushed the thought out of his mind. There were three more traps to be dealt with. Auroch and Long Eel picked up the huge river trout and placed it on the sled. It twitched, its body beating against the wood and antler frame in a desperate last attempt at remaining conscious. The men watched it die before heading off once again across the ice.

"A fine woman, Egret. Old Heron was a good man. I would expect he would have wanted a good man to put a child inside his daughter!" Long Eel said, cheerfully. "If I didn't have three women in my ear already, I would consider it myself!"

Auroch flinched at the thought of Long Eel and Egret. He said nothing but sulked silently as Long Eel prattled on about his wives, who seemed nothing but a nuisance to him as far as Auroch could tell. The pair repeated the process for the second trap, this time with no result. After another march across the ice, they checked the third. Only a small fish this time. Auroch, who had been impressed with the method, began to realise it was far less precise than it initially appeared. They began the walk to the fourth trap. This one was further away, and the island was close now. The ice felt thinner underfoot, although Auroch wasn't sure if that was his own reservations about ice fishing fuelling his increasing nervousness. He looked over the island. The trees grew tall, and their broad, snow-covered branches obscured the ground. Long Eel chipped away at the ice below the fourth pole.

From the island came an awful, inhuman howl. It echoed off the ice and bounced around the desolate, open space of the lake. The sound of Long Eel attacking the ice stopped. The lake fell silent once again. It was like no animal Auroch had ever heard, and the screech seemed to push its way into him, wrapping itself around his heart. Panicked, Auroch looked to Long Eel. The large, rugged man seemed to shrink into the ice, avoiding Auroch's gaze.

"What kind of man or beast was that?" Auroch demanded. The sight of Long Eel cowering unnerved him.

"Neither. Both. It is the Black Wolf. It haunts us."

Auroch paused. He had heard of this beast. The body and cunning of a man, but the head of a great Black Wolf, its grinning maw ready to feed. It stalked the night, when men were most connected to their ancestors and could rip the souls from bodies with its sharp fangs.

"Let us leave," Auroch said, panic overcoming him momentarily "Come down the river, away from its hunting grounds."

"I have lied to you, Auroch," Long Eel said mournfully. "I do not need your help, but the help of your wise woman. I needed you out here on the ice while we took her and the child."

Auroch gripped his spear. He could kill the man here and now. He saw himself driving his spear through Long Eel's neck, watching as he flopped about on the ice in a bloody puddle just as the fish had. A voice inside him was telling him to do it. Don't make the same mistake as at the Skull Eater camp! Kill while you have the chance!

"What wickedness has befallen Egret and the child?" Auroch asked, his demeanour calm but demanding.

"No harm has come to her, I swear by First Eagle, who crafted us from the peat! Nor shall I harm the child. We have need of her, but once she has performed her duty and communed with the world of spirits, we will provide the canoe you need and supplies we can spare."

"What possible need do you have of her, in this life or the next?" Auroch asked, still ready to pounce.

"We lay our dead to rest in a cave on the island in the middle of the lake. It is where we celebrate midsummer and shelter when the current of life bashes us into rocks and scrapes our belly on the sandbank." He looked at the island before once again averting his gaze as if whatever had made that terrible howl would meet his eyes if he looked too long. "After the massacre, we brought our canoes to the island shore, but something terrible awaited us. Something that raved and raged would steal our souls if given half a chance."

Auroch guessed the outcome of the conversation. "Where are your dead?" he asked. He was furious that his own stupidity had trapped them. What way was there out of this bargain now?

"On the shore." Long Eel said, "In a pit. No way for folk to lie in death. They must be moved to the island, but first, the Black Wolf must be driven out. Your Egret is our only chance."

"She may refuse. What would make you think that she would help you?"

"By now, we have taken the child and hidden it away. If she does not aid us, it will be smothered."

Auroch was taken aback by his bluntness. Despite the violence of the last few moons, the callousness and desperation in his voice shook him.

"We have no choice then," Auroch concluded. He hoped Egret had come up with some kind of plan, as by now, the situation must be clear to her. However, he would play along for now "I will ask one question, however, Long Eel of the Riverfolk."

"Yes?"

"On the night the Skull Eaters came, why were you the only riverman to survive?"

"I hid. I watched it all, but there was nothing I could do. They would have wrung my neck like a hare and stripped the flesh from me." he uttered.

"A coward then," Auroch said coldly. "You should throw yourself into one of your fishing holes and drown in order to avoid further shame."

Chapter 22

Egret, flanked by two elderly men, appeared from across the ice. Auroch stood and watched as the trio trudged towards him. He had no doubt that she could have run or fought off the two ancient guards, who must have seen well over one hundred summers between them. Auroch locked eyes with her across the frozen, crystal surface of the lake, communicating silently their conundrum.

"I promise you; no harm will befall the child!" Long Eel shouted, squirming on the spot.

Egret said nothing, instead shooting him a death glare. One of the old men swung a bag from over his back and handed it to her.

She looked inside, silently examining the contents. Auroch watched as her lips noiselessly counted the items inside. She seemed satisfied.

"Is there anything else you need to cleanse the island?" Long Eel asked. The veneer of politeness covered the words of a desperate, craven man. Auroch wondered what would happen if they failed to exorcise the spirit of the Black Wolf. Would they let them go on their way? Or would they take the child and abandon them on the frosty shore? Or even worse, kill them here on the ice.

"I have everything I need. I will cleanse the isle. Then we will return, you will hand us the child, give us supplies and a canoe. If you break this bargain, I will curse your three women with rotten wombs. From them, your children will be crippled and sickly. They will die in infancy." The threat hung in the air.

Without looking back, she walked across the ice towards the island. Auroch followed confidently, mirroring her stride. He hoped she had given them something to think about. When clearly out of earshot of the figures shrinking in the distance, she slowed and allowed Auroch to catch up with her.

"I am sorry. They took your brother before I realised." she said, notes of genuine apology in her voice.

"You are not to blame. We shouldn't have allowed ourselves to become separated. You were right to think they had impure motives." Auroch replied.

"How are your fingers, Auroch?" She asked, quickly changing the subject to avoid the topic of their collective naivety. He removed them from his glove and showed them to her. Egret said nothing, but her face gave away her concern. Perhaps she had some more ointment she could give him? Or the Riverfolk may have something to help him? He knew that another, more drastic, solution would be much more likely.

"Will I have to lose them?" He said, for the first time vocalising the thought that had been swimming around his head for days. She said nothing but continued to march across the ice towards the island.

It was almost evening now, and a thick fog began to creep across the lake's surface. Egret produced two torches from the bag, and after several attempts, Auroch managed to light them. The damp air made his clothes feel heavy. They were almost at the island now, and the darkness enveloped them. The trees loomed high above the pair. The moon and stars were dull, and the only light seemed to come from their torches. Auroch felt panic rising in the back of his throat about the nature of their task. This was Egret's world, not his. What good could he do? He couldn't fight an ephemeral foe. Nor did he know what combination of words and signs would banish it.

They stepped off the ice and onto the bank of the island, the snow crunching below their deer-skin boots. There was total silence, as if the isle itself were dead. The mist rolled across the ground, the only movement against a backdrop of complete stillness. Egret set off into the interior of the island without making a sound, and Auroch followed, spear in hand. They crept slowly through the trees, Auroch placing each step carefully so as not to disturb whatever lurked just out of sight. Egret seemed relaxed, as if she had settled into a trance. The calmness with which she walked between the boughs made her seem ancient, as if she had done this a thousand times before.

Before long, the pair came to a clearing. The trees formed a neat circle, and in the centre was a large flat rock. Its distinctive natural features marked it out amongst the trees, and instinctively Auroch sensed this was what Egret was looking for. The stone was recently daubed with ochre, and thick grooves covered it, created by hands hacking at it with stone tools. There was something ancient and gaudy about it. Auroch wondered if the old men of the hills had looked over the stone as he and Egret did now. Egret rummaged in her bag, producing a small, wooden, carved figurine. It was a man, his shoulders back, standing tall. Where the figure's head should be was the grinning face of a wolf. Auroch shivered. He knew these totems. They could be used to trap evil spirits. He had seen them among Morning Mist's possessions. He remembered at seven summers old asking the crone if any of hers contained spirits.

"Not just the peaceful spirits that walk the woods at night, but demons that rip your soul from your body and devour it, gulping it down with nary a morsel spare." The old woman had said. It had frightened Auroch so much he had cried, and he remembered that Father had caught him leaving the old lady's canvas tent in tears and beaten him for softness.

"Are you going to trap the spirit in that vessel?" He asked Egret, who was busy crushing some dried mushrooms and winter berries with her antler pestle. She nodded silently, indicating she wished not to be disturbed while she worked. Auroch decided that he would guard the little circle of trees while she battled her metaphysical foe. He paced around the tiny clearing, spear at the ready. The flatness of the lake allowed the wind to rush across it, hitting the island at a speed that caused the trees to creak and bend all around them. The swaying was so violent that Auroch began to worry one might fall, either on top of them as they stood on the island or onto the lake, cracking the ice and stranding them here with the strange spirit. The bushes moved, and Auroch jumped. Was there something in them? It was just the wind, he reassured himself.

He looked to Egret. She had finished her paste and placed a small slate on top of the rock as an offering of food for the spirit's journey.

Taking two pieces of sandstone from her bag, as well as a small wooden bowl, she began to rub them together. She shielded the sandstone from the wind with her body, letting the small flakes fall into the bowl until she had enough rubbings. Producing a lump of sharpened flint from her bag and still nursing the rubbings, she made her way over to the other side of the clearing where a small frozen puddle stood. She began to chip away and crack the ice until enough had been cleared to pull a small chunk. Taking off her reindeer hide mittens, she put her arms under and up inside her thick tunic and began to rub the ice between her hands, a warm refuge against the wind and frozen world that surrounded them. Auroch watched her face, brow furrowed with concentration as she warmed the ice until it was melted. She placed it in the bowl and produced a horsehair paintbrush. Gripping its wooden handle, she dipped the brush into the bowl and mixed the sandstone with the water until it produced a white, chalky paint. Auroch watched as she began to paint along the carved notches on the stone, accentuating the gaps in the altar. She painted over the most recent daubings with her own ochre, creating a striking clash of grey, white and red.

There it was again! Movement in the bushes! He was sure it wasn't just the wind. The Black Wolf. It must be! An ear-spitting howl drowned out the noise of the wind. It was here! But where? Egret, also reacting to the noise, began to daub the stone faster.

"Turn your back now, Auroch," she said calmly. "You mustn't watch."

She dropped to her knees and began her incantation. Knowing that it was forbidden to watch while the wise women performed their magic, Auroch turned his back to her.

"First Eagle, White Owl, hear my summons! A beast roams here, scowling, screeching. The Black Wolf writhes and howls madly. A man transformed into an animal, cursed to roam the world, eating the flesh of the dead, devouring the souls of the living. The man inside him diminishes every day, and the beast inside him expands, crawling inside his flesh and turning his blood black with rot. The soul grows ever dimmer. Pull the beast from the man, trap it inside this totem, so that the man may grow back into his flesh, so that he bleeds his red blood. Help him vomit up the souls of the trapped…"

Egret was abruptly cut off, her desperate plea to the ancients replaced with a scream. Auroch instinctively turned to see a dark shape, on two legs, covered in dirt and muck, with tangled long hair, dragging her by her ankle into the bushes. Auroch sprinted towards the attacker, thrusting his spear at the mass of angry hair and flesh. It recoiled as the spear struck, letting go of Egret's ankle. The torches, now dying on the ground did nothing to expose the figure, and in the almost darkness, Auroch wasn't sure if he was looking at a beast or man. The Black Wolf was both. The creature howled again before retreating into the undergrowth. The clearing was once again silent. Auroch helped Egret to her feet.

"Auroch, you turned!" she said breathlessly, her voice agitated. Auroch knew what he had done. The ritual had been disrupted, but she was right. He had turned to look when he heard her scream. This was a serious crime. Banishment was normal for this offence.

"Did you finish, at least?" Auroch looked mournfully at her, the gravity of this transgression now setting in.

"No. I need something to draw the spirit out into the vessel." She looked at him, a great sadness in her eyes. "Auroch, there is little I can do for you. You must leave now or...."

Auroch knew what would happen now. Flesh was the only price that could be paid to avoid banishment. He removed the mitten on his left hand, looking at his two blue, frostbitten fingers attached to his hand for the last time. He placed it slowly on the altar. Egret took his blade from him and placed it across his fingers. She looked him in the eye, her gaze soothing him. She kissed him gently on the mouth as if to share some solidarity and sympathy through physical contact. Auroch experienced a moment of spine-tingling elation before she brought the blade down hard. Auroch yelped, suppressing the instinct to scream. They had not been severed. She brought it down again, and again, and again. Tears ran down his cheek. He doubted his heart was hard enough for Father's approval.

It took several blows for Egret to absolve him of his crime. He fell backward to the ground, staring at his hand in disbelief at the bleeding stumps where his two fingers had been. Gently, Egret rolled him over, so he was no longer facing the altar before tightly wrapping his wound in a heavy, plant fibre cloth. He plunged his hand into the snow, letting the feeling of cool wash over the gap left by the impromptu surgery. He lay there listening to Egret's footsteps as she danced around the rock.

"Binding blood now stains the altar!" she cried, "A man has lost a part of his flesh here, this day. To be absorbed by this totem." Auroch heard a thud. He guessed she had slammed the wolf-headed statuette down on the bloody mess left by the amputation. "Watch now, as it seeps into the base and imbues the figure with the scent of man." The wind intensified. From the trees came another howl. Unlike the previous screams of the beast, this one seemed pained, scared. It was working!

Egret continued to shout and beseech the ancestors to fill the vessel with the soul of the wolf. Auroch closed his eyes, terrified that if he opened them, he might catch a glimpse of the beast, or the ceremony performed behind his back. The shouting, dancing, and howling seemed to go on forever. The wind smashed through the trees. His hand ached.

The first rays of light began to creep over the lake. He pulled his hand from the snow and found it soaked with blood. The snow was crimson all around him. He tried to move but felt lightheaded. How much blood had wept from the wound? He realised the wind had dropped, and he couldn't hear the rhythmic footsteps of Egret's dancing or the howling of the Black Wolf. A hand touched him on the shoulder.

"You can rise now."

He turned to see a tired but smiling Egret. She grabbed him by the shoulder, pulling him to his feet. In the half-light of dawn, he saw the little figurine on the altar, its base red where the viscera had bled into the legs of the little wolf-headed man. Auroch looked at what had been his fingers. Egret hadn't cut them cleanly, and the meaty, sanguine chunks were barely recognisable as his digits. He felt queasy. He sat down on the ground again, this time with his back against the large rock. The morning sun filtering through the trees hit the back of the little wolf-headed statuette, casting a long shadow on the ground before him. Egret dropped down beside him and slowly unwrapped the bandage around his hand. Auroch expected to see a great lump of gore protruding from his hand, but instead, the wound looked cleaner than expected. She had sliced through the flesh and bone just above the knuckle, meaning that he had two small stumps where his two frostbitten digits had been. Without saying a word, she took his hand and began to rub balm into the wound, before redressing it in clean cloth.

"Do you think the Black Wolf is dead?" Auroch asked earnestly.

"Sealed in the figure. I know not what happened to the man it possessed."

The two rose, and after taking a second to orient themselves, they headed back in the direction they had arrived under cover of darkness. The island was quiet now, and Auroch felt the pressure on his chest begin to lift despite his injury. Was it because the spirit was now sealed in the tiny figurine nestled in Egret's bag? They walked down to the island's shoreline, neither of the pair feeling like venturing straight back across the ice, despite the success of Egret's exorcism.

"What is that?" Egret pointed to a small group of objects hidden below a small rocky outcrop within a few strides of the ice.

Auroch strode over and examined the modest scene. The remains of the small fire, extinguished and blackened, lay next to a small pile of fish bones. They had been picked clean by whomever had lit the fire. Below the overhanging rock was a bed of tattered old furs, which appeared to have been slept on recently.

"Does the Black Wolf shelter here?" Auroch asked, "I thought him a beast? Not a creature that tires and cooks fish?"

Egret said nothing but began to search the bedding. After a few moments, she produced a necklace. Thin chord held together painted rocks, and at the end was a long flat piece of mammoth bone, calved with the image of a fawn. A child's necklace.

"Did the Black Wolf take this? Did he eat the child? Take its soul?" Auroch continued to probe.

Egret did not respond to the question this time either. The pair started onto the ice, where they spied a figure lying on the surface, as motionless as the frozen landscape all around them. As they approached, Auroch could make out the body of a man. He was strewn on his back, and his long, dark, uncut hair was wrapped around his face and upper chest. The man would have been naked if not for a loincloth and boots, and his body was smeared almost black with dirt and mud. There was a red gash on his abdomen that Auroch recognised as the place where he had driven the spear into him the previous night. It was the Black Wolf.

"He looks like a man," Auroch said, unsure of what to make of the pathetic, frozen corpse before them.

"The wolf was trapped in the totem," Egret replied. "All that remains is the man."

Auroch noted a hint of hesitancy in her voice. She was lacking her usual assertiveness. But she was a Spirit-Maiden and knew ancient secrets he had no hope of understanding. The pair crept closer to the body, the wound in his abdomen easier to see now. Auroch had done a lot of damage with his spear, and the sharp point had obviously ripped through his skin as the pair had struggled.

"I did not think I could kill him. Our weapons cannot injure or kill spirits?" Auroch asked, puzzled.

"They cannot," Egret replied more confidently now. "The fatal wound would only have killed him after we trapped the wolf. Once this body was free from its influence."

The pair stood over the corpse; his pained, twisted expression more indicative of fear than any malicious intent. Egret knelt over the body and efficiently searched his corpse, before pulling something on a sting from around the dead man's neck. She held it in her mitten, examining it in the morning light. Auroch inched closer, looking over her shoulder. In her hand was a mammoth bone pendant, the same as the one found by the camp on the shore. She turned it over in her hand slowly, the growing light penetrating her fingers to cast shadows on the small piece of jewellery. On it was an adult roe deer, etched in the same style as the fawn. A father's necklace to be matched with a child. Egret placed it back on the body, and the two continued across the ice.

Chapter 23

True to his word, Long Eel was waiting for them on the shore. His wives stood next to him, the youngest of whom cradled the baby. He twitched nervously as the pair approached him, crunching across the ice, faces full of thunder. Noticing the anxious, fearful reaction from Long Eel, Auroch wondered what the pair of them looked like now. Had the last two seasons shaped them into something violent, something frightening? The large man whom Auroch had first met only two days ago seemed diminutive now, only having power over them by virtue of a stolen child. When they were only a few strides away. Egret produced the wolf-headed figurine from her bag and threw it at the feet of the woman holding the baby.

"It is done. The back wolf is trapped in the totem. It's living vessel is destroyed, and the island is free for you to bury your dead."

A noticeable relief washed over the faces of the assembled Riverfolk. Despite his anger, Auroch almost felt a sense of pity and kinship. He agonised over the fate of his mother and had prepared to travel far just to name the child. He understood this man's impulses. But would he have taken a child to ensure this? He decided not to answer his own question.

"You have done us a great service, Egret. And you also Auroch." Long Eel said gracefully as if there had been no threats of violence had they refused. He motioned to the woman holding the baby, who swiftly handed him back to Egret. The Spirit-Maiden didn't allow her stony expression to change. The child reacted warmly upon seeing Egret, gurgling and laughing as he was placed in her arms. Auroch watched her stern expression and realised that Egret wished to gather the child up, to coo and kiss him, but knew now was the time to project strength rather than love.

"The canoe" Auroch said forcefully, reminding the Riverfolk of their demands. "Food and Skins."

"Please, with me." Long Eel gestured for the pair to follow him, his agreeable tone not matching the intensity of loathing that was emanating from Egret and Auroch.

He watched Egret retrieve the statuette from the floor and place it securely back in her bag before joining the small band moving along the pebble beach. The group walked beside the lake for some time, following the natural curve of the shoreline. Auroch gripped his spear tightly, ready for a double cross, but none came. There was little said as they worked their way around the icy water.

This was the second time he had been betrayed in as many seasons. Blooded Thistle's refusal to flee with him stung more than the Riverfolk's trickery, but all the same, he couldn't believe that it had happened again. Egret had at least been wary of the Riverfolk, whereas he had swallowed every word they had said. Was he naïve? Had he spotted Bloodied Thistle's entanglement with the Skull Eater girl earlier, could he have intervened? What would drive a man to betray his kinfolk as he had?

They left the shoreline and walked inland before re-joining the river that ran from the glacial lake. From the safety of the shore, Auroch could see the ice here was thinner and, as they made their way down the path, began to take up less and less of the river's surface, until there was a clear, narrow path for a canoe to travel down the centre of the river, hemmed in by a thin layer of frozen water touching the shore on each side. The group scrambled over a small, slippery rockfall. Auroch and Egret cooperated instinctively to pass the child back and forth to whoever had the most purchase.

On the other side sat a boy, perhaps no more than eight summers old. He nervously paced back and forth in front of several dugout canoes, a spear held at the ready in his small hands. The Riverfolk hadn't been lying then! The canoes were there!

"My Son!" Long Eel shouted to the boy. His tone was sing song, and the boy looked happy and relieved to see him. "You have done well to guard the canoes!"

The boy ran towards Long Eel, hugging him around the waist. Long Eel reciprocated. His arms covered the boy's head as it pressed into to his navel. He turned to Auroch and Egret.

"I wish things had been different, Auroch and Egret of the Summer Valley. I really did intend you no harm. Perhaps when tempers have simmered, we may see each other on the great plains next winter. We may eat reindeer and fish together as kinfolk under the same sun."

"You won't travel to the plains?" Egret asked, attempting to maintain her cold demeanour.

"It is too late now. Spring will be here soon. The solstice is imminent. I fear the season for feasting, trading, and taking wives is almost over."

Auroch nodded. Long Eel had put into words his greatest anxiety, the unspoken worry that the pair had silently decided not to talk about. They were, most likely, out of time. The banished would be close to the great cavern if they weren't already there.

Gracefully, Egret placed herself into the canoe and the baby in her lap. One of Long Eel's wives handed her a bag of supplies. Egret went through it efficiently, examining every item to be sure they weren't being short-changed.

"Everything you asked for is there." Long Eel said earnestly, watching as Egret checked the fresh supplies.

She nodded to Auroch, who began to push the canoe from the shore into the gap in the ice by the bank. Long Eel, rather than watching him struggle, moved him to the side, and together, the two men pushed the dugout canoe holding Egret and the baby into the water. Auroch jumped forward, landing torso first in the canoe. A quiet murmur of laughs came from the bank. His pathetic display had broken the tension amongst the Riverfolk. He swivelled himself around, so his feet pointed in the correct direction and orientated himself into a more natural sitting position. The laughing subsided.

"Take this!" Shouted Long Eel from the bank. He threw a long, flat, bone paddle to the boat. Auroch caught it deftly. The wide pelvis bone of an elk had been chipped away at until it was flattened and then halfted to a strong pole fashioned from antler. Auroch placed it in the water and used it to propel himself forward. He needn't have bothered. Before the pair could take a moment to get accustomed to the tiny vessel, the current took them. Auroch turned to watch the small group on the side of the bank shrink as they got further and further away from the lake and onwards to the great plain.

They were gaining speed now, and Auroch vigilantly used the paddle to push them away from floating clumps of ice and rocks. The little canoe, while sturdy, was clearly built for better weather, and every small bump or unpredictable swell caused the little boat to sway violently from one side to the other, threatening to capsize them. Auroch marvelled as Egret, her back to him, fussed and doted over the child to keep him calm, rewrapping the child in new, distinctive swaddling clothes provided by the Riverfolk. He noticed her hands grabbing tightly at the wooden sides of the boat occasionally, her fingernails digging into the wood. Under her composed exterior, she was terrified.

He was not enjoying the journey. Little ice was on the river now; the strong current had taken care of it. Rocks, on the other hand, had become more frequent. Auroch used the paddle to push the boat away from any potential dangers jutting from the water, but it was what lay underneath the swirling black mass that worried him. Twice, they felt the bottom of the boat scrape over some large debris at the bottom of the river. Twice, he gritted his teeth and waited to feel the cold, wet embrace of water rushing into the bottom of the boat. It never came.

Before long, the small river gave way to a larger one, and the violent waters to calmer currents. Leaving the tributary, they found themselves in a wide river, hemmed in on either side by a low ridge.

The ridge had very few trees, and Auroch realised they were pushing forward at quite a pace now back onto the steppe. They had already covered maybe a day's walk in the canoe. He felt elated but decided to keep it to himself. They still had a long journey down the river and across the open plain in the winter. It was cold enough when the group crossed in autumn. In winter he expected it to be much more difficult. The prangs of worry he felt for the child once again surfaced. Could they make it?

The herds of reindeer that sustained the tribes who met on the plains during winter would be long gone by the time they arrived. They had missed the window, setting off at least two moons later than normal. The mass of hunters guiding and corralling the herd into the killing pits in late autumn was quite a sight. The vast quantity of meat harvested from the dead and dying reindeer impaled on the short spikes at the bottom of large trenches sustained them during the winter. Auroch remembered his first trip to the cave at the bottom of the solstice rock, where it was dried and placed in the ice that formed naturally at the bottom of the shaft.

Auroch was shaken from his thoughts by movement on the bank. Something was rustling and snapping the dead branches while moving between the trees. He listened, the lapping of the water against the side of the boat fading into the background of his mind. Another glimpse, a flash of red and brown hair. Horses! Egret turned to look at him excitedly, having heard it too. He could pry a sole horse away from its herd if he was quick and clever.

"Shall we come ashore here?" she asked quietly.

Auroch shook his head, "They are likely moving with the flow of the river." He used the paddle to stab the soft mud on the bottom of the river, slowing the canoe. Silently, they floated down the river, eyes keenly watching the bank. There was little doubt there was at least a small band of horses. As they got closer to the side of the small canyon, Auroch could hear the distinctive sound of hooves pushing through the powdered snow. Auroch felt like he was now getting a handle on the canoe, using the paddle to slow them to almost a dead stop at certain points. His glove irritated the terrible wound of the night before, but he had become accustomed to the pain. Egret, speaking only in whispers, asked after it several times, but he replied only in grunts. From her position in front of him, she couldn't see the blood beginning to defy his bandages and seep through his mitten.

Auroch began to tire of watching the sparse treeline above them with the requisite intense gaze of a hunter. A wave of lethargy was beginning to fall over him, and the throbbing in his hand was coming back. He hadn't slept or even really examined his wound since first light. They had been following the horses for much of the afternoon now.

He turned his attention briefly back to Egret. Her long, black hair looked surprisingly healthy and clean despite their weeks on the move. She had unfurled it, and it clung to her back, running from her neckline down to her waist, where its end draped over Auroch's feet at the bottom of the canoe. She had kissed him on the isle, exploring his mouth with her own. It was a gesture reserved for lovers, and Auroch relished the memory despite the amputation of his fingers moments later. Auroch felt a knot of anxiety thinking about the feel of her lips on his and realised he was frightened by the possibilities that her affection represented. Should he raise it with her? She was singing softly to the child now, keeping her voice low enough not to scare the horses that trotted just ahead of them, out of sight on the bank.

The lullaby began to affect him in a way intended for the child, and his eyes began to droop as his chin collapsed to his chest. He shook himself awake again. In a few seconds, he could feel his head sink to his chest again. Stay Awake! His eyes closed. He tried to fight it, but he had barely slept for two days. He was jolted out of his state of lethargy as the canoe slammed into a rock.

"Auroch!" Egret shouted, turning just enough to see his eyes shoot open and his head fly up from his chest.

Auroch had enough time to register the anger and disappointment in her gaze before the canoe slammed into another obstacle protruding from the river. A third rock was dead ahead of them, but Auroch had just enough time to use the paddle to deflect the boat away from it. The child was crying now, and the loud whining accompanied heavy, wet tears. Egret turned her back to Auroch, her annoyance with him becoming a second priority to the weeping child. His stupidity would startle the horses! He pushed them away from a lump of floating ice and inadvertently splashed the occupants of the canoe with freezing water as he pulled the paddle back to the boat. Egret made another angry sound, partially muffled at the last moment for the sake of staying silent.

The canyon walls began to slope down, and Auroch looked along the river to see it flattened out. Auroch could make out the figures drinking from the water at the point where the river met the dip in the shore. The herd was there. He watched as curious heads rose from the water and looked toward the canoe. He had mere moments. As soon as they got close, the baby's crying would spook them, and they would be gone. He pulled himself into a crouching position in the back of the boat and placed the paddle down beside his feet. He retrieved a long dart from the same position, grabbed his atlatl from his belt and balanced it on his hand. He had to move swiftly. The boat was nearing where the horses had been drinking until a few moments ago. They looked at the scene quizzically; he could see their muscles tense on their legs as the herd waited for the first horses to bolt. When one went, the others would follow.

Steadying himself, he rose so that he was standing upright in the small dugout canoe. It rocked back and forth violently, and he pushed his right foot against the side to brace himself. Pulling his arm back, the atlatl across his wrist, he balanced the thin spear along his arm. He had one chance. He saw his chosen horse twitch and then turn; a great swell of powdered snow launched into the air as thirty beasts spun on their axis to escape the strange object in the river. Auroch pulled and flicked his wrist forward; the dart cut through the cold afternoon air, twisting as the momentum from Auroch's wrist propelled it across the water's surface and then squarely into the neck of the fleeing horse. Egret and Auroch watched as the animal stumbled, neighing and crying before shock and blood loss overcame the horse, and it fell to the ground. He had hit the carotid artery with uncanny accuracy despite his fatigue.

Auroch wasted no time getting the canoe ashore. Making use of the leverage the thick mud that lay at the bottom of the freezing river provided, he propelled them towards the bank with the paddle, taking care not to rock the boat as he dropped once again to a sitting position. With one hard push, he beached the canoe, and hopped ashore making sure he avoided getting his feet wet. Once he was on the bank, he pulled the canoe, still carrying Egret and the child, ashore. The thrill of the kill distracted him from his increasingly painful left hand. Egret dismounted elegantly and handed him the tools he would need to butcher the animal. Smiling triumphantly, he took the flint scrapers and bladelets from her. What a display of hunting prowess! She blushed as his right hand touched hers.

Moving quickly, he descended on the carcass, carving the largest cuts of meat first, ready to be delivered to Egret's bag. It was bloody work, and by the time he had skinned the beast, he was already covered in a viscous red-black fluid. Despite the late afternoon cold, he felt woozy and hazy as he worked. The initial elation of the kill had worn off and was now replaced with the ache of his fingers, the pounding of his head. Egret could sense his discomfort. She watched as his shaking hand missed the muscle on the horse's hind leg, badly butchering the available meat.

"Here, let me," Egret said gently, taking the blade from him and placing the fur bundle carrying the child on the snow.

He stood up and walked a few paces away from the carcass. Looking down at his torso and arms, he realised he was covered in the beast's blood. He had been careless and clumsy. Bloodied Thistle had taught him better than this. The dark blood of the horse was mixed with a brighter crimson. He followed its source up to his wrist and into his glove. Pulling the mitten off his left hand he stared horrified at the pulsating mass of gore. The neat bandaging of the previous night had come undone, and the stumps where his two missing fingers should have been had become raw and bloody.

He punched a hole in the snow, cooling his injured hand just below the surface. A pulse of sickness followed. From behind him the thwack of flint on bone and flesh fell silent, to be replaced by a strangled chocking sound. He spun around to see Egret on the floor, twitching and throwing her arms around uncontrollably. Not now!

He ran over the girl and rolled her on her side while she thrashed and flopped around. The spirits were speaking to her! Morning Mist had told her this was a great gift, but Auroch suspected that Egret thought of it more as a curse. He held her head, preventing her from smashing it on the frozen ground. The child began to cry again. She was strong in this state, and it took every bit of his diminishing strength to hold her. Was this related to the spirit she had vanquished? What was she being told by the ancestors?

After what felt like a lifetime of struggling, she fell limp. She existed now in a half-awake state, confused moans the only speech she was capable of. Auroch was barely able to stand himself. He spied a small cave one hundred or so strides away from the riverbank and began to pull her slowly but surely into the entrance. She was panting and huffing, and he could hear the child crying. Her body spasmed, and he relaxed his grip on the thick winter clothing that covered her shoulders.

"Auroch? Where are we?" she exclaimed loudly, her voice trembling. "Oh! The river!"

Auroch helped her from the floor and, taking the baby in arm made it to the cave. They sat, the two recovering from their ordeal, watching the sunset through the entrance. He tried to stand, but his hand, still raw and bloody, was exposed, and when it touched the floor, he howled in pain.

"Stay still," Egret instructed calmly; it seemed she had recovered from her episode.

She grabbed and helped him scoot along the floor to a flat rock so that he could sit up without much effort. Producing some cloth and herbs from her bag, she began to dab the wound with dried moss, the dark green turning crimson as Auroch's blood seeped into it. Taking the baby out of her back sling, she placed him on the ground next to Auroch.

"Wait here."

He was in little position to argue, so silently watched as she scurried out of the cave and back down to the river, mildly embarrassed that she had recovered so quickly while he still clung to consciousness by his fingernails.

The baby had stopped crying, and Auroch used his uninjured hand to tease and tickle the child, who giggled in delight at the playful interaction. Egret returned with a leather bladder of cold, fresh water from the river. Taking his hand, she washed it in the water before rubbing an herbal mixture on it and then bandaging it again. Auroch lay against the rock, watching her. Something was wrong; tears were forming in her eyes and began rolling down her cheeks.

"What is the matter?" Auroch asked gently, putting his right hand underneath her chin and raising it so she was looking at him.

"The setting sun. Today is longer than yesterday. The spirits told me on the riverbank," She stammered "I didn't realise it was one of the days just past… I thought we would have more time."

Auroch gulped. They hadn't made it to the plains in time. Nor had she prepared anything on the day of the solstice. She had been delivered a message that she had failed, that she had forsaken her ancestors who imbued her with magic.

"With no tribute given, I will be stripped of my power by the ancestors!" she wailed, "The sun will rise for others but not for me! I can sense the magic of the woodland flowing from me back into the earth!"

"Are we certain that yesterday was shorter?" Auroch said, hoping that the spirits who had visited her had been lying. She helped him to his feet and to the entrance of the cave.

"Look," she pointed to the night sky. The stars were coming out. Auroch was unsure of how long it had been dark. "I have been awake from sunrise to sunset. They told me Auroch! They showed me!" She said through angry, disappointed tears. "I can feel the ancestor spirits pulling their power from me!"

She collapsed into Auroch's arms, shaking and crying. Between a tumultuous few days, the exorcism, and the canoe ride, could they have been so wrong? Would she really be punished for her transgression? Auroch knew the significance the day had held for Morning Mist. He had seen all the Spirit-Mothers and their wards disappear to pay their mysterious tribute on the day of the solstice. He held Egret, his hand still throbbing, listening to her sobs as the sun set over the river.

Chapter 24

A melancholy had overtaken Egret the next day as they packed the bounty from the horse onto the canoe and began to once again paddle down the river. She barely said a word to him, and his attempts at conversation were met with little more than a grunt. She continued to play with the child, but Auroch wasn't sure if she would be able to perform the naming ritual. He dared not ask but instead began to concoct a contingency plan. If a child was a foundling, it could be named by another tribe and then raised by them. They could, perhaps, leave it at the entrance to the great cavern. The child would be safe there at least and named. Auroch didn't think that having another people name the child with their strange customs would help Mother across the river to her ancestors. Again, he dared not raise the question with Egret. She sat with her back to him, and in the few instances she did turn around, he could see her eyes were still wet with tears.

The grim morning turned into a grim afternoon and then a grim evening as the pair beached the canoe to find a place to sleep. Egret sat, hunched over the fire despondency, as they chewed through the horse meat.

The next day was much the same. The river's ice flows had become more frequent as it began to thin, making their trip downstream harder. Yet again, Egret would sit silently in the evening, staring at the flames. He cleaned and wrapped his hand, but there were no mumbled blessings, no prayers. The day after proceeded much the same, and then next. Auroch didn't know what to say. The comfortable silence that had characterised their journey had turned into a miserable one. He watched as the stumps on his hand, stitched together with a tiny bone needle and fibre, began to heal themselves.

On the fourth day with the canoe, the waterway became no longer navigable. A great birch had fallen across the mouth of the river into the smaller estuary, slowing the river to a snail's pace. The slow water and build-up of detritus had caused the water to freeze over. This ice hadn't broken apart like the chunks upstream.

"We can walk on this, I think," Auroch said, testing it with his paddle.

It seemed solid. Pulling the canoe next to the birch, he pulled himself over the tree and onto the ice. It shuddered below his feet but held. He pulled his nervous gaze from his feet and looked up. The scene took his breath away. From his elevated position, he could see a short way up the river to where the sloping canyon walls opened out on the smooth rolling hills of the great plain. And beyond them, a gigantic, tall, lone rock. Its great natural spire protruded from the ground, casting a huge shadow over the plain in the afternoon sun. He knew that below it, he would find a massive cave entrance, and there, a hundred fires burned, with members of all the great plains tribes meeting, rutting and trading next to them. The smoke from the fires was channelled upwards and out of a hollow chimney of rock calved out before time by the elements. The frozen river ran all the way to this rock, filtering into a basin in the cave network where it froze, providing the tribes that met on the plain a place to store the reindeer acquired by chasing the herds into the killing pits.

He turned back to the boat and, steadying it with his foot, he helped Egret and the baby ashore. She gasped as she saw the scene in front of them.

"We are almost at our journey's end!" she exclaimed, the first real emotion she had shown in days. Taking the baby from the cradleboard around her back, she placed him in Auroch's hands. A tear rolled down her cheek. Auroch knew what was coming now.

"This is where we must part ways, Auroch. I cannot help name the child. Not now I have severed my connection to the ancestors."

"You cannot survive out here on your own." he replied, choosing each word carefully so as not to provoke.

"Then I shan't survive. I still have value to them as Old Heron's daughter. As soon as they see me, I will become something to be traded, to be fought over. At least out here I will die free."

Auroch opened his mouth to respond, but before he could utter a word, the unmistakable whizzing noise of a spear disrupted his thoughts. Egret jerked and stumbled forward, making only a small grunt of pain. A splodge of crimson began to grow on her thick tunic as she fell to her knees. From her right shoulder blade protruded a long, wooden spear, its lovingly whittled shaft only appearing to Auroch from Egret's back as she fell on the ice.

The attack was accompanied by a shout. A man stood on the bank, screaming at them in words that Auroch only half understood. He recognised the headdress that adorned his face, the antlers, and the white markings that covered his cheeks and lips. It seemed so long ago since that first confrontation with the Skull Eaters, but here they were again, as they neared the conclusion of their journey.

Auroch had one distinct advantage. Their attacker had thrown his only spear. He watched as the man produced a blade and began to lollop through the thick snow of the bank. He had mere moments. The baby, still in Auroch's hands, was placed carefully inside the foxskin bag that hung from his side. Pulling his atlatl from his belt, he balanced his own thin spear over his wrist, nestling it in the small piece of bone that would throw the projectile. He aimed at the man moving from the bank onto the frozen river. He held his breath. Flicking his wrist forward, the spear flew at the man, connecting with his neck just below his chin. He fell to the ground, the ice creaking dangerously as his momentum pulled him across the frozen surface of the lake. Auroch breathed out.

Egret! He bent down and grabbed her shoulder. A loud, angry groan came from her body. She was still alive! Auroch examined the wound. It was deep, and her back was stained crimson, her winter hides heavy with blood. But she was alive for now. Pulling the bag around from his back, he checked momentarily on the baby before placing the warm fur bundle containing him on the ice. Egret needed immediate attention.

"Auroch, what have you done!" The voice carried itself across the lake.

Auroch looked up to see the Master Huntsman of the Summer Valley dressed in the Skull Eater garb. Bloodied Thistle was thin and malnourished, and the antler headdress caused his head to dip and bob. In his hand, he carried a flint spear. He brandished it towards Auroch, the baby, and the injured Sprit Maiden.

"Help me with Egret." Auroch pleaded, "We aren't far from the meeting ground; we can get help there."

Bloodied Thistle said nothing but began to circle towards the dying Skull Eater, making sure not to exert too much force as the ice shifted and moaned beneath him. Both hunters knew they would normally scoot across dangerous ice like this on their bellies, but the standoff forced them to remain on their feet, avoiding any stance that would leave them prone to attack.

"I'm sorry Auroch. I've been instructed to wait for you here. I can't let you reach the plains."

"Is that the will of your new chief?" Auroch spat at Bloodied Thistle, "He killed our people! Destroyed the valley! My family!"

"I know. But I cannot change what has been, and they have offered me a new life. These people were maltreated by the tribes of the plains. The man who provokes the bear cannot complain when the beast lashes out at him."

Auroch had heard enough. He pulled his blade from his belt and ran at Bloodied Thistle, throwing his full weight into a dive, aiming for the man's head. He had forgotten how fast the Master Huntsman was. He swung his spear around, hitting him in the gut with the side of the shaft. Auroch crumpled and skidded across the ice. He felt it heave and crack underneath his weight.

"Please Auroch…" Bloodied Thistle said, but his assailant was already on his feet, ready to throw himself against the man a second time. "Take Egret. Leave this place. She may still live. You cannot venture to the meet under the great rock. Even if you were to dispatch me and make it there Grey Stag would kill you on sight."

Auroch couldn't even understand what Bloodied Thistle was saying. He just wanted the traitor dead. All the bottled rage that had accompanied him through the night of the massacre, his time as a captive, and his long journey with Egret poured out of him now, channelling itself into the fist clenched around the handle of his blade.

"Grey Stag sent us here to intercept you, but he never said we had to kill you." His former friend pleaded. "I have watched you grow, Auroch. I have watched Egret blossom from a girl into a woman. I have no desire for either of you to die."

Once again, the words fell on deaf ears. Who was this man who could start his life anew so casually? The rage began to solidify into an appraisal of the situation. He was going to kill Bloodied Thistle, not in defence or an accidental scrap. Auroch was going to smash in his brains. But how? Bloodied Thistle's spear held him at bay; getting close enough to him for a killing blow was impossible. Could he retrieve his spear? No. The Antler head had likely snapped off inside the Skull Eater; it was little more than a stick now. Perhaps the one that had grievously injured Egret? No. Bloodied Thistle would see him going for it and stick him with his sharpened piece of flint. The Ice! There must be some way to get the man in the water. He used the bottom of his foot to feel the surface beneath him. Glancing down for naught but a moment, he saw the cracks beginning to form. This was the spot! But how to lure him? He would need more weight.

The man who had thrown the spear at Egret lay a few strides away from him. Auroch began to circle towards him, taking care to step on the fractures already forming beneath his feet. He pushed at the ice with his leg muscles, relishing every crack and groan from the frozen surface of the lake. Bloodied Thistle circled opposite him, maintaining enough distance to launch his spear if needed. Auroch was standing over the man now, the crimson of his blood seeping into the cool blue of the ice. Now, the difficult part, the sleight of hand. Without taking his eyes from Bloodied Thistle he crouched down over the man and pretended to check for breath with the back of his hand.

"Still alive." he said, adding a purposefully cruel sneer to his voice. "We shall have to correct my earlier mistake."

He pulled a lump of unknapped flint from his bag and positioned himself ready to deliver a blow to the man's head. Bloodied Thistle sprung into action, lunging toward the pair. Auroch's gamble had worked. He kicked off with his feet backward, using his outstretched from the faux blow at the dead man's head to grab the ice behind him. He watched the spear cut through the air just in front of him as Bloodied Thistle lept forwards. As his feet hit the ground, he felt the reverberations through the ice. It was too much for the already weakened surface, and the small area around the three men gave way.

Auroch's premature jump had pushed his arms clear of the break in the ice, and he used every fibre of his strength to pull himself out of the small hole that had formed as the hunter had hit the surface. Almost as soon as his knees and ankles touched the frigid water, Auroch was clear. The other two were not so lucky. The Skull Eater, already dead, rolled in quietly, sinking into his cold dark tomb without fuss. Bloodied Thistle went under, only to emerge shivering, teeth chattering from the small hole at chest height, his hands grabbing at the ice to find some purchase.

The rage that Auroch had held at bay was back once again, throbbing through the rock in his hand. He stood over the shaking Bloodied Thistle, the man's stature and hunting prowess meaning nothing now as he fruitlessly grabbed at the ice by Auroch's feet. Auroch could see the fear in his eyes, the realisation that even if he hauled himself from the hole, it would be hard to dry himself fast enough to survive, that even if he hauled himself out, his fight with Auroch would continue. Auroch saw the will to live in his eyes. This man wished above all else not to die. It was why he had drunk the concoction made from human flesh, why he had joined with the Skull Eaters, and why he had tried to stop them from reaching the plains. Bloodied Thistle begged silently for mercy with his eyes. Auroch gave none. He did not hesitate. In a single swift motion, he brought the flint down on Bloodied Thistle's temple. It bounced off his head, but not before smashing through hair, skin, and bone. Sanguine spray danced across the ice, adding colour to the monochrome landscape. Then Bloodied Thistle went limp, his relaxed body sliding smoothly and quietly into the hole, disappearing beneath the surface.

Auroch stood over the hole for a moment, shaking. He half expected his former friend to bob to the surface, but instead, a solemn silence had fallen over the river. The child's cry cut through the air, snapping Auroch back to reality. He walked back towards Egret and the child, careful to avoid further damage to the already weakened ice.

The child was in distress, but he didn't have time to comfort him. He slung the baby over his back and then bent down to examine Egret.

Her back was sticky with blood, but she was breathing, if only semi-awake. She murmured and stirred. Pulling some plant fibre cloth from his bag, he braced his arm against her back and gripped the spear with his right hand. This was going to be extremely unpleasant, and he silently hoped she wasn't conscious enough to feel it. He pulled hard on the end of the spear while bracing the part of the shaft closest to the wound. Most of the shaft broke off, falling to the surface of the frozen river. Egret screamed, her voice echoing across the ice. Birds lifted themselves from the trees and scattered, terrified of the unearthly cries of pain from the young woman's mouth. She once again slipped into unconsciousness as Auroch tried his best to dress her wound. The head of the spear couldn't be removed from the wound yet as it was preventing blood loss. There was little he could do. She was already in the death trance, the state of transition between this world and the next. Some could come back to the world of the living at this stage, but it was rare.

Auroch glanced up at the sweeping vista of the plains and the huge, solitary rock formation in the distance. How far would he walk if he moved quickly? Half a day? Until dawn? Egret had saved him more times than he could count. She had saved the child, nursed him back to health, and sacrificed everything to help them return to the plains. They would undoubtedly recognise her tattoos if he took her to the meeting place. Would she really rather die than become a pawn in tribal politics once again? Bundling her up in his arms, the child on his back, Auroch began to walk, then jog, towards the huge rock in the centre of his vision.

The rest of the morning went by as if it were a dream. He scrambled across the plains, the dying girl in his arms causing him distress with every missed breath and every grunt of pain. Would he make it? He didn't pause to take in the harsh beauty of the rolling hills. He didn't pause to take in the winter brooks with their cool, clear drinking water. He didn't pause to take in the magnificent sight of the lone rock towering over the plains. He just kept on moving. Before he knew it, the afternoon sun was setting, and the day turned into night. Looking up, he could see fires illuminating the base of the structure. The baby had been crying for most of the afternoon. He knew the child was hungry, as he was, but there was no time to stop, no time to eat. They were so close. With every step, the fires were closer. Auroch could imagine their heat, could imagine a swarm of wise women from other tribes grabbing Egret from him and performing their magic. Without realising, he reached the bottom of the slope that ran up to the great rock. His legs burning, he pushed on, almost throwing himself towards the summit.

With one great heave, he pulled himself on top of the hill at the entrance to the great cave. The fire had melted the snow here, and he gently placed Egret down in a sea of slush and mud. He could hear himself shouting for help, the drumbeat of blood pulsating through his ears. After what felt like an age, a crowd of concerned faces began to appear out of the darkness of the cave. A group of older women ran over to him and relieved him of the crying child. Egret was looked over and was taken away for healing. Heavy hands grabbed his shoulder, pulling him to his feet. Auroch scanned the crowd, recognising some of the faces from previous winters, until he settled on the figure of an old man, staring at him from a fire lit near the cave entrance. The old man's lips contorted into a cruel smile as he gave the exhausted boy a nod of approval. Grey Stag and the Skull Eaters had made it here well before them. A shiver passed through Auroch as he realised that despite reaching the meeting on the plains, the journey was far from over.

Spring

Chapter 25

A continual, slow barrage of water droplets dripped on Auroch's head, preventing him from sleeping. It had been one droplet at first, occasionally, but now they had become regular enough that it was impossible to ignore. Somewhere above him, there was melting snow, and the water running off the ceiling of the great cavern was now falling in an irregular pattern onto his face. He sighed and pulled himself out of his deerskin sack. He wasn't getting much sleep anyway. Between his nightmares, the child's crying, and his worries about a visit in the dark from Grey Stag or one of the other Skull Eaters, he barely slept anyway. He had set himself and the child up at the opposite end of the great cave from the Skull Eaters, pitching some pieces of red deer hide he had managed to wrangle in trade up between some sticks as a screen. He mostly kept to himself. Although the grand cavern was huge, there were many Skull Eaters, and it was easy to find himself face to face with one of the shouting women, cruel children, or angry men from his time as a slave.

The night he arrived, he had been pulled before the great fire of the clan chiefs and had been ordered to explain what had happened to the Summer Valley and Old Heron, his seat now empty. Grateful for the opportunity, Auroch had held nothing back, describing the encounter in the meadow, the attack on the valley, his enslavement, and the journey to the meeting place. There were three Grand Chiefs present, as well as an assortment of lesser ones. They had listened patiently, asking the appropriate questions and giving Auroch time to give a full account. Auroch had noticed the jewellery they wore around their wrists. Some of it was made by his own hands, crafted by the river in the autumn months. Grey Stag was brought before them soon after and unsurprisingly denied any involvement.

"Haven't I been generous!" The old man had said, "What goods I have brought to you, I have come back, so many winters since I was banished, bearing only good will and gifts."

He had accused Auroch of fantasy, delusion, and even potentially of killing Old Heron himself. This had gained a frustratingly large murmur of approval. One of the Spirit-Mothers who had been treating Egret's injuries had approached Brown Colt, the Grand Chieftain of the Horse Hunter tribe, and whispered something in his ear.

"The woman you carried across the plain was a Spirit-Maiden! Old Heron's daughter!" Brown Colt spoke to Auroch, although the announcement was more for the benefit of the crowd gathered around them. "She is still in the death trance, although it is possible she may still live. If she does, we shall hear her story without any hushed words from you as to what has been said this evening. We shall give her until the spring's dawn, and then her words will guide our judgement."

It had been at least a moon since then. Egret was sequestered and guarded in another part of the huge cavern. Auroch was unaware of what state she was in, if she was conscious, what she knew of the current situation. Auroch suspected that their fate wasn't to be decided until the time at which the tribes began to depart so as not to bring discord into the camp and allow for at least a moon's more trading. The drip, drip, drip of the water onto the cavern floor told him all he needed to know. It was almost spring.

He heard the unmistakable trumpet of Great-Tusk, the Mammoth. From what he had gathered, Grey Stag had made quite an impression, reaching the cave astride the animal, his entourage of Skull Eaters in tow. Only about two-thirds of the group that had set out from the river had made it by Auroch's reckoning. He wondered what grisly fate had befallen them, but the brief questions he had been able to ask members of the other tribes who were present when the Skull Eaters arrived had received no answers. As far as they were concerned, this was the full tribe of the banished.

He picked up the child and exited his little screened-off area. The cavern was grand, and the shouts of the various tribesmen and women echoed across small fires as they jostled and bartered for goods. In the centre of the chamber was the great fire, its embers still smouldering this time in the morning, ready to be relit when the evening began to draw in. Auroch walked across to an area where a group of older women were preparing reindeer carcasses, the last stragglers of the yearly migration. Auroch was thankful that he didn't have to repeat yesterday's work, hauling the carcasses out of the pits on the plains and carrying them up the long hill to the entrance. He was handed a flint scraper by a stern woman with a bright blue otter tattooed across her face, and he set to work skilfully removing the layer from the beast's hide. It was easy work, and he was good at it. The child was handed to the otter woman's daughter, only nine or ten summers old herself. He watched from the corner of his eye as she teased the gargling infant with some painted bone fragments on a string or used her hands to hide her face, only to reveal it to delighted squeals from the baby.

Around midday, he decided to briefly rest. The otter woman assured him she would watch the child, and he wandered around the cavern, looking at the different objects laid out on furs, ready to be traded. He passed silently by those belonging to the Skull Eaters, recognising some of the ornate bladelets and jewellery. Still, after giving a great deal of it to the Grand Chief in order to negotiate their way into the meeting, there was such a great amount of goods produced by himself and the other Skull Eater slaves that he thought that it was unlikely that they would be able to trade it all away. Perhaps they planned to bury it nearby in preparation for trade at the next winter solstice.

Circling around the great cavern, he kept to the shadows. He watched as Grey Stag, surrounded by two of his entourage, chatted up Brown Colt and several other minor clan chiefs. From this angle, he could also see the guarded area where he guessed Egret was recovering. He had thought many times about sneaking in to check on her but was wary about jeopardising the Grand Chief's judgement. He watched for a little while, imagining himself stealthily moving past the guards and making his way under the stitched deerskin screen blocking his view when a voice called him out of the dark.

"Calf. Come to me, wretched child." The man was shrouded in gloom. The afternoon sun bathed the secret corners and alcoves in darkness, obscuring him to Auroch's eyes. "Over here."

Auroch dutifully followed the voice into the corner. His eyes adjusted almost immediately, and in response, his stomach tightened and curled itself into knots. The man was sitting against the wall, a skin placed underneath him. His legs were splayed, and his arms lay across his lap in a way that someone might lay them if sleeping. Auroch recognised the cruel smile on his face and the large scar across the hole where his pupil used to sit. The one-eyed man, Red Fox.

"Come closer, boy. I can't move," Red Fox said. Auroch had presumed him dead after the elk had attacked him, and his sudden reappearance was an unpleasant surprise.

"Here in the shadows, I could slit your throat. Nobody would see." Auroch said calmly, channelling the same cold, calculated rage he had unleashed onto Bloodied Thistle.

"I would welcome it." Red Fox replied in his strange accent. "I am a dead man already, but for my head." Auroch recognised the slump. The man was crippled, presumably by the elk.

"Then I will leave you to your suffering," Auroch replied. He turned to go, but an audible objection from Red Fox stopped him.

"I will help you, boy, if you promise to kill me." The man pleaded. "I will help you banish my father once more if you promise to plunge your spear into my chest."

"Your father?" Auroch hadn't spent a moment considering the relationship between the one-eyed man and the leader of the Skull

Eaters. "Grey Stag is your father?"

"He is," Red Fox replied. "I am his second seed. And the arrogant fool will not leave me to die. Even when so many were killed on the route."

"Tell me about him," Auroch asked, hoping for some solid information at last.

"I will tell his story, and I will help you banish him once more when the Grand Chiefs debate. But I require one thing. You must vow to kill me. Free my spirit from this useless vessel. And don't allow any of my compatriots to feast on my flesh. I need my strength to meet the ancestors."

Auroch thought for a second. What had he got to lose? As much as he wished to inflict the maximum amount of pain possible on this man, perhaps it would be better to utilise his services in the upcoming judgement, then allow him to go peacefully to his sleep. He wanted to hurt him, though. He wanted the man to suffer. Auroch considered that for all the trials he had faced, he still felt indecisive. What would Father do? He could enact his vengeance in a small way now, to this broken man, in the corner of the cavern.

His thoughts were interrupted by the smell of urine. The skin that Red Fox lay on began to darken as his water began to seep into it. The one-eyed man looked at it, only realising what had left his bladder as he smelt it.

"I wish to die, boy. I wish to be killed rather than dragged on a sled by a coterie of women and children."

Auroch had made his decision. He nodded. He sat down beside the man, taking care to avoid the urine-stained fur. "Tell me Grey

Stag's story."

"Grey Stag was of the Riverfolk more than forty summers ago. He fell in love with a young woman, Little Vole. At least that is the name you knew her by before she was renamed when she was taken as wife and Spirit-Mother by the leader of your tribe. You knew her as Morning Mist."

Auroch had figured out the bones of this part of the story at least. He cast his mind back to the verbal history he had drilled into him. Morning Mist was the former wife of Wet Bittern. Leadership had transferred to his brother, Egret's grandfather, after he died, and then again to her father, Old Heron, in turn.

"When the tribes met in midwinter, Father rekindled their love in secret, until a baby was conceived. What a surprise for my father when he encountered the Valleyfolk the next year and Little Vole, now called Morning Mist, returned with a baby boy. The two made plans to run with their child, to live as clanless. Once again, they rekindled their love. But this time, they were caught by Wet Bittern. They fought, and my father won. He killed your chief. The uncertainty over the parentage of the child put the leadership of your people at risk. And so, the child was killed, thrown from a rock. And Grey Stag was banished."

"But what of the other Skull Eaters!" Auroch cried. "They have not just sprouted from the ground."

"Where do you think the majority of the clanless come from?" Red Fox shot back, "The plains, valleys, and hills are crawling with men who have done little but upset the Grand Chieftains. Those accused of theft after a long journey with little food! Those who challenged the full bellies of the clan leaders while they traded what little goods they had for morsels of preserved meat. Those who didn't appreciate being traded like fint between tribes in order to keep the peace!"

Auroch's thoughts turned to Egret. "He wants revenge on the tribes?" he asked.

"Revenge? No. Revenge is for short-sighted fools. Great men plan. He wandered the plains with Great-Tusk for years. He never forgave, and he always carried the pain in his heart. But he was aiming for a higher purpose. He gathered the clanless, the banished. There were other women, such as my mother, but he never forgot his Little Vole, his Morning Mist. He vowed to lead the clans away from the gluttonous rule of the Grand Chiefs so that no woman would be traded, nor a bastard child killed, nor an innocent exiled ever again. That there would be a fair trade at the winter solstice."

"But you eat the flesh of men!" Auroch shouted. A few men and women looked in his direction. He was causing a scene.

Red Fox shrugged. "We absorb the power of men through their meat. Almost half our number died before we could make it to the plain. We consumed them and carried their vigour forward." He paused before continuing his story. "There are some who still remember Grey Stag. My party was despatched to find them before we could return to the winter meet."

Auroch realised he was shaking. "And what of the Valleyfolk …my parents, my sister, my brothers."

"We thought Old Heron might raise an objection to his uncle's killer being welcomed back into the fold. Our meeting in the meadow only solidified the plan. We couldn't allow you to carry news of roasted man flesh to the plains, knowing that the other tribes think it an affront to the dead. Better to deal with any conflict before the solstice."

The casual dismissal of the slaughter as part of Grey Stag's plan once again caused anger to bubble to the surface inside Auroch. How could he be so cruel to wipe out the Summer Valley? He felt his hand reaching to his belt for his blade. These people were monsters. They deserved nothing but death. His vow meant nothing. He should slay this one-eyed monster here in the gloom.

Shouts interrupted the pure white hot rage aching to escape his body. A young fisherman of the coastal tribe, his dark scalp covered by a woven fibre net with various seashells attached, was causing a commotion towards the cave entrance. Auroch looked at his hand curling around his flint. He needed this creature alive if only to destroy Grey Stag. He turned on his heels and walked towards the entrance, worried if he spent any more time with Red Fox, he would kill the cripple. There was a crowd gathering around the fisherman now. Auroch could make out his hurried gesticulations from a distance. He had a thick, hard-to-understand way of speaking, like the rest of the coast dwellers, and whatever had been spotted must be of some importance because outside of the dried fish they brought to the solstice, they weren't to be trusted in matters of hunting or tracking.

"Just like that one!" the boy shouted, gesturing down the rolling slope to where Great-Tusk stood, gnawing on the grass exposed by the melting snow.

Auroch had gathered that the mammoth had caused quite a stir when it first arrived, and there had been no shortage of people who had wished to kill the animal. Grey Stag had cut a powerful figure as he approached atop it and had sent children running and screaming as Great-Tusk trotted up the hill. However, after the initial fear had worn off, the Mammoth had become an amusing sideshow. Plainsmen sat and watched it, throwing dried shoots and leaves and watching it gnaw on them. Some of the braver children would go close to Great-Tusk and touch his trunk before jumping back, laughing. Auroch had noticed that the beast looked noticeably thinner, perhaps malnourished, compared to when he had first seen it in the autumn. The boy from the coast continued to point down the hill.

"Ten mammoths!" He shouted, "Ten! A Matriarch, a herd with juveniles! Spotted just east of here, not far!"

A murmur spread through the crowd. This was rare. There were tales of men frequently hunting mammoth in the distant past of the great freeze, but they weren't seen now with any frequency on the plains. Brown Colt began organising his hunters.

"The effort of many tribes is required!" He shouted, "Able men, grab your spears! We can drive them into the killing pits!"

The crowd began to peter out as men from various tribes went to fetch their tools. This was going to be a big hunt. As the plainsmen drifted away from the entrance, he could see Grey Stag, standing across from him, his face as white as snow.

"Grey Stag!" Brown Colt approached the man and slapped him on the back. "Time for you to test this beast of yours! Can it help herd its own kind into the pit? A true test for your band of banished men!"

Chapter 26

Auroch checked on the baby, quickly negotiating away some of his share of mammoth fur in exchange for the Otter woman and her daughter to look after his brother while he participated in the hunt. Soon, he was assembled along with the other men by the yawning mouth of the cavern. A nervous-looking Grey Stag was helped astride Great-Tusk. The hunt began.

The various tribesmen sang and whooped as they made their way across the plains. The melting ice and snow had made the surface muddy underfoot, and Auroch squelched through the dirt with difficulty. As valued as his spear was, the mystery surrounding the Men of the Summer Valley's disappearance had placed a veil of suspicion over him, and there was little said to him as they marched towards the killing pits. Isolated, he felt apart from the others, even as a member of a hunting party. He wished Egret were here beside him; even her stony silence or occasional foul moods seemed preferable to suspicious glances. Auroch wondered if he would ever attend the solstice again. He had been so focussed on getting to the meeting that he hadn't considered what came next. He had failed in his task of naming the baby, he had failed to stop Grey Stag, and he wasn't sure if he would ever see Egret again. He wondered what happened when they all left. Was he clanless? Where was he, Egret, and the baby to go?

He was pulled from his thoughts by the sight of several moving lumps on the horizon. The mammoths. They carefully considered their angle of approach, noting that if they could drive them far enough south, the sloping plains narrowed into a gorge with killing pits at one end, that were used by the tribes to funnel reindeer to their deaths in late autumn. The mammoths could not climb, even from a shallow hole. The men stopped and quickly devised a plan. Grey Stag riding Great-Tusk was to position himself in front of the herd at the end of the gorge while some of the hunters moved behind their prey, driving them toward the trap with dogs. They would startle and throw spears at the mammoths, who would then barrel down the gorge toward the pits. Another group of hunters, including Auroch, would be on the side of the gorge, ready to rain spears down onto the fleeing mammoths. The mammoths, seeing Great-Tusk safely beyond the killing pits, would make a break for him where they would fall the height of a man into the pits full of sharpened flint spearheads and jagged rocks and trees, ready to be finished off.

It was a simple plan, but Auroch was weary of bringing Grey Stag's trained animal into the proceedings. The old man looked equally panicked about the prospect. Still, the mammoth had been touted to the plainsmen as a great hunting aid. Therefore, there was much expectation and hubbub surrounding his inclusion in the pursuit.

Before long, Auroch found himself overlooking the gorge with about three dozen other men. He looked to his right to see the figure of Grey Stag, astride his mammoth, below him. How close was he? Auroch thought about the distances involved for a moment and speculated that he was likely within throwing range. Could he do it? In the chaos and confusion of the hunt, a rogue spear could make its way into his side, either killing him outright or causing the old man to fall from his mount. It occurred to Auroch that he had been placed where he was precisely because of this. If Grey Stag was hit, it would be obvious who was to blame. He watched as the great beast searched around for shoots and small plants to strip on the floor of the gorge. He could do it. Throw the spear now, and this ordeal could be over. He may not make it back to the cavern alive as there were at least seven Skull Eaters with them on the hunt, but the ordeal would be over, his parents avenged.

A hunting cry pierced the air. The carefully planned chaos was about to start. From over the rolling hillocks came the barks of lively hunting dogs and the shouts of their masters, followed by the deep rumble of the mammoths as spears were thrown into their rear and back. They appeared over the rise, howling in fear and anger. The first saw Great-Tusk and made a beeline for him, squeezing himself down the narrow gorge formed by an ancient river that had long since vanished. The rest of the mammoths followed, and not before long, there was a queue of gargantuan beasts barrelling towards the killing pits. A shout rose, and the men loosed their spears, hurling them at the animals. Auroch looked at Grey Stag once again. Could he do it?

The hunters following the mammoths were right behind them

now and using longer, flint-tipped spears to poke and prod at the beasts, preventing them from turning around. One managed to turn its head just enough to catch a hunter with his tusk, sending him flying. Auroch pulled his arm back, his atlatl firmly in place, the spear balanced on top of it. He looked again at Grey Stag. Great-Tusk was bellowing and thrashing around in distress as he watched the herd of mammoths take spear after spear into their side. The old man was clinging on for dear life and had clearly given up any attempt at attempting to marshal Great-Tusk. There was nothing he could do now but hold on and hope his ancient frame wasn't flung against the rocks of the canyon walls.

Auroch launched his spear, hitting the broadside of an adult mammoth. In a panic, its tusks smashed into the beast before it. The matriarch at the head of the column misplaced her foot, and the first of the ferocious animals fell forward into the killing pits. Her terrified wails echoed through the valley as her foot was pierced by the sharpened wood pikes. The massive weight of the creature caused her to topple sideways, a second wooden spear piercing her gut. She struggled to move, but the pain and shock proved too much, and she collapsed in agony. She was shortly joined by a second mammoth and then a third. Auroch watched as the hunters at the back skilfully allowed some of the young females back out of the gorge while keeping the others moving with vicious prodding and stabbing. The four females didn't run far, cowering and screaming as the older animals were herded into the pit. It was mostly pointless to kill those at an age they could give birth; it was better to let them wander off to have more children, then one day become prey when they were old.

Auroch watched Grey Stag clinging to Great-Tusk's matted fur, struggling to regain control. Had a similar thing happened to the orphan mammoth that had then been found by the banished, grieving Grey Stag?

Another mammoth fell into a pit. Then another. One of the older females managed to get enough space to turn around and charged the hunters tormenting them with spears, easily swatting two into the side of the gorge. A hunter to the side of him signalled to Auroch, and the pair launched themselves down the slope of the gorge, skidding on their rear into the narrow passageway. Auroch grabbed one of the discarded spears, its head still intact, and took up the position previously occupied by the man lying on the ground to his left. The mammoth in front of him was attempting to follow the lead of the beast that had escaped and make the turn. Auroch ran to its head and jabbed his spear violently at its eye. It roared and shook its head angrily, smashing its tusks into the smooth rocks which formed the walls of the gorge. They had it! Auroch and a man from the Fen pressed forward toward the pit, giving the mammoth no quarter. All the mammoths but one lay struggling and dying in the pit now. Just a little further, keep it scared! Auroch watched as its misplaced foot missed the edge of the dirt hole, and its huge frame tumbled into its grave.

Cheers and whoops rang out across the plains from the hunters. They had done it! Kills of this magnitude were rare, and the wave of euphoria that swept across the men was contagious. Auroch found himself shouting along with the others. The men gathered around him and the Fen man to slap them on the back and congratulate them.

This was a great day, thought Auroch, not because of the hunt's success but hopefully, it would give him some standing in the judgement. He had driven the last of these beasts into the pit and secured some recognition from the Grand Chieftains. Meanwhile, Grey Stag had flailed around, barely in control of his animal. Auroch watched as a group of four hunters whispered amongst themselves and glanced at Great-Tusk, who was now acting in a more sedentary fashion, albeit with occasional whimpers of distress. The day was won.

Chapter 27

Auroch sat on the slope of the gorge and watched the dying mammoths struggle in the pit. There was work to be done still, but not just yet. Great-Tusk stood at the side of the pit and wailed at the mammoths, who in return howled back in their deep guttural language. One by one, the beasts fell silent, succumbing to the grievous wounds caused by spears and the sharpened wooden stakes and rocks in the pit. On the horizon, a caravan of people approached; men, women, and children were arriving to begin dismembering the animals. Auroch spied the otter-faced lady and her daughter walking in the evening sun, holding his infant brother. He lifted himself from his perch, feeling the soreness in his legs, and headed over to them. The woman congratulated him on the hunt and handed the infant to him. He was to rest while they worked. Auroch did not protest, nor did the other hunters, and the new arrivals began to poke at the still-living mammoths in the pit with flint-tipped spears from the safety of the edge.

Darkness descended as Auroch watched the group work. It was a long process. One by one, the butchers jumped into the shallow pit, avoiding the deadly traps left for the mammoths, and began to work on the corpses with flint flakes and blades, cutting the meat precisely. It was a novelty to butcher a mammoth, and only a few of those in the pit had done it before, but all relished the work. Large chunks of meat were removed and placed on sleds, then dragged back to the great rock in the moonlight. Although the chill of winter had not just left the air, Auroch didn't feel cold, and the child in his arms slept soundly. The baby was wrapped in thick swaddling leather of the Riverfolk, and Auroch's battered furs he had received at the turn of winter kept them snug as the others worked.

It was almost midnight by the time the first beast had been completely stripped of usable meat and organs. Bones were removed from the carcass where it was possible for it to be shaped into jewellery, spears, and other tools. The rest would have to wait for now; the meat was more important, and he was sure that groups would be scurrying between the mammoth and the cavern for the next few days at least. The group in the pit moved onto their next carcass and began the process again. Auroch, the child in his arms and his back against rock felt his head nodding before falling into a restful slumber.

It was dawn when he awoke. He rubbed his eyes, brushing away the dreams of Egret, Bloodied Thistle, and his family. He was present once again, watching the group, who had been working since nightfall, dismember the kills. He assumed the second group would be there to relieve the workers soon, and then he would have to join in the butchery. He glanced across the pit at a haggard-looking Grey Stag beside the still restless Great-Tusk. Had he spent the whole night soothing him? Why hadn't he led him away from the pit? Auroch realised he had very little control over the beast. Great-Tusk wanted to stay and mourn the mammoths, and there was little that Grey Stag, for all his boasting of having tamed the beast, could do about it.

A shout came from behind him, and Auroch turned to see the second group not far away across the plains. A cheer of relief came from the pit, and people began to lift themselves out, exhausted and bloody. As they clambered up the sides, a sudden terrified bellow came from one of the smaller carcasses in the pit. Auroch hadn't been able to see previously, but with some of the mass removed, Auroch could make out one juvenile, crushed between two adults, that had somehow survived the night despite its horrific injuries. The noise startled the workers, and Auroch watched as the otter-faced woman and her daughter pulled themselves onto the side directly beside Grey Stag and Great-Tusk. The beast reacted to the noise by rushing to the pit and trumpeting loudly. Grey Stag grabbed at its side and tried to calm it, but it reacted violently, thrashing and stomping.

"Calm, my friend!" The old man shouted, "We must be calm!"

The words had no effect on Great-Tusk. The old man was faster than Auroch suspected and dived to the side, dodging the gigantic tusks. The Otter-faced lady tried to pull her daughter away from the beast, but it was too late. The beautiful, painted ivory of his tusks smashed into the little girl, and she flew through the air, bouncing off the side of the gorge before falling limply to the floor. Great-Tusk bellowed again and turned around, sloping off up the gorge, Grey Stag in pursuit. The second group had arrived and, much like the crowd that stood by the pit, were frozen by events. The otter-faced woman ran over to her child, cradling her and weeping, cursing her ancestors and begging them with every other sentence. Auroch had seen before the cries of a woman who had lost her child. He watched as others broke out of their shock and ran to help. There was nothing to be done but howl and caress the cheek of the dead girl.

Chapter 28

The days after the mammoth hunt were tense and fraught with speculation. Great-Tusk was gone, chased off into the plains by Grey Stag. Or so the old man had said. There was little appetite to go after the beast, so the issue was allowed to fester. The weather had changed dramatically, bringing the first rainstorms of early spring. The plains turned into a quagmire of mud from the melted snow and ice, but the dividends paid by the mammoth hunt relieved the usual pressure this time of year to begin the long journey back to the summer hunting grounds. The mammoth meat had been stored in the icy cave underneath the cavern, ready for transportation when groups left in the coming days. On a normal year, spotters from the Summer Valley would be at the mouth of the river, where Bloodied Thistle had died, waiting for the signs of red deer migrating to the foothills where the stags would come down in time for the rutting. The rest of the tribe would be alerted, and that's when they would leave, following the herd home. There was no spotter this year. Auroch thought any attempt by himself to monitor the river would be futile.

He largely kept to himself. The atmosphere inside the camp had improved towards him and worsened for Grey Stag. Whispers that the Skull Eater never had control of Great-Tusk and that he had caused the young girl's death had begun to circulate. Auroch didn't wish to be overconfident, but he was beginning to feel that with his and Egret's testimony and help from Red Fox, he may be able to persuade the Grand Chiefs to banish Grey Stag. His optimism gave way to worry. Egret, having lost her magic as a Spirit-Maiden, could be no help in naming the child, even if they did escape punishment. Auroch had to decide soon. The child could be named by the Spirit-Mother of another tribe, but Auroch would have to leave the baby, and it would be passed to a barren woman or an old couple in the new tribe. Mother would still not be allowed to cross to her ancestors, but at least the child would be safe in this life. What about himself? Could he persuade someone to take him and Egret under their wing? No doubt they would be separated. Egret would still be considered a valuable commodity despite losing her connection to the ancestors.

It was mid-morning when the news of the great oak's first green made its way through the cavern. The lone tree stood on a nearby hill signalled the official end of the winter meeting. By the time Auroch reached it, painters had already begun daubing it with pictures of reindeer and mammoths, the bounty of the winter hunts. There were other pictures as well, fish, rhinos, hares. Auroch added his own red deer to it, although he wasn't sure if he would ever hunt the animal again. He did it anyway, the customary symbol that would normally bring him success in the year to come. No sooner had he done this a young girl of the Horse Hunter tribe informed him that the judgement would be held at midday underneath the great tree. Auroch became anxious. He had fallen into a routine now and having to wait for his judgement had given him time to reflect on the year before. He certainly enjoyed the doldrum life in the great cavern far more than walking all day or backbreaking labour as a slave. A tingle of excitement was mixed in with the anxiety. He was going to see Egret! He wondered how she was feeling, if her injuries were healed, if she would be angry with him for carrying her to the gathering.

He waited under the tree for the Grand Chieftains, and one by one, they emerged from their busy work in the cavern. Brown Colt of the Horse Hunters was first; the handsome man was only twenty or so summers old and looked resplendent, his wrists and neck covered in mammoth bone jewellery. Wise Shrew was next, of the Fen dwellers. The man was a misshapen and tiny, standing no taller than a child. He had an enormous green tattoo on his back as did all his people, but his head, disproportionally large for his body, carried an additional circular tattoo on his temple. Auroch had met Wise Shrew on several occasions as a child and knew that the man's head was so large in order to hold all his wisdom.

Next to arrive was the Coastal fisherwoman, Graceful Seal. Her wiry dark hair was platted through a net, which on it sat painted seashells. The coastal people were strange, and her dual role as Grand Chief and Spirit-Mother for the Coastfolk didn't sit well with many of the other tribes. Although unprecedented within the other groups, they had been reliably informed that there were previously women leaders at the Coast, and so the other groups had begrudgingly allowed her to sit with the other Grand Chieftains from about five summers hence. The final two Grand Chieftains were missing, Pike of the

Riverfolk and the Old Heron of the Summer Valley. Auroch realised he had not asked after the leader of the Riverfolk when he encountered them on the frozen lake but had presumed him dead with the majority of the other men.

Auroch sat in respectful silence with the chiefs, waiting for the judgement to begin. A hand touched his shoulder and he found Egret standing behind him, a sly smile on her face. Maintaining the silence, she looked around at the chieftains and spectators from a mixture of grand and lesser tribes before sitting cross-legged next to Auroch. She held the respectful quiet, but Auroch felt her warmth. He was glad to have her sitting nearby, to be able to reach out and brush her skin with his hand if he wished. She was already wearing summer attire despite the warm weather not quite reaching the point where most were comfortable with it. An ugly new scar sat on her back, just below the left shoulder blade. Auroch quietly wondered whether it had been his doing when he snapped the spear shaft. Other than that, she looked well. Her hair had been cut shorter and was a little haphazard and messy rather than the neat braids she normally kept during the winter months, but clearly, she had been cared for and fed. Auroch wondered what he looked like, living day to day in the corner of the cave. He had done nothing for his appearance and wore no jewellery, unlike the three Grand Chiefs that sat before them.

From behind them slunk Grey Stag. The old man looked tired and crestfallen as if the day's events were already predetermined. He sat down next to Auroch. His presence made his skin crawl, but Auroch knew the three had to sit in judgement together under the tree. Brown Colt was the first to speak.

"We have spoken with each of you individually and heard your tale of seasons past. We have reason to believe the banished man now returned, Grey Stag, has inflicted harm upon the Men of the Summer Valley and potentially the Riverfolk. It is likely two Grand Chieftains were slain by his hand or the hands of his tribesmen. Consequently, Grey Stag has argued that the banished are not responsible, and that the fates of the two are unknown." The man's jewellery jangled as he recited the accusation.

Auroch exhaled. They were sympathetic! As a chieftain, Grey Stag would be the first to speak.

"I have come this way bearing many gifts for the other tribes. Valuables were all given in kindness by my people to yours. I was banished many years ago for slights against former chieftains. I and have come in good faith back to you. I could have lived with my riches in the valleys to the west, but instead I made the perilous journey here to share and communicate with our ancestors under the winter moon." He paused and searched the crowd for approval. There were a few nods of appreciation. "I am sorry for any terrible events that have overtaken the Riverfolk and the Men of the Summer Valley, but they are not of my doing."

Graceful Seal spoke next, directing her question at the Valleyfolk sitting cross-legged on the floor. "You claim that other than yourselves, all the men of the Summer Valley are dead? And most of the Riverfolk as well?"

"Yes. Auroch said that he was enslaved with several of Wise Shrew's people, along with our own men." Egret replied confidently before Auroch could answer, "The Skull Eaters feed on the flesh of men. I have seen it myself in the summer and Auroch witnessed one of our fellow tribesmen, Black Alder, have his body defiled and consumed. There is no sign of the remaining slaves, so we can assume they were killed. Bloodied Thistle, of the Summer Valley, was killed by Auroch while trying to save my own life." Her voice quivered as she finished her statement.

Despite the terrible memories unearthed, it felt good to hear her voice after so long, as firm and collected as ever, despite the loss of her magic.

Graceful Seal shot back at the leader of the Skull Eaters. "You deny any knowledge of these men?"

"I do. All but Bloodied Thistle. It is true that this pair killed him. He had been banished himself from the Summer Valley and joined us on the journey. This pair killed him where the plains meet the river."

A murmur spread over the crowd. Auroch hadn't expected Grey Stag to admit to knowing Bloodied Thistle. Why would he? What game was he playing with the Chieftains? He glanced at Egret, his brow furrowed, and she returned the look.

Now was the time for the deformed Wise Shew to ask a question. "You did not think to tell us before that you had met Bloodied Thistle, Grey Stag? Why not?"

"I judged it unimportant. When a man is invited into the fold of the banished, his past ceases to matter. He was not a Man of the Summer Valley, he was one of my children." The old man smirked. "And he told me something about the Spirit-Maiden Egret. I didn't know at that time what fate had befallen the Valleyfolk, so I didn't think much of it. Now however…" He trailed off, glancing at Egret, his eyes full of malice.

"Speak, man!" said Wise Shrew.

"The Spirit-Maiden Egret rejected her responsibility. Summer past she ran from the Valley, wishing not to dedicate her life to becoming a Spirit-Mother and aiding under another tribe. She and her lover, Auroch, wished to flee into the forest, to abandon years of training and ignore the rites of our people."

"Is this true?" Graceful Seal interjected, her voice carrying notes of sympathy. Egret said nothing in response.

"That's not the end of the tale!" Grey Stag continue, now growing in confidence. "She ran and was recaptured! Perhaps the boy Auroch freed her and killed the Men of the Summer Valley! He has already admitted to killing his fellow huntsman!"

"The man lies!" Auroch shouted over the noise of the murmuring crowd. "His men destroyed the Summer Valley!"

"The baby's swaddling clothes! Was it not the stitching of the Riverfolk? They met them and were aided by them by their account! Perhaps they stood in the way of these wayward murderers! They only appeared here when the girl was grievously injured after murdering Bloodied Thistle! The last who could confirm my story!"

Brown Colt leaned across the other two chieftains and said quietly. "Perhaps they only sought us out to aid the girl's healing?"

"This man had my father killed in front of me!" Egret stood up, dismissing the conventional manners displayed normally at such an occasion. "Old Heron was your equal as a Grand Chief! My father was a man you feasted and danced with!"

Brown Colt didn't press her on her infraction. Coldly, he replied,

"Did you forsake your duties as Spirit-Maiden?"

"I ran once during the summer months, but I returned. I was present when they burned the camp and killed my people."

"And you still walk the path of the ancestors? You still have access to the earth's magic?"

Egret paused again. What was she to say? She hung her head in shame. Auroch's heart sank.

"No. I failed to make the offerings for the winter solstice. I have been denied access to powers I once had. I did not wish it, but the incantations I hold in my head no longer can influence the will of ancestors."

"You see!" Grey Stag shouted, "These two have rejected the first men, rejected First Eagle! They killed their family and ran and wish to blame me because of feuds long past and since forgotten."

Auroch was quietly panicking. The crowd had been built up to a frenzy now, and he heard hecklers shout both for and against the pair. Even if they didn't believe Grey Stag's accusation that they had murdered both the Men of the Summer Valley and the Riverfolk, Egret's apostasy could get them killed. He had no choice now but to call on the man that had caused him so much pain, Red Fox.

"Please, can we hear Red Fox speak?" Auroch shouted over the commotion. "The son of Grey Stag."

The colour drained from the old man's face. He hadn't expected this. Graceful Seal nodded, and several Horse Hunters disappeared into the cavern. Auroch watched tiny beads of sweat begin to form on Grey Stag's forehead as the group waited for the cripple. Egret sat with her head in her hands, anticipating the next set of lies. Auroch gave her knee a reassuring squeeze. After a short wait, Red Fox appeared, dragged on a sled. He was pulled up the hill and into the seated position beside Egret and Auroch.

Grey Stag didn't waste any time. "My boy, my sweet broken boy. Tell them we wish no harm. Tell them we only wish to trade and worship the winter moon here. Tell them…"

"Quiet!" shouted Wise Shrew. "Please speak, Red Fox." There was a gentleness from the tiny, misshapen man towards the other cripple. A quiet understanding.

Red Fox sat in silence for a few agonising moments as if he was choosing his words with great care. "I have killed men, women, and children in the name of Grey Stag. I killed the family and tribe of these two young Valleyfolk. I have feasted on the flesh of our enemies. I have taken slaves. I have committed deeds most foul in the name of my father." The statement electrified the crowd, and the jolt jumped to those involved in the judgment. Egret looked up, and as if transactionally, Grey Stag placed his head in his hands.

"Why would you reveal this." Wise Shrew replied softly, detecting no word of a lie in the one-eyed man's testimony.

"I am crippled, a useless half-man now. I cannot move outside of my head, and despite this, he refuses to kill me, to leave me to die." He started to get angry. "This man wanted me to watch his triumph, for him to be accepted as a Grand Chieftain. Then he was to usurp you, to destroy you!"

Brown Colt butted in, "What for? We have done nothing to you!"

Grey Stag laughed. "You become rich and fat with gifted spoils, banish any who confront you, and trade people like painted beads.

You have not changed, your inherited positions given to you by your forefathers, not for any great feat of leadership or courage." He turned the crowd, addressing them directly. "Why should they get the pick of the best meat? Why should they get showered with gifts and adulation? Why should they make judgements about life and death?"

The crowd began to murmur and stir in response. Grey Stag laughed again, before spitting at the feet of the three Grand Chief.

"My son, I should have killed you when you asked." he said mournfully to the crippled Red Fox. "I could have roasted you and licked your bones dry."

"You admit you eat man's flesh?" Graceful Seal interjected "It grants you the power of the body that was consumed? As the old men of the hills once did?"

"I suppose" the old man replied, "Mainly I just enjoy the taste." He began to laugh, loudly and manically.

Auroch sensed a fight was about to break out. Cleary Brown Colt felt the same way. He leaned over to the other Grand Chiefs and whispered to them. There was a nod of agreement before they turned back to address the crowd.

"Grey Stag is judged to be a wretched killer, a liar, and little better than a rabid beast. He is responsible for the banished men, and we will show mercy. Skull Eaters, take your belongings, your share of the mammoth hunt and this old man, and flee to whatever dank cave you came from. Do not return here, and there will be no conflict."

Auroch breathed a sigh of relief. For all his feelings of hatred, of revenge, he was pleased that the ordeal was over. Grey Stag's plan had been disrupted, and he would be sent back to his little caves along the river a failure, all his violence coming to nothing.

However, Brown Colt continued. "Egret, you were anointed Spirit-Maiden by Morning Mist of the Summer Valley. This is a great honour, and you were asked to carry the weight of departed souls and ancient knowledge of your people to other tribes, to be the bond between this earth and the world of spirits, the bridge between the living and the dead. You have rejected this and forsaken your duty."

Without her usual confidence, Egret replied quietly, "I never chose that life."

Brown Colt stood up, his muscular frame towering over Auroch and Egret. "You were never expected to choose. What you wish for is of little importance. The ancestors chose for you this task, and you have abandoned it." He paused, "Therefore, you must die."

The terrible worry that had just left Auroch's body with the pronouncement of Grey Stag's fate returned in an instant, but this time, its immediacy overwhelmed him.

"You banish this beast, this eater of man flesh!" Auroch pointed to Grey Stag as he unleashed his fury. "But you kill Egret! Victim of this monster, who has come all this was to tell you of the bear you invited into your cave!"

"Quiet Calf" Brown Colt shot back. "She was a Spirit-Maiden raised in the ways Summer Valley. She has betrayed you just as she has betrayed the first Spirit-Mother, White Owl. She would have taken your people's knowledge far and wide when she was sent to another tribe as Spirit-Mother."

"A curse on your Spirit-Mothers," shouted Auroch, throwing himself at the large man. Brown Colt batted him aside, and two spearmen pinned him to the floor.

"Attack me again, and you will also be killed." Brown Colt said.

"Perhaps she doesn't have to die," interjected Graceful Seal, looking to defuse the situation. "My mother spoke of such a situation, of the honour of the ancestors defiled."

"You fulfilled your duty," Wise Shrew volunteered "What sympathy have you? I remember when you left the Fen as a girl of sixteen summers. You knew what needed to be done!"

"Still," replied Graceful Seal. "There is a way she may live. We all have doubts at one time or another. If she reconnects with her ancestors, then she may return to her duties and live as Spirit-Maiden once more."

Egret looked up from the ground, her eyes full of tears. She hadn't wanted any of this. Auroch wondered if she dammed him silently under her breath for bringing her here, for forcing this fate on her. She could have lived out her time in the world with the elderly clanless couple, brought up the child, and lived her life free.

"What must be done?" Egret said weakly, "To reclaim the gifts of the spirit world."

"The river you must swim is not a calm one." Graceful Seal replied, "You must unleash a dark spirit and battle it in its own realm. But where first to hunt such a spirit? What caves or deep woodland contain one to grapple with?"

Egret said nothing but slung her bag over her shoulder and rummaged around in it until she found what she was looking for. She produced the small figurine, the wolf-headed man from the frozen lake. There was an audible gasp from the several Spirit-Mothers and maidens in the crowd. She handed it to Graceful Seal, who examined it before handing it back to Egret.

"Yes, I believe that will do."

Chapter 29

Auroch and Egret sat with the child on the slope underneath the tree and watched as the Skull Eaters departed, hissed and booed by members of the other tribes as they slumped off across the plains. The Skull Eaters looked less than happy with the old man, who was limping as he led them away. Egret rested her head on Auroch's shoulder as the last few disappeared with their sleds over the top of the rise, only to reappear again, further away, on the crest of the next hillock. Feeling some peace in the current moment, Auroch decided to say what had been weighing on his mind for the last few moons.

"I wish I had never asked you to follow me here," he said, unsure of the response he would receive.

"You didn't compel me. I decided to come, knowing what could happen to me." she replied.

"Before, when your father had you captured, you would have rather died than become a Spirit-Mother. Would you have rather I left you to die on the ice?"

Egret said nothing. The child was sleeping peacefully, and the cool springtime breeze blew past them, causing Auroch to shiver a little.

Finally, after what seemed like an age, Egret replied to the question.

"I am not certain. I don't wish to be sent off to live with the Horse Hunters or the Fenfolk. But I suppose the Men of the Summer Valley are dead now. If I am to become a Spirit-Mother..." She picked her head up and looked Auroch in the eyes. "If I am to become a Spirit-Mother, I don't wish to leave you again," she said softly. "I would like you there tonight, at the ceremony. Someone will need to break the vessel containing the Black Wolf. I want you there, whatever happens."

The pair sat, hand in hand, for much of the afternoon before trudging back to the cavern entrance. Taking animal fat lamps, they made their way to the back of the cavern and, crouching down, began to slide through the passage towards the icy cave where the meat was stored over the long winter. The continual dripping of water rang in their ears as the passage narrowed before they emerged in a large cavern, still encrusted with melting ice. The glacial pools at the bottom of the cavern reflected the lamplight, and Auroch noted they were as high as he had ever seen them. He had been told in times of spring rains, the cavern often flooded. Although the Men of the Summer Valley, to his memory, had not stuck around long enough to see it, usually following the deer back to the valley as they appeared on the plains.

The pair walked down the incline into the heart of the ice cave, crossing a natural bridge carved by water into the rock. The air was musty and wet, and he could hear the water dripping, trickling down stalactites, dropping into the pools of water forming from the rapidly melting ice below. In the back of the cave, he could make out a group comprised of men, women, and children carefully painting images onto the wall to project good fortune for the year to come. As they got closer to the group, who stood in a silent state of meditative grace, the painted images became visible under the soft light of the lamps. Auroch watched as children, on the shoulders of adults, blew ochre through reeds onto the cave wall, using their hands as a stencil. Adults did the same at a lower level, carefully bending their fingers down to specify their wishes for spring and summer to the ancestors. Five fingers meant a healthy herd to follow, four a release from the pain of injury. Auroch held up his mutilated left hand and wiggled his three remaining fingers. Three for resolution and freedom from grief.

Without a word, Egret handed him a reed and bowl of ochre. He placed his mutilated hand against the wall and blew on it, creating a red outline that was almost immediately lost in a sea of similar handprints. Auroch directed the lamp up to a huge visage of First Eagle, the first Grand Chief, departing this world. As was the custom, he was depicted as a bird-headed man, with his true avian soul sitting just away from the figure, on a rod, ready to fly to the stars where all men's souls would go after they departed the earth. He was chased by death, depicted here as an enormous bison, its guts dangling from its belly as it charged the bird-headed leader.

Egret gave Auroch some small fragments of mammoth bone taken from the killing pit. He placed them as gifts inside crevices in the rock face. Egret handed him the baby and followed Auroch in completing the same ritual. She curled two fingers of her hand down and blew on it, creating another image of a three-fingered hand next to his. Then, carefully, she placed the bones into the rock before mumbling a prayer. Auroch sensed she didn't care if the ancestors could hear her or not.

Taking out a small stone bowl, Egret moved to the side of the rock face, where some low-lying stalactites were at arm's length due to a downward buckle in the sheer rock of the ceiling. Auroch followed her with the lamp, watching as she began to chip away at the soft, wet rock closest to the ground. Soon, her bowl was full of the crumbly, damp calcium. She leaned over and sniffed it before affirming to Auroch that they had what they needed.

The two left the cave within the cave. They followed the winding maze of passages before finding themselves in the grand cavern once again. It was warmly lit by the entrance; they could smell the smoke pouring through the natural chimney above them and feel the heat from the various fires scattered across its massive interior. The pair sought out Graceful Seal, who was cheerfully playing some kind of game with her children on the far side of the cavern. Auroch and Egret watched as her two boys of seven summers and daughter, no more than four summers at most, ran around the cavern chasing each other with a large stick. Whoever received a gentle whack on the ankle was the next person to take the stick and the role of chaser. Auroch watched as Graceful Seal, laughing, ran purposely slow enough so her daughter could catch her and then feigned injury when caught. Auroch understood why she had been so prized as a Spirit-Maiden by the coastal people she led. She looked quite beautiful now, laughing and smiling, in stark comparison to her severe demeanour at the previous day's judgement.

"I am ready now, Graceful Seal," Egret interrupted, in a manner that Auroch thought could perhaps have been interpreted as hostile.

Graceful Seal ceased her play and began to walk towards the pair, her expression darkening with every step. She stopped in front of Egret and put a hand on her shoulder.

"This could mean a fate worse than death, little bird," she said solemnly. "To battle with a dark spirit, not for another's soul, but for your own, is a dangerous path. Are you sure you would rather commit to this struggle than have a quick death?"

"I wish to reclaim my connection to the ancestors," Egret replied in a line that had been clearly rehearsed. Auroch watched her clenched fist shake with fear. That's it! Take the fear. Push it down inside you! Let it drown in your resolve! At that moment, he knew of the woman standing before him could do anything. She wouldn't be doing it for Graceful Seal, Old Heron, Morning Mist, or even Auroch. There was only one person to whom she needed to prove her mettle.

"As you wish," Graceful Seal replied. "Please follow."

Egret and Auroch followed Graceful Seal to a small group of women who were busy crushing mushrooms with wooden pestles.

"The boy can't watch!" said one, the Spirit-Mother of the Horse Hunters.

Graceful Seal grabbed Auroch's mutilated hand and held it up so the injury was visible to the whole group. The grotesque scarring on the stumps where his fingers used to be seemed accentuated by the golden afternoon sunlight.

"This man has already given his flesh in service of the ancestors. He is here as Egret's companion, to guide her back to the world of the living if she wanders too far. All he needs to do is to agree to whisper naught secrets of the ancestors over something for which he would gladly die." Graceful Seal looked down at the baby. Auroch nodded and held out his hand. Taking a small, sharpened flint flake, Graceful Seal cut directly across his palm, drawing blood. Auroch winced despite knowing it was for the best.

"You are ready." Graceful Seal said gently. Auroch handed off the child to a waiting Horse Hunter woman. The troop of old crones, young witches, and Auroch left the cavern and embarked on the short walk to the lone tree that had witnessed the judgement the previous day.

The sun was slipping below the horizon now, and Auroch felt the cool night air rush in without the warmth of day to heat it. The group walked in silence; the only communication Auroch needed was Egret giving his uncut hand a gentle squeeze. He squeezed back, offering what comfort he could, but he knew she would be embarking on a journey that he couldn't follow nor hope to understand. The group reached the tree, and one of the young Spirit-Maidens began drawing a circle in the earth with sticks in front of the oak. Egret wouldn't be allowed outside of this little ring; she would have to endure the entire ordeal without help from the other women now busying themselves on the hillock.

Auroch watched as the final preparations were made to the bowl of dark liquid containing mushrooms, stalactites, and other ingredients to which Auroch was not privy. Egret sat in the centre of the circle on her own and produced the wolf-headed figurine from her bag. She placed it in front of her and stared at it while rhythmically tapping the ground with her palm. Now standing evenly around the circle, the women began to hum a strange, haunting melody. Graceful Seal stepped forward, the broth in hand, careful not to break the circle.

"Egret, daughter of Quick Coot and Old Heron, you wish to be reclaimed by the ancestors and to once again feel the power of the earth flow through the soles of your feet and up through your body as if moisture through the roots of the tree." Graceful Seal asked, looking not at Egret but at the sky behind her.

"I do."

"You have forsaken your role as a Spirit-Maiden, but you can earn your way back into White Owl's favour. You must free this trapped spirit and battle it on the shores of the great river, vanquishing it to the next life."

"I understand" Egret repeated. Auroch noticed the stars had come out and could now see the great milky river above them, cutting a swath through the sky overhead. Graceful Seal turned to Auroch.

"Auroch, Egret has instructed you to be her champion, to guard her body in this life while she battles the Black Wolf in the next. Do you wish to honour her?"

"Yes."

Graceful Seal walked to him and handed him the bowl of black liquid. Its peculiar, decaying smell caused him to wrinkle his nose. He took the bowl graciously and waited for the next instruction.

"You may enter the circle," Graceful Seal said before grabbing him by the arm and looking him dead in the eye. "If you leave the circle, then Egret's choice of champion was misguided, and her judgment too far clouded to be salvaged. She will be killed."

Auroch nodded and passed over the threshold carrying the small bowl. He sat down opposite her, crossing his legs to mimic her seated position. He held the bowl out, and she accepted it. She began drinking from the bowl, gagging and retching between gulps. The singing had ceased now and replaced with a tune from a small flute, played by the youngest Spirit-Maiden of the group, a Fen girl of only around eleven summers old. Egret placed the bowl down, having drained the broth.

"Please destroy the Black Wolf's vessel, Auroch," Egret said quietly, gesturing to the wooden figurine.

Taking a heavy flint blade from his bag, he held the figurine on the ground and steadied the base with his hand. He took careful aim at the monstrous wolf head attached to the figure, slightly angling his hand so that if the blade slipped, he wouldn't bring it down on his fingers. He looked to Egret, who gave him a small nod. He brought his hand down hard, the head of the little animal man split asunder by the sharp flint. The wolf head now consisted of splinters scattered about their feet, and a heavy gash ran through the statuette's torso down to its midriff. A cool breeze blew over the hillock and across the group watching the ceremony. Auroch shivered, and observed some of the women who surrounded the circle do the same. It wasn't summer yet, and the winter's last stand continued to chill the night air.

The flute playing intensified, and Auroch watched Egret drift from her usual hyper-alert state into a dreamy half-sleep. She lay back on the grass, and Auroch saw her eyes roll back into her head as the broth began to take hold. Her hands grasped and then released the wet grass beneath her fingers as she drifted into a state of unconsciousness. Auroch had seen her take trips to the world of the ancestors before, but never to do battle. He watched impotently as her soul temporarily left her body for the bank of the great river. Auroch looked up towards the streak through the sky, comprised of an incalculable number of stars. Could he see her? He squinted fruitlessly, but as he had been told before, it was so vast, so far away, there was no hope to see any of its earthy visitors. He wondered if Egret would see his mother on the riverbank, waiting patiently to cross.

"Has my child not been named? Could you not do it? Could my son not help you?" Auroch tried to imagine Mother questioning Egret, but he struggled to remember her. He tried to focus on her face and found that her features had lost their detail. He racked his brains for her comforting smell and voice when she sang but came up short. She was fading away from him, lost in a sea of clouded, traumatic memories. Tears began to wet his eyes, and he realised he had started to weep softly at the thought of his family, his last image of them in his mind, their bloated, rotten corpses rolled and laid to rest in the long grass.

The flute music had taken on a malevolent, angry tone, now and Auroch watched as Egret lay, her head jerking and to fro as she did battle in the next life. How long would she fight? How could one know if she won? After a while, she stopped moving and fell limp. Auroch looked at Graceful Seal, who was swaying lightly to the tune of the flute. Was he allowed to check on her? Graceful Seal gave him a subtle nod. He lay across Egret, placing his head on her chest. Her heart was still beating. Good.

Sitting down restlessly, he imagined what might be going on above him. Egret, replete in a Master Huntsman's bearskin and holding a spear, stepped in a semicircle around the opposing beast. The Black Wolf, his features fuzzy and difficult to make out against the darkness, stepped in concert with her, ready to pounce on the young woman. Auroch imagined Egret's dark eyes, hungry for violence, watching the beast for any twitch, any movement that could give away its intentions. The Black Wolf growled and threw himself at the girl. She pirouetted and jumped aside, thrusting the spear into his back. The monstrous wolf howled and swiped at her, but she was too quick, using her legs to push herself through the air away from the massive claws. The river beat at the shore, an incalculable number of stars hidden just below the water's surface as the pair once again slowly circled each other, each waiting for their opponent to make the next move. Blood flowed from the beast's back into the river, diluting it with the cursed, inky black liquid that pumped rhythmically from the wound. The wolf moved as if to jump again but finally pulled back in a feint at the last minute. Egret fell for it, moving out of the way of the potential path of the creature and into a prone position. The animal jumped, for real this time, landing on the girl and pinning her to the ground, his howls and angry gasps now just a hair's breadth from her face. The howls turned to squeals and cries as the beast recoiled, dragging himself across the shore, his guts hanging from his shaggy hide. Egret lay, her hands covered in blood, exhausted. She had impaled the animal as it jumped on her, spilling its innards all over her bearskin clothes and body. She sat on the shore as the dark spirit choked and died, screaming for help from the ancestor wolves that watched from the opposite shore, bathed in starlight from the river below.

Auroch was pulled out of the imagined battle by the sounds of choking from the girl on the ground, gargling and coughing, her body convulsing and thrashing. Auroch, already at her side, grabbed her jaw and pulled it down. She had vomited, and as the stench hit his nostrils, he felt himself gag in response. Despite this, he acted quickly, placing his fingers in her mouth and digging the regurgitated food out before throwing it onto the grass. She coughed again and inhaled, sucking in a lungful of air, seemingly briefly conscious for the moment before slipping back into the world of dreams. Auroch rolled her on her side, her mouth facing the floor to prevent further accidents. He watched as her breathing became more regular and her sleep more peaceful. Despite the sweating and illness caused by the distress of her journey to the world of the ancestors, the vomit on her chin, and the large ugly scar across her back, Auroch thought she looked more beautiful than any woman he had ever seen. He thought back to the previous summer and their journey to find the red elder. She had given everything to help him; he had betrayed her, and still, she had journeyed here with him despite it running contrary to all her desires. Hers was a rare bravery, deeper and brighter than the man who stared down a charging bison or climbed a wall of sheer ice. Auroch couldn't let her go.

It was dawn now, and the first rays of sun began to poke over the plains, casting light onto the tired faces of the women. They had been dancing and singing all night, and it had taken its toll. Auroch watched as the Spirit-Mothers grasped their aching backs and legs, drained after the unbroken prayers and spirit song needed for Egret to battle the Black Wolf. Auroch looked at Graceful Seal; her normally pleasant face looked haggard, her light maroon skin sagging around her eyes. She gestured at Auroch to look at Egret. Her eyes were open, and she was spitting vomit into the ground. She sat upright before examining the small, broken figurine that lay on the grass, turning it over in her hands to examine the damage where Auroch's blade had split the little man in two above the neckline. Auroch scooted himself over to her. The singing became louder again before building to a blistering crescendo and then a full stop. It was quiet once again, and all Auroch could hear was the distant sound of the morning routine from the cavern entrance.

Graceful Seal stepped forward. "You were victorious, Egret?"

"Yes" replied the woman transformed the by experience and thought into a Spirit-Mother. "The beast lies dead on the shores of the great river, and my innocence with it."

Chapter 30

Egret took much of the next day to recover. Graceful Seal stayed by her side, giving her regular sips from a small wooden bowl, a herd of bison carved around the rim. Auroch watched as the mighty beasts migrated to her lips and then down again as she gulped the cool water. At regular intervals, Graceful Seal would hand Auroch the bowl and ask him to make his way down to the caves to collect some of the liquid formed by the rapidly melting ice. In the early afternoon, the rains started. The violent storm hurled water deep into the cave entrance as hurried shouts rang through the great cavern, causing men, women, and children to brave the rain, moving their belongings into the back of the massive chamber. The water, dipping through the natural chimney in the centre of the winter home, fell onto the remnants of the great fire, causing it to hiss and crack.

Auroch stood at the mouth of the cave, watching as the bison bowl filled with rainwater. On the horizon, he noticed movement, a flash of red amongst the torrent of rain pouring over the plain. The deer? Were they only making their way back to the valley now? Later than usual. He turned to take the bowl back to Egret and Graceful

Seal, but a voice called out from the cavern's entrance, muffled by the storm.

"Calf!" Auroch recognised the voice and felt a pit open in his stomach. He had thought that the Skull Eaters had taken Red Fox with them as they departed. Auroch could make out his one eye glinting in the darkness.

"Pull me in, boy. Please!" he shouted over a thunderclap, clearly struggling with the torrential rain battering his immobile body. "You made a promise to me!"

Arouch set down the bowl and approached the man, the wind battering his arms and legs as he took him by the underarm and began to haul him into the cavern. Red Fox's clothes were soaking, and his useless legs were covered in mud where the rain had turned the first spring grasses into a brown mush. Auroch pulled him clear of the storm and dragged him behind a rocky outcrop, out of view of the rest of the cavern dwellers who had migrated to the back, away from the storm.

"Father left me," said Red Fox, pitifully. "I thought he might kill me, but he took one look and left."

"He knows how to torture and punish," Auroch said coldly. "It is better than you deserve."

"You vowed to me, Auroch. You vowed to me that would rid me of this broken vessel."

Auroch looked sheepishly at the floor. He just wished the man to suffer. Why did he drag him into the cave? Why not watch as he struggled and died fighting against the storm, unable to move even a finger in defence. He imagined himself plunging a spear into the man, watching his guts spill out, smashing his head open with a flat stone and laughing as his brains trickled onto the stone floor. It felt good.

"There's a bag." Red Fox sensed Auroch's desires. He motioned to a small sack that sat in the rain. "A weapon."

Auroch pulled the bag over and rummaged around it, finding a small knife carved from a piece of mammoth tusk. He turned it over, carefully examining the ornate carving on the ivory blade. A mammoth, Great-Tusk, rendered in exquisite detail.

"Grey Stag gave this to you?" Auroch asked.

"When I was a boy." Red Fox nodded tears in his eyes.

"Did you kill a family with it? By the brook in the valley? A man and woman, a girl and boy, a baby?"

Red Fox slowly nodded, knowing what confirmation would bring him. Auroch watched, fist clenched as he looked across the rain-swept plains. The cloud had moved away from the cavern now, and the pair could see the deluge in the distance, the heavy pitter-patter on the grass standing out against the now silent cavern entrance. The sun had started to come out.

Holding the blade firmly, Auroch stabbed the one-eyed man in his heart. He did it again. And again. And again. Red Fox's one blue-green eye rolled into the back of his head as he passed from his body and into the arms of his ancestors. Auroch didn't stop. Crimson stained his hands, but every stab felt like ecstasy. Time became a blur, and he found himself back in the Summer Valley, examining the bloated corpses of his family. He launched a new frenzied attack with the knife for every pang of pain in his heart. He didn't care that Red Fox was dead or the man had asked for this. Father was avenged. Little

Wren was avenged. Boar was Avenged. Even the baby, Burgeoning Yew, was avenged. Mother was… Oh, Mother. Egret was Spirit-Mother now; the child would be named, and Mother would be ferried over the river.

At some point after he killed Red Fox, he found himself sitting, wet with blood, at the dead man's feet. It was over. He scanned the horizon and settled on a location to leave Red Fox's corpse. He had at least, been allowed to prepare his family death and thought it would be only fair to return the favour. He picked the man up so that he was holding him across his torso, his limbs dangling lifelessly just as they had been when he had been breathing. He struggled out of the cave, aware of the crowd forming behind him. Nobody was going to stop him. The rain had caused the grassland to transform into something akin to a swamp. Every step was a struggle as the ground grasped at his ankles. He headed for the spot he had picked out in the distance, the dead man seeming to weigh more and more with each step.

He walked until the sun began to sloop below the edge of the plains, the adrenaline from his act of violence pushing him onwards until he came to a small hillock with a few larger rocks upon it, creating a natural shelter. He climbed it slowly and deliberately, his ankles and arms throbbing under the weight of Red Fox, until finally he reached the top.

He dropped the body and sat beside it. His hands had the distinctive smell and look of butchery, a dark brown where the one-eyed man's blood had been violently expelled from his body. He wiped them on the still-wet grass, smearing them with the rainwater until the stains were almost gone. He examined his mutilated left hand, wiggling the two small stumps where his fingers used to be. Auroch tried hard to take himself back to the previous summer, sitting with Bloodied Thistle and Father, full of deer and happy and whole. It seemed like a distant dream now, like the memory was a glimpse of another life. A drop of water landed on his head. And another. It began to rain again, and Auroch sat there, shivering and wet in the dark. Where was there to go? What was there to do?

Red Fox had allowed him to tend to his dead family, and Auroch returned the favour, hauling the corpse under a rocky outcrop of stones. Here, he could lie. Perhaps he would be disturbed by some animal, but Auroch didn't much care. He thought about leaving the man his father's knife but decided against it, instead leaving him the rest of the small bag he had produced it from for the next life. He reflected on the cruelty of Old Stag, the Great Chiefs, and the chain of events of violence and revenge reaching back to before he was born. He wondered what future killing he had unleashed by his actions today. Did Red Fox have a child? Was that child to become a man and hunt him down? Would he win and kill Auroch, perhaps leaving Egret or his baby brother to hunt down his killer and begin another bloody tale anew? No. Tomorrow, he would ask Egret to help him name the child under the tree, then pass him into the care of Graceful Seal. The last child of the Summer Valley.

Chapter 31

Auroch sat with Red Fox's body in the dark, sheltered from the storm for some time. It beat at the rocks above him, drowning out the noises of the night, but for the sound of voices in the distance, getting closer and closer. It seemed unlikely that a hunting party would be roaming around at this time. The Skull Eaters? They could be back!

Auroch crept from under the overhanging rock to see a group of figures standing at the bottom of the slope on which the vast stones rested. The moon was obscured by clouds, and it was hard to determine what was happening below. A huge, shifting mass moved with them; Auroch could feel the vibrations underneath his feet as it moved and rumbled. Great-Tusk, the Mammoth. He could just about make out a figure in the gloom atop the beast. Grey Stag! The figure was shouting something, but Auroch couldn't hear through the wind and rain. The intent was clear. They were going to attack the men and women in the cavern, using the storm as cover.

He looked across the plains, trying to make out detail against the darkness. The lack of starlight makes it challenging to intuit a direction. How did he approach the hillock? He ran his hands over the rocks, remembering where he had come from. The setting sun had been in his eyes as he approached Red Fox's final resting place, so he needed to head east, opposite the overhang, to return to the cavern and warn them.

He turned on his heel just in time to see a hand holding a stone smash into his temple. Dazed, he fell to the floor as four strong arms pulled him to his knees. They dragged him down the slope to the waiting crowd through the mud. Auroch tasted the sweet tang of a mixture of rainwater and blood flowing down his face from the gash on his head. Blinking the mix out of his eyes, he was confronted by a pair of grizzled knees, creaking as their elderly owner bent down to come face-to-face with him.

"Fate, truly, to find you here, rather than at the cavern with the rest of the servile plainsmen." Grey Stag cackled through the rain.

Auroch struggled to find words, so he opted to spit at the old man instead. The gesture amounted to nothing as the liquid projectile was immediately snatched from his lips and smashed into the ground by the rainfall. Just within the cone of his vision, a Skull Eater bent down and shouted into Grey Stag's ear. They must have found Red Fox. Grief passed over the leader's face for just a moment, just long enough for Auroch to see it, before he collected himself and continued.

"My boy is dead up there. I suppose you killed him? His body was dead already. I am thankful that you have sent his soul to our ancestors." Grey Stag continued.

"Don't attack the cavern," Auroch begged, "You will be massacred. Most haven't left to return to their summer hunting grounds yet."

Grey Stag laughed, "Those fattened hogs haven't the fight in them." He pulled him close, whispering in the boy's ear, "My own people think I have led them to destruction and misery. I won't survive the long journey back across the mountains. Better to die by a thrown spear than a slit throat in the night."

"Please…" Auroch began but was dealt a heavy blow to his stomach, winding him.

Grey Stag stood up and spoke to the Skull Eaters who had gathered around the scene. "Keep him alive. When the Grand Chiefs are dead, I'm going to bring the woman and the child here and eat them as he watches."

Auroch heard the deep vibrations of Great-Tusk as he moved off, stomping across the plains towards Egret and the child. Another pair of arms grabbed him and began to bind his legs and arms tightly, cutting off the blood flow before unceremoniously dropping him into the mud, unable to move. He could still hear voices, quieter and gentler than the shouts of the men. They had left him with the children and the infirm as the rest of the Skull Eaters assaulted the cavern. He twisted around to see a young woman standing over him, Red Fox's ivory dagger in her hands. They were shaking, and just below that, he could make out a small pregnancy bump through the rain, no more than a few seasons.

"If you move, I will take the rest of your fingers," she said, failing to seem anything other than wet, cold, and terrified.

Auroch squinted at her familiar face. The Skull Eater women had kept to themselves in the cavern. He was sure he didn't know her from there. That was it! He thought back to his time as a prisoner and remembered her blushing as she washed down Bloodied Thistle. How she had fed him and lay with him at night. She had a glow about her then, different from the miserable creature that threatened him now.

"Who is the father?" Auroch asked weakly, hoping that he had guessed the answer already.

"Quiet," said the woman, choking back tears. Auroch had openly admitted to killing Bloodied Thistle at the Judgement. She knew what he had done. It was a slight chance, but it was his only one.

"I can stop the bloodshed," Auroch said, spitting rainwater and mud from his mouth. "Just let me go. I can stop Grey Stag."

The woman seemed to consider his proposal before a few angry shouts from behind put her back on the defensive. Auroch managed to heave himself onto his back so that he could see her in full. His tied hands sunk into the ground, and he could feel as every inch of his body became seeped in water and mud.

"They're all going to die," said the woman out loud, bursting into tears. It wasn't clear if she was addressing Auroch, the Skull Eaters, or her ancestors. "They will die in the attack, and we will be left out here, banished and starving."

"I wish Bloodied Thistle had walked a different path," Auroch pleaded. "He was my friend. I knew him since the day I was born and I dream of him every night, along with the others who have died. Please don't add your child to the deceased. Let me stop the attack."

The woman circled him with the knife and placed her soaked footwrap under his chest. He obliged her, and she used her foot to flip him onto his front.

Bloodied Thistle's pregnant bride squatted over him, holding the knife with unsteady hands. She paused, and Auroch could sense the blade only inches away from the back of his neck.

"What are you doing?"

It was a man's voice. Older. Scared and shaky. One of the infirm left behind by Grey Stag's raiders.

"He can warn those in the great cavern! Without the advantage of surprise, our men will be forced to retreat." The woman shouted back through sobs.

"Foolish girl!" The old man's voice began to acquire a new strength. "There is no way backwards for a man like Grey Stag. There will be no retreat, no contrition. The man will take death as his bride and us alongside him."

Auroch listened for movement, but there was none, only the deafening sound of rain. He dared not breathe, imagining the conflicted face of Bloodied Thistle's lover standing over him with the knife.

"Release the boy, and he will murder us here, on the wet earth." pleaded the old man.

A moment passed. The ropes loosened around his wrist and fell away, as did the ones binding his feet. He heard shouts of impotent protest directed at the pregnant woman as he scrambled to his feet.

He took in a pitiful sight of around twenty elders, women, and children huddled in the rain, fearfully waiting for either the signs of victory or defeat. Auroch turned to the shaking woman and slowly prised the knife from her grasp. She let it go willingly, flinching as if he would turn it on her. Auroch felt his audience panic in anticipation of a massacre, waiting for the young boy to overpower them, slaughtering them here in the rain.

They watched, jaws agape, as the boy turned on his heel and sprinted back towards the cavern.

Chapter 32

The rain battered his face and made it impossible to see anything but the dim glow of the fires from the cavern. Distant shouts and screams occasionally penetrated the deluge. Auroch was under no illusions that the attack had now begun. His shin struck a rock, and he stumbled before righting himself at the last minute to continue sprinting. He was close now. The dull light had become brighter and now stretched in a thin amber line across his field of view. Through the storm, he heard howling and trumpeting and knew it meant only one thing. The light from the fire was blocked by a huge, angry shape thrashing around and bellowing from its massive trunk. Auroch could see the cavern now and several figures, shrouded in firelight, jabbing spears in a futile counterattack.

Dead men lay at the entrance, their bodies covered in either stab wounds from Grey Stag's attack or their bones crushed and broken from fending off Great-Tusk. There were Skull Eater bodies mixed in, but only very few. The majority of the fallen were from the plains tribes. Auroch recognised two of the figures fighting Great-Tusk. Adorned with jewellery, Brown Colt, spear in hand, screamed as they tried to get underneath the mammoth's maw and stab at him. Behind him was a collection of men and women desperate to defend their homes. Amongst them stood Egret, Auroch's antler-tipped spear in hand, thrusting at the beast. They had managed to push it from the cavern, and it began to slip and slide as its back feet made contact with the quagmire outside the entrance. It roared again and reared up before smashing a heavy leg down onto the ankle of Brown Colt. The great chief screamed and fell backward, his ruined leg collapsing from under him.

Auroch ran at the animal, putting his full force into a blow to its backside with his blade. He pierced flesh, but it was unclear if the beast felt anything as he continued to swing his tusks at his attackers. Another Horse Hunter was caught too close, and the momentum of the mammoth's tusks slamming into him sent him flying, careening down the hill. Auroch ran to the man, realising his arm was twisted and broken as he got close, the exposed bone gushing blood onto the muddy hillside.

Callously, Auroch grabbed the man's spear and took a second run at the animal. He locked eyes with Egret, who stood at the back of the formation. She bobbed her head in acknowledgement, and a surge of confidence overtook him. He plunged the spear into the animal's backside, causing it to violently kick back at him. It missed and, in frustration, turned part of the way towards him. It was all the defenders needed. Diving under the tusks, Auroch watched as Egret and a man from the Coast, unaccustomed to spearing beasts of the plains, thrust up into the Great-Tusk's neck. Their spears sliced through the meat and gristle. The beast howled and reared, but the pair held their spears tight, and as he fell, the momentum drove them deeper, crushing his windpipe. Great-Tusk's front feet landed with a thump as he flailed around, in his last moments trying to injure his attackers with what little time he had left. Egret gracefully rolled out of the way of the beast's trunk and ivory, but the Coastal man wasn't so lucky. A trunk wrapped itself around his waist and rolled him violently across the ground, smashing him against the rocks dislodged by the heavy rain.

Great-Tusk finally fell, his frame landing with a wet thump in the mud. The animal lay there, his laboured breathing growing shallower and shallower. Auroch felt a familiar hand on his back and tuned to see a panting Egret standing behind him, her light summer tunic covered in blood.

"How many of them?" Auroch asked before remembering that mid-afternoon, Egret had been barely conscious. "How can you stand? Where is Graceful Seal?"

"It's hard to say. They began killing while we slept. They followed Graceful Seal and the others into the ice caves while we fought the beast." She replied, brushing off the question about her health.

"My brother?"

"In the caves. Graceful Seal took him."

The pair's exchange was cut short by shouts from one of the fallen men. Brown Colt lay on the floor, his leg crushed and useless, the bone protruding where the mammoth had stomped on the now-ruined limb. He beckoned the pair over, and they knelt with several men and women who had survived Great-Tusk's onslaught.

"The majority of our people have fled into the rain," the wounded man said, gritting his teeth through the pain. "Graceful Seal and Wise Shrew have taken many, some into the depths of the cave, and Grey Stag's wretches have followed. I ask you, as Grand Chief of the Horse Hunters, to follow them into the caves and act in their defence." Auroch looked around at the small group of survivors. They were six strong, three men, himself, Egret, and a small, shaking Fen woman who tightly gripped a spear, clearly unused to the violence that had engulfed the camp. Without a word, the group began to rummage in the wreckage of the small structures dotted around the cavern, looking for the animal fat lamps they would need as they descended into the caves.

A frightened snort came from his left, and he realised Great-Tusk had not yet died. The beast lay, fear in his eyes, shivering and wheezing as rain battered him. His trunk moved a little, searching for something, anything, in a vain attempt to find a comforting touch in his last moments. Auroch wondered if his last thoughts were of Grey Stag, who had rescued and raised him, or the other Skull Eaters who had exalted him. He was the only mammoth that man had mastery over. It mattered little, Auroch thought, a pang of pity cutting through the blood pounding in his ears. Just like those driven into the pits, Great-Tusk would die the same way, terrified and alone in the mud.

The group lit their lamps and descended into the narrow passages that led to the ice caves. Rainwater fell through the cracks and seeped through the walls, tricking through every crevice and nook visible by the dim light. The first body they came across was that of a Skull Eater, lying in a pool of dark red death at the end of the first passage. The next was a Horse Hunter, whom Auroch vaguely remembered to be called Yellow Grasses. Shouts echoed throughout the maze of tunnels. Many people were down here, not-so-silently stalking each other in the dark, narrow labyrinth. The first living souls the group encountered were at a junction in the dark, the passage splitting into three, the thin middle tunnel decorated with pictures of reindeer, leading visitors down to the ice cave where Auroch and Egret had carefully painted their hands on the wall. A woman and her terrified children grabbed at their ankles as they approached, begging them to help the others.

"We were scattered throughout the passageways." She wept from sheer fright as she spoke. "They are like demons, hunting us down here in the dark."

A quick decision was made to split up, and a wood pigeon call to be mimicked if they stumbled on a group of Skull Eaters. In the darkness, Auroch felt Egret squeeze his hand, and then the pair were off, down an adjacent passage, the damp walls closing in on them as they searched. Auroch paused as he heard voices ahead and cupped his hands around the flame of his lamp, plunging them into darkness. Egret touched his shoulder in tactile confirmation that there was someone dead ahead.

The voice mumbled on, and Auroch realised he wasn't listening to a conversation, but a man lost and angry, stumbling around the caverns. He passed the lamp back to Egret, careful to shield the passage ahead from the small flame. Creeping forward, he pulled Red Fox's knife from his belt, making as little noise as possible as he approached the voice. From the shadows, he saw a young man, replete in the antler headdress of the Skull Eaters, pacing back and forth in a small chamber, deciding between two passages. He stopped and turned, moving his finger back and forth between his two possible routes while reciting some kind of rhyme or prayer.

Auroch had no choice. He threw himself silently at the young man, plunging the knife into the back of his neck.

Auroch felt a tinge of guilt as he turned his head away from the dying boy. He called back to Egret, and she followed through the passage, a steady hand on the lamp.

"Which way?" Auroch whispered, desperately trying to ignore the pained last gasps coming from the space around his feet.

Egret pointed to a great beast painted across the contours of the roof above them. "The bison. It lays out for us the path to our ancestors," she said quietly, as if not to disturb the boy's final moments lying gurgling on the floor.

Without a word more, the pair began down the passage. The water rushing down the walls and pooling around their feet formed a solid stream until they splashed ankle-high through a torrent of freezing water. The ceiling lowered, and they began to crawl, hands and knees slipping off the polished, slippery rock. Auroch felt himself fall several times in the darkness, and their lamp went out abruptly as Egret slipped, accidentally extinguishing the flame in the shallow water. Panic overcame him for a moment, crawling through the flooded passage in absolute darkness, but Egret continued ahead, refusing to stop.

Then, out of the darkness, a dim light appeared ahead, growing brighter as they moved towards it. Auroch resisted the urge to rush towards it, grabbing Egret's belt to indicate to slow down, but she continued her pace, confident about where they were going. The passage widened, and Auroch accelerated until the pair were shoulder to shoulder. The light became brighter and brighter, and he threw caution to the wind. Finally, out of the darkness! The pit in his stomach turned to a feeling of nausea as he put his hand down to find nothing below him. Swaying, he almost fell forward but for Egret's hand on his shoulder. Balancing himself, he shunted back from the sheer drop, cringing as he loudly splashed around at the top of the waterfall created by the rainfall. The two were on a ledge overlooking the main chamber.

Below them stood Graceful Seal and the other survivors, waist-deep in water, their backs to the handprint stencils. There were perhaps thirty people in all who stood against the wall, scared and soaking. Graceful Seal held Auroch's brother in one arm and her fat lamp in the other. Her children, the water line across their chests, were gathered at her feet, and behind them, an assortment of women and the elderly. Auroch opened his mouth to shout but felt Egret's palm shoot in front of his face. Another light emerged from the entrance at the other end of the flooded chamber. Auroch silently hoped that Grey Stag hadn't caught up with the group, praying for all but a moment before the gaunt, hollow visage of the old man emerged from the passageway. Graceful Seal passed the lamp to one of her daughters and produced a small knife, brandishing it at Grey Stag and four Skull Eaters behind him, who in turn raised their weapons from across the walkway, hidden by the rapidly rising water.

"Stay back!" Graceful Seal screamed. "You have yet to experience the fury of those born during a coastal storm!"

Grey Stag stepped forward and spoke softly and calmly. "The Grand Chiefs must die, and the tribes must be scattered to the wind. No more leaders to decide to move people around like rocks in the dirt. I wish your children no ill. Come with me, and I will kill you quickly. I expect Brown Colt is already dead, killed by Great-Tusk. And is that the cripple I can see back there, hiding with the children?"

He craned his neck to see Wise Shrew hidden in the crowd. The tiny man gasped and stepped out next to Graceful Seal, brandishing an antler-tipped spear cut to his size. Graceful Seal herself said nothing, handing the child off to one of the Spirit-Maidens standing behind her before wielding her small flint blade again.

Grey Stag placed his hand on the shoulder of the Skull Eater to his right and whispered in his ear. The man, spear in hand, began to advance menacingly towards the two Grand Chiefs. It was impossible to see where the small natural bridge was from Auroch's ledge, but he steadied his mind and tried to think of his visit to the sacred ice cave before. The man was only a few strides from Graceful Seal now. He had to act. He looked at Egret, the dim light below them only partially illuminating her face. She didn't need to say anything. Her eyes urged him to go.

He threw himself from the ledge, the ivory blade raised over his head, and screamed, throwing just as much energy into his warcry as he did ensuring he would strike his target. The Skull Eater advancing towards the crowd turned for just a moment. It was enough time to see him. Auroch saw a look of fear and confusion cross the young man's face as he barrelled into him, stabbing and slashing as they fell into the ice-cold water. Auroch couldn't see a thing, but he felt the freezing deep penetrated by whisps of warm, thick liquid. The man thrashed violently for a moment before becoming still as he succumbed to the frenzied attack. Auroch mused on how at ease he felt with killing a man now. He held the man, feeling the last energy in his body drain from him as he died before letting him go and swimming upward to the surface.

He found the side of the natural bridge with his hands and pulled himself up, emerging from the water. He screamed again, guttural and angry, remembering the Black Wolf of the isle. The three men behind Grey Stag stepped back in fright, wary of the beast that had appeared in front of them. Auroch's spear flew from the ledge above them and struck a Skull Eater in the shoulder, sending him tumbling into the water. Auroch glanced up to see Egret hunched over above them, having thrown it accurately without the aid of an atlatl. The man she had hit pulled his head out of the water and cried for help, but none came. The three remaining men were focussed on Auroch and the group now huddled behind him.

The two remaining men that flanked Grey Stag looked strong. Auroch recognised them from his time in the Skull Eater camp. They were prone to kicking and shouting at the prisoners and doled out punishment with little hesitation. He looked past their leader and addressed them directly.

"Where has this man led you? Many of your number are dead. The source of his power, Great-Tusk, is dead, killed by our Spirit-Mother." He gestured at Egret and watched as the men cowered. Auroch noticed his booming voice was drowning out the sound of the man injured by Egret's spear throw. "Let these people pass, drop your arms, and abandon Grey Stag, who has guided you to death and destruction. This is your choice. If you chose another path, you will be killed. Let me take the life only from this old man, who has given you nothing."

The two men looked and each other in silent, swift contemplation before hurling their spears into the deep. The wounded man cried out as they pulled the spear from his shoulder before hauling him out of the water and disappearing back up the passage towards the surface.

Grey Stag now stood alone. Auroch felt Graceful Seal and her band pass by him, whispers of gratitude in his ear, as they walked around Grey Stag and then headed through the same passage that the Skull Eaters had disappeared through.

A stunned look passed over the old man's face as he stood, spear drawn, facing Auroch. The water was at Auroch's chest now, and he found, as he moved, he bobbed around. This foolish old man had lost everything but his life. He was no match for Auroch's youth. Grey Stag moved slowly, ensuring he didn't put a foot wrong, taking care not to fall off the narrow path below him obscured by water. The old man reached over to a column of natural rock jutting out of the water just above head height and placed his animal fat lamp on its flat head so that he had two hands on his spear.

"You are going to die in this cave, Calf! I won't die without my hands around your throat!" spluttered Grey Stag, laughing and cackling as he moved, tapping his foot to not step off the narrow walkway.

Auroch had heard enough taunts and empty threats. He jumped through the air towards the man, snarling like a dog, and slashed at him. The old man moved deceptively fast in the water, and Auroch, having misjudged the water resistance, fell short. His foot missed the elevated platform, and he slipped from the side. He was swimming now, desperately looking for purchase with his feet. He found none. He watched in horror as Grey Stag raised his arm, spear in hand, to throw at the now prone Auroch. He let loose, and Auroch pulled himself below the surface. He felt the spear slow as it pierced the water and then the sting of contact as it struck his arm. Had he been stabbed? No, just a graze. The spear had cut him but was now lost in the murky depths. He held his eyes tightly closed and breathed out slowly. Grey Stag would be expecting him to come up immediately, so it better to wait as long as he could, gain the element of uncertainty. His lungs began to strain, and he exhaled again. Just a few moments longer!

After what felt like a lifetime, he relented and pulled himself up to the surface to find nothing. It was pitch black in the cave. The water level must have reached the lamp. Other than the surface of the water, there was nothing to indicate up or down, left or right. It was impossible to stand in the chamber now. Auroch floated in the nothingness, waiting for some indication of his foe's location. He could hear the rain pouring into the chamber, the dripping of incalculable drops from the ceiling and walls falling onto the water, splashing into the air and falling again, sending vibrations through the surface. A symphony of action and reaction. Above the din, Auroch heard a splash to his left. There! He pulled at the water, grabbing at walls and rock face to reach the noise, but was met with nothing, only empty, wet blackness. Again, to his right! He moved like lightning but was met with only the cool touch of a wall where his foe should be.

A strong hand grabbed him from behind and forced him underwater. Auroch felt the old man's beard on the back of his neck and his fingernails digging into his skin. The two were underwater now, locked in a grapple. Auroch managed to turn and face Grey Stag, but the old man's death grip squeezed around his throat, choking out of him his last few breaths. He slashed wildly at Grey Stag, stabbing him over and over again, but it made no difference. The old man has decided to die here with Auroch and was using every last ounce of strength in his body to kill him. Auroch stabbed and stabbed, but it did nothing; he would not budge. Once again, the chill in his body was temporarily abated by the sensation of warm blood diluting with the water as the two sunk toward the bottom of the flooded cave. Darkness swept into his body as pain became merely an inconvenience. His lungs stopped burning as he fell into a sweet, calm state.

Auroch was seven summers old again, stood at the top of a hill overlooking a temporary autumnal camp. The group was about halfway through their yearly journey to the plains and had stopped for two days to hunt. His back to the river, the young boy surveyed the scene below him at the bottom of the little hill. He watched as woodsmoke drifted lazily into the afternoon sky and listened to laughter and barking dogs, the cacophony of camp life. He heard the slightest of footsteps behind him and then a heavy hand on his shoulder.

"That was a good kill," Father said, rubbing the back of the boy's neck with his palm. "You showed little hesitation for your first."

"What would have happened if I had hesitated?" Auroch looked up at the gigantic figure of Father. "Or been unable to slit the deer's throat?"

"Nothing." replied Father, in a kindly manner that Auroch didn't think matched with his usual gruffness. "We exist in concert with the deer and the other animals of the woods, river, and plains. We play our tune, and they play theirs. They are not our enemies, and we should not wish for their suffering or death. It is natural for you to hesitate, to regret, to feel guilt. If you had not been able to kill the deer, we would have tried again."

"Oh," said Auroch quietly, unsure if there was something wrong with him, for he had slit the deer's throat easily and without much remorse.

"I hesitated the first time I killed a deer." Father said softly. "I think it matters little what your first instinct is. What matters is control, to use your own mastery over yourself to do the best for your people." He ruffled the boy's hair before thumping him playfully on the arm "Now, come along, my bones are weary, and I wish to see your mother before dark."

He dropped his hand from Auroch's shoulder and began to walk down the slope back towards the camp. Auroch looked into the eye of the deer carcass held over Father's strong shoulders. The cool autumn breeze made him shiver, but the thought of familiar faces, song, and laughter warmed him. He started down the hill after Father, excited to reach the sounds of life below.

Auroch felt as if he was out of time, as if he was beyond the borders of the physical world. The hands wrapped around his throat had gone, as was the knife he had used to stab the old man. There was no up or down, just the endless cold void. His lungs came alive again, agony shooting through his body. His mind slipped back to Father, to his family, to Egret, and he felt a sense of calm. He had escaped death many times now. He could not evade it forever.

Above him, a distant light penetrated the gloom. It seemed like it was simultaneously above him and a day's walk away. It wasn't bright enough to illuminate objects in the dark water but enough to indicate direction to Auroch. Up. His feet found rock, and he pushed himself towards the surface, throwing what was left of his strength behind his kick. Closer, closer. The light was right before him now, and he gave one more almighty punt, pushing at the water with everything he had left. He broke the surface, and air came rushing back into his lungs. He felt giddy and sick, but before he had time to take more than one breath of air, a hand grabbed him, pulling him up by his armpit. He blinked the water out of his eyes to see a familiar face. Egret. He was within arm's length of the platform on which they had entered the chamber, and with one mighty heave, he pulled himself onto the ledge. Egret, her little lamp relit, gave him only a moment's respite before she began leading the way back through the maze of passages.

Chapter 33

What normally would feel claustrophobic instead felt to Auroch like being on the wide-open plains. Crawling through the narrow passages felt like a dream, as if he was still at the bottom of the flooded cave, tricking himself with visions of escape. He couldn't remember much of the way out. His mind was scrambled, but he followed the Spirit-Mother as she led the way confidentially through the drowned passageways. He was jolted back to reality as he saw the body of the boy he had knifed earlier, now floating face down in ankle-high water that had since rushed into the chamber. No more. Nobody else was to die.

The pair emerged from the tunnel and entered the great cavern just in time to see the sun's first rays shining through the entrance, illuminating the night's death and destruction. Auroch paused a moment to shower himself the with dawn's warmth, just happy to be alive. Graceful Seal, babe in arms, was calming a crowd of tribesmen as they emerged from the caverns. Auroch watched her mouth fall agape before quickly reciting a prayer under her breath as she strode over to them, as confident and collected as possible.

"You live," she said, unable to quite find the words.

"Yes." replied Egret. "We live, and the monster Grey Stag is dead. What of the others? How many are safe? What about the Skull Eaters?"

Graceful Seal gestured to a huddle of a hundred or so faces gathered around a large fire in the centre of a chamber. It was no longer raining, but Auroch could see how cold and wet many who had fled onto the open plan were. Tired and scared faces, desperately trying to warm themselves by the fire, reunited with those who had descended into the caves. Behind them, laid on the uncaring ground, were the bodies of the dead, around thirty. Auroch noticed that the Skull Eaters had been unceremoniously left in the positions they fell, scattered around the entrance next to the fallen body of Great-Tusk. Graceful Seal handed the baby to Auroch, who, for the first time in days, cracked a smile as the child giggled and laughed at the sight of him and Egret.

Graceful Seal motioned for the pair to follow her, and they walked past the huddled mass of people, past the dead, and out the entrance. Auroch looked at the dead mammoth lying slumped in the mud. Grey Stag's power over his men been drained the moment the animal died. The old man had been lucky to find the infant mammoth alone and scared, but in the end, he had little control over the beast. He never had. Auroch remembered the faces of the men as they fled, regretful and terrified. The same faces confronted him as he left the cave, as scared and upset as he had last seen them.

About thirty men, women, and children were kneeling in the mud outside the cavern, watched over by a group of eight armed Horse

Hunters and Brown Colt. The Great-Chief sat on a mound, a wooden splint visible along his bandaged leg. Auroch watched him wince as they approached, the pain clear above his stoic exterior.

"Auroch. Egret." he grimaced, "You killed the old man?"

An Audible gasp rose from the group on the ground, and Auroch nodded. He watched as the realisation of their predicament passed over the band of Skull Eaters. The pregnant woman who had freed him was sobbing quietly into her palm, her other hand stroking the small bump on her stomach.

"We caught more of these wretches skulking around just over that rise," Brown Colt continued, "Trying to see what became of their attack. Some ran off, as did some in the caves, but we got most of them."

He picked up a small rock and threw it, hitting one of the captured men from the tunnel square in the mouth. His lip began to bleed profusely, but his hands were tied behind his back, and he could do little but groan in pain.

"What now?" Egret asked, plainly embarrassed by Brown Colt's show of cruelty. She didn't look at the Great Chief, and Auroch felt his annoyance as her eyes scanned the row of prisoners rather than meeting his gaze.

"I thought we would kill them now." Brown Colt said plainly. "They worshiped that man and his beast. They cannot be left to live. I thought you may wish to see them before they died, given what they did to the Summer Valley."

He raised his hand to his men, who in turn raised their spears, ready to begin the slaughter. The pregnant woman was crying harder now, and an old man, his face covered in faded grey tattoos joined her, weeping silently into the mud.

"No," said Auroch, fully in control of the commanding tone that left his throat. He glanced at Egret, and she nodded in encouragement. "These people were led astray by a man, hurt and seeking revenge for wrongs done before you suckled at the teat. You say some have run? If we kill these men and women, those who ran they may return, hurt and angry as Grey Stag was."

"Merciful," laughed Brown Colt. "They have eaten the flesh of plainsmen. Who is going to turn them back from animals into men? You?"

"Our valley is silent now," Auroch continued, ignoring Brown Colt's taunt. "We will take them there. They can live as we did, to hunt the red deer and live for First Eagle and our ancestors."

A heartbeat passed. Then another. Brown Colt looked him dead in the eyes. Auroch could see them watering, holding back the pain of his ruined leg. The Great Chief lowered his hand slowly. The Horse Hunters relaxed, their spear shafts resting on the ground by their feet.

"Very well, take the beasts and make people of them. I hope I live long enough for their souls to be worthy of crossing the great river."

"Our Thanks, Brown Colt," Egret said, remembering her manners. "We shall talk of your mercy in the valley."

"You won't be joining Auroch," Brown Colt laughed, "I wish to take you as my bride, Egret." He waved his hand towards the cave. "Auroch, take Jumping Mare, our Spirit-Maiden. You will lead this group now, and you two can make many babies."

Auroch watched as Egret balled her fists before uttering a quiet,

"No."

Brown Colt laughed again, looking Egret dead in the eyes. Graceful Seal, who until now had been listening from afar, crept closer as if she were ready to intervene.

"I killed Great-Tusk and battled the Black Wolf on the shores of the Ancestor's River. I am willing to never return to this place, so be it. I saw my own path as the one that winds back to the Summer Valley when I visited the world of the ancestors. With the Men of the Summer Valley, I will stay. You are but a living man and know nothing of the world beyond. Who are you to question White Owl's will?"

"Foolish child." Brown Colt spat into the dirt by her feet. "Do not presume to tell me your place."

Graceful Seal stepped forward, her calm demeanour forming a protective aura around Egret and Auroch.

"The floods have wiped the caves clear, Brown Colt," she stated. "A new start. The Men of the Summer Valley have been torn down, and now Auroch will rebuild them. Egret lost her status as Spirit-Maiden but was born anew underneath the spring's first growth, here, at the place for all peoples. She does not belong to the Men of the Summer Valley, just as she does not belong to any tribe. As a clanless Spirit-Mother, her fate is not yours to set."

Brown Colt mumbled a response, but Auroch didn't hear it. Egret squeezed his hand, and the pair looked at the child, who gurgled and laughed. They were free to live as they saw fit, as Valleyfolk or clanless. The morning sun illuminated the whole world around them, the wet grass glinting as it caught its rays. One more task and the journey was over.

Chapter 34

It was mid-afternoon the next day by the time Egret was ready for the ceremony. The pair watched as the Horse Hunters departed across the plains, ready for the long journey north to the tundra they called home. Brown Colt shot them one last scowl as the sled he lay on was dragged across the wet grass, over a hillock and out of sight. It was hard not to breathe a sigh of relief. They had spoken to the captured Skull Eaters at length. They had agreed to accompany them at least to the Summer Valley. There, they would decide whether to sloop back to the shallow river where Auroch had been held prisoner or stay with the pair.

The ceremony was sparsely attended, but Auroch was quietly relieved. Graceful Seal had helped Egret, laying out the entrails around the base of the flowering tree in the appropriate way according to the new Spirit-Mother's direction. Auroch sat on the wet grass with his back to the pair as the two women did their work, the child asleep in his arms. In the far-off distance, he could see Bloodied Thistle's pregnant bride sitting alone, observing the scene. He silently wondered if she held any resentment for him, if he had managed to break the cycle of violence that had started in that cavern so long ago. He said a quick prayer to First Eagle under his breath before bending down to whisper it in the baby's ear.

"Soon Mother…" he said quietly.

A soft hand touched the back of his neck. Egret was ready. For all its buildup, the ceremony seemed simple to Auroch, but he quietly told himself that he knew nothing of Egret's magic and the importance of doing it here, at the turn of winter to the dawn of spring. He was directed to place the baby in the circle of hare guts. He sat at the edge of the circle as Egret danced around the baby, in a mesmerising display of grace. Her long, light, summer tunic bellowed in the wind around the shape of her body as she sang and chanted of a new life, of a child born and the feats he could accomplish, of the people he could meet, or the stories he could tell his own children. Her song was a haunting one, and as she danced, Auroch found it hard not to think of the naming ceremonies he had seen before. He was suddenly sitting in the sun with his family, watching his younger sister be named. He felt ugly tears well up in his eyes and a heavy lump making its way up his throat but suppressed it.

As soon as it began, the ceremony ended. Egret scooped the entrails from the floor and made a little sign of a bird on the child's head, placing him under the protection of White Owl. Kneeling, she whispered into the child's ear so that the name would not be heard by another first and claimed. A sense of relief passed through Auroch as he knew the ceremony was over. Mother had reached the other side of the torrent, bravely swimming across the rapids, taking care not to catch her feet on the stars that lay below the water. He imagined her pulling herself out of the river, running into the waiting arms of her family.

The child began to cry, and Egret picked him up and began nursing him, cooing and pulling faces to make him laugh. She brought him over to Auroch and sat down next to the new tribal leader, relieved that the task they had set out on several seasons ago was now complete.

"He is named?" Auroch asked, trying to sound nonchalant despite his curiosity.

"The name of the boy is Green Sapling. To grow in the Summer Valley."

Summer

Epilogue

Auroch held his breath and steadied his aim. His new band of hunters, hidden in the grass next to him, waited for his command and the sound of the spear leaving his atlatl ready to meet the soft flesh of the red deer in front of him. His party of five men was small, and they were yet to acquire dogs or become one cohesive group, acting on instinct as one lethal symbiotic arm. But they were learning, and Auroch had high hopes that by the turn of next year, they would have become the killers he wanted. His arm was completely still, and he knew that when he released his spear, it would hit the deer closest to him, a young doe, with pinpoint accuracy. He swung his arm and breathed out, watching the projectile strike its target.

The warm afternoon took its toll on them as they carried the four deer through the birch forest at the bottom of the valley and back toward camp. It wasn't too bad in the shade, but when the trees cleared for a moment, the sun stung his arms. He wondered if Egret could produce some salve from her bag to slather on himself and cool his burns. As they approached the camp, they could hear women's chatter and children's laughter, running around and tiring themselves out in the afternoon sun. Their number was small enough that it made little sense to divide themselves into male and female camps. As well as that, he had found many of the Skull-Eaters to be nervous and jumpy and felt that the communal group was best to put them at ease. The return journey to the valley had been a tense one, as the former Skull-Eaters had grown to accept Auroch as the new Grand Chief and Egret as Spirit-Mother.

They reached the camp, and Auroch spent the afternoon in a comfortable silence with the others, skinning and preparing the meal. Periodically, people would return from the woods, baskets laden with berries, mushrooms, and whatever other plants they could find. Some had left the group when they arrived in the valley and either went their own way or headed back across the mountains, but most had stayed, won over by their new leaders or impressed with the bounty of the valley. There had been little discussion regarding eating the flesh of men, and Auroch had felt a silent sense of relief at the passing of the custom. He had broached the subject with Bloodied Thistle's bride, and she had dismissed it as a custom associated with Grey Stag. Auroch had decided to wait until times became leaner, before considering the scourge eradicated. The old customs seemed to have died with the ancient man, and Egret had no issues inducting the new folk into the various joyful dances and ceremonies that accompanied the summer solstice in the valley.

The stars were coming out by the time their work had finished. Feeling weary, Auroch decided that he required some solitude and began walking up the valley away from the camp. The evening chorus of birds ringing in his ears, he emerged into a clearing in time to see the great river bloom in the sky above him. Saying a silent prayer to his ancestors, he sat on the ground in the clearing and watched the stars, each of them a light from a faraway fire lit by those who came before him. He imagined his own family, laughing and sharing food. He looked forward to seeing them when his work was done on this earth. The birdsong died down, and against the clear sky, he could see woodsmoke rising in the distance from the camp. The sound of the night insects set in, and Auroch felt at one with the valley. Footsteps, crunching through the dry twigs and leaves, came closer and closer until a familiar figure emerged from the wood and joined him in the clearing.

Egret looked healthy. The sun had given her a glow that radiated from her and permeated everyone and everything she was near.

"No dancing tonight?" he asked, half joking.

"Not tonight." she replied before adding, "Your brother is with the other children."

Auroch nodded. He was crawling around confidently now, examining the worms and other tiny creatures that could be found in the grass. Auroch lay back down, and Egret lay close to him, as they had when huddled in the freezing, tiny caves over the winter. She kissed him deeply on the lips, as she often would since their return to the valley. He reciprocated tenderly, still not accustomed to the pleasant warmth of her affection. The night sky was alive tonight, and the pair watched a star shoot across the ethereal vista above them, burning red and white.

"It looks so close, the world of our ancestors," Egret said after a while.

"I suppose it is close. Only a few moments away." Auroch replied. He thought for a short while and then asked something he had been meaning to ask Egret for much of the year just gone. "The vision that Morning Mist showed you of the world of ice. Is that still to come? As it was for the Old Men of the hills?"

Egret watched the stars for some time, plainly ruminating on the answer. Auroch picked a long strand of grass and placed it in his mouth, chewing rhythmically and grinding it between his teeth. Egret buried herself into his chest.

"The world before us and the world after us shouldn't concern us. We shall see it all in the end, gathered around the stars forever. Right now, we are free." she said, her eyes closing as she began to drift from the birchwood forest into the world of dreams.

Auroch yawned and allowed himself to follow her. The smell of distant smoke from the campfire gently caressed his nostrils as he drifted to sleep. Somewhere behind him, an owl hooted, beginning its night-time hunt for a grass snake. A deer, having lost a number of its herd to Auroch's hunters earlier that day, took a cool, refreshing drink from a stream before melting with ease into the lush woodland of the Summer Valley.

END

About the Author

Francis Roberts is a debut historical fiction author with a passion for archaeology and the outdoors. When not crafting his next novel, he can be found roaming England's beautiful West Country. Francis resides in Gloucestershire with his partner and two miniature schnauzers.

Follow him on Twitter @author_franc1s and on TikTok @theworldbefore6 for updates and insights into his creative process.

Made in United States
North Haven, CT
07 October 2024